ery Series

THAT TOUCH OF INK

"A terrific mystery is always in fashion--and this one is sleek, chic and constantly surprising. Vallere's smart styling and wry humor combine for a fresh and original page-turner—it'll have you eagerly awaiting her next appealing adventure. I'm a fan!"

— Hank Phillippi Ryan,
Agatha, Anthony, Macavity and Mary Higgins Clark Award-
Winning Author of *The Other Woman*

"All of us who fell in love with Madison Night in *Pillow Stalk* will be rooting for her when the past comes back to haunt her in *That Touch of Ink*. The suspense is intense, the plot is hot and the style is to die for. A thoroughly entertaining entry in this enjoyable series."

-Catriona McPherson,
Agatha Award-Winning Author of the Dandy Gilver Mystery Series

"A fast-paced mystery with fab fashions, an appealing heroine, and a clever twist, *That Touch of Ink* is especially for fans of all things mid-century modern."

— ReadertoReader.com

"Diane Vallere...has a wonderful touch, bringing in the design elements and influences of the '50s and '60s era many of us hold dear while keeping a strong focus on what it means in modern times to be a woman in business for herself, starting over."

— *Fresh Fiction*

PILLOW STALK

"A humorous yet adventurous read of mystery, very much worth considering."

— Paul Vogel,
Midwest Book Review

D1559268

That Touch of Ink

That Touch of Ink

a mad for mod mystery

Diane Vallere

HENERY PRESS

THAT TOUCH OF INK
A Mad for Mod Mystery
Part of the Henery Press Mystery Collection

First Edition
Trade paperback edition | April 2014

Henery Press
www.henerypress.com

ISBN-13: 978-1-940976-09-9

Printed in the United States of America

To Devon Marbury

ACKNOWLEDGMENTS

A special thank you to the people who inspired me, helped me, and/or believed in me while I worked on this book:

Ramona deFelice Long, Brenda Errichiello, Margery Bubinak, Hank Phillippi Ryan, Catriona McPherson, Gigi Pandian, Brad Holcomb, Sgt. Derek Pacifico, Dennis and Cheryl O'Hagan, the Secret Service, and the FBI.

Marc at HighDenomination.com for permission to use the image of the five thousand dollar bill on the original cover. I've spent way too much time on your website while writing this book!

The Guppies and Sisters in Crime-Los Angeles, both for providing a supportive community where I'm not the only weird one who talks about murder.

Mom and Dad, for always encouraging me to do what I wanted, Kendel Flaum, for a friendship that surpasses anything that either of us set out to accomplish, and Josh Hickman, for more than I have room to say.

ONE

The money arrived on a Tuesday. Five thousand dollars, wrapped in a sheet of newsprint. It wasn't a stack of carefully counted bills. It wasn't a check. Nobody owed me money. But the fact that this sum of five thousand dollars came with the rest of the mail, in the form of one bill, made the situation all the worse. Only one person in the world would send me a five thousand dollar bill.

Brad Turlington. The man I thought I knew better than anyone I'd ever known in my life, until the day I learned he was a stranger.

The five thousand dollar bill was in good shape inside a clear plastic sandwich baggie. I flattened it out with the side of my hand. Under the bill, a phone number was scrawled across the newsprint. The familiar area code did little to soothe my mounting anxiety. It was the same area code I'd had when I lived in Philadelphia, before I'd moved to Dallas. I looked at the envelope. It was addressed to me, Madison Night. The address was mine, the handwriting his, the postmark Dallas. If it's true that money talks, then I didn't like what this five thousand dollar bill told me: Brad was alive, he knew my price, and he had found me.

To my untrained eye, it looked like Monopoly money. I set it on my dining room table and stared at it like it was going to do tricks, though the mere act of arriving in the mail, uninsured, in a plain white envelope should have been trick enough. The fact that it delivered a message from a ghost was the cherry on top of the sundae. Or the straw that broke the camel's back. Sometimes, when you're trying to justify your past to your present, it's hard to tell.

I put the bill into a new business-sized envelope and sandwiched it between the pages of the latest *Atomic Ranch* magazine. There would be time to question Brad's motivation later. Right now it was time to repaint my living room. I pulled a slightly damaged pink hat over my light blonde hair and tucked a few of the longer strands under the band like I would a swim cap. The hat was vinyl, cracked in several places. I'd picked it up at a local secondhand shop for a dollar. It was too beat up to wear outside, but it was the perfect complement to my painting attire: white overalls and a T-shirt printed with yellow and pink daisies.

Two gallons of daffodil-yellow paint, aluminum trays, rollers, and trim brushes sat at the ready.

Rocky, my fluffy caramel-and-white Shih Tzu, bounded out of the bedroom. Sunlight filtered through the window and highlighted stains that had appeared as if by magic on the once new apartment-grade carpeting. As long as I was redoing the walls, I might as well have at the floors too. Considering I owned the building, my decorating therapy was tax deductible.

I turned on the TV and pushed the furniture to the middle of the room. A weatherman predicted the ten-day forecast. Seventy degrees in February. I'd been in Dallas for over two years now, and I'd never get used to it.

After a couple of commercials, a local newsman reported about a traffic jam on Loop 12, a domestic abuse case, and finished with a human interest story about two boys who had found something special while picnicking at the Dallas Arboretum. It was a piece of a five thousand dollar bill.

Repainting the living room was going to have to wait.

The reporter gave a brief history of the bill. First printed in 1928, it remained in circulation for forty-one years, until 1969 when the secretary of the treasury announced that the Federal Reserve would stop distribution of high-denomination bills. At the time the bill was retired, the government had explained that secure transfer technology eliminated the need for large bills, which were originally intended for bank transfer payments. But it was widely rumored that the decision was actually part of President Nixon's efforts to interrupt the dealings of organized crime. The reporter added the irony that James Madison himself had renounced the value of paper money, but was the president pictured on one of the most coveted bills on the collector's circuit.

He turned his attention to the boys. "Now, which one of you found the bill?"

The chubbier boy pulled the microphone from his brother's hand. "We had a picnic. I was cleaning up. I found this stuck to one of the plants near the trash cans."

The other boy took the microphone. "Dad said it was play money. We spent hours looking for the rest of it, but our parents said we had to leave."

"Do you know what it's worth?"

The boys shook their heads.

"I'm sure your parents will help you find that out. Can you hold it up for the camera?"

The chubby one held the scrap in front of him. The reporter straightened up and addressed the camera. "The James Madison bill is one of the more collectible units of American currency. Hard to say what a piece of one is worth, but if this had been a complete bill, it might be worth one hundred thousand dollars."

I felt as if someone had turned the temperature down twenty degrees. It was too much of a coincidence, these boys finding a piece of a five thousand dollar bill the same day one had arrived in the mail. A coldness snaked over my bare neck and down my spine. Coincidence, I could have handled.

I moved to the desk chair. A Google search confirmed what the reporter had said about the value of the bill, but even Google couldn't tell me why Brad had sent the $5000 bill to me in the first place. The only place I could look for answers was my past, which meant dredging up memories. Memories I'd learned to block, to ignore, to pretend had never existed.

"I have one, you know. In the back room. Framed. Mr. Pierot must have gotten it in one of his estate buys, but it's not exactly mid-century, so he never displayed it. If you want it, I'll buy it for you."

"Keep it. If you ever need me, and I mean, really, really need me, you know my price."

A tingling sensation radiated from the center of my chest to my fingers and toes, replacing the chill. I didn't want to accept the truth even though it sat right in front of me. The $5000 bill meant one thing.

Brad really, really needed me.

I closed my eyes, and the memories played through my mind like a classic movie that's been watched enough times to be familiar.

"Are you saying you can be bought?"

"Under the right circumstances, with the right motivation, anybody can be bought."

"Sure, but you're not just anybody, Madison."

Memories flooded back to me. The sheets, on the dark cherry wood double bed in the back of Pierot's, the furniture and interior decorating business in Philadelphia where we first met. The bed was part of the store's inventory until Brad and I christened it. One night, he carved our initials into the wood, a silly gesture that slashed the resale value. Two perfectly good apartments, two consenting adults, and we spent three nights a week in a double bed in the back of a mid-century modern furniture store like a couple of teenagers in the back seat of a soccer mom's SUV borrowed for a date.

I shook my head to make the unwanted memories go away. Rocky danced around my feet. I ruffled the fur on top of his head and leaned down to plant a kiss in the middle of it. "We're okay by ourselves, right Rocky? Our life is perfect just the way it is."

"That's too bad. I was hoping you'd be happy to see me."

The voice was as familiar as if I'd heard it yesterday. I straightened up and turned to face the front door. Brad Turlington—former love of my life, former breaker of my heart—leaned against my open front door with a fist full of daisies.

I was suddenly awkward. I reached for the ladder for balance and knocked the gallon of yellow paint over. I fumbled to right it but failed, spilling most of it on the drop cloth, the carpet, and myself.

Brad set the daisies on the desk and stepped into the room to pick up the paint can.

"You're the only woman I know who looks good in overalls." He put a hand alongside my face and brushed his thumb against my cheek, smearing a trace of yellow paint. I didn't want to look at him, didn't want to fall into his dark brown eyes, hidden behind square tortoise shell frames, but I couldn't look away.

The last two years had been good to him. The planes of his face were still angular, and a few more strands of silver had threaded their way through his curly black hair. Top Brass had always been his styling product of choice, and it gave his thick mane a glossy appearance. Today was no different.

"It's been a long time, Madison," he said. "I've missed you."

I pushed him away. "I can't do this."

"This?"

"This." I motioned back and forth between his chest and mine. "Us. I'm not the same person I was then."

"Neither am I. But you can't deny how perfect we are for each other. I bet I'm still the one person who knows you better than you know yourself."

"I think you should leave."

He stood in front of me, smiling, waiting for my anger to subside. He would be waiting a long time. I said nothing more.

"I'm not letting you go a second time, Madison. I promise you that." Finally, he stepped backward into the hallway and left.

Yellow paint was splattered over the drop cloth. A daffodil-colored pool of semi-gloss soaked the carpet. I poured myself a large glass of cold white wine and pulled *Atomic Ranch* off the desk. I pulled the five thousand dollar bill out of the center of the magazine, turned it over, and then set it back down.

Brad coming back into my life was too much to process. Two years ago, Brad had lied to me. I'd turned off my emotions and had built a whole new life. Only recently had I learned the lie was the lie. He'd been protecting me from dangerous men who were after him, and he needed me to leave in order to know I'd be safe.

I didn't know what to do with the emotions his return had triggered. I didn't know where he'd been for two years. But I knew this: if he'd sent me the bill, it was because he was in trouble. I couldn't ignore that. I picked up the daisies from where he'd left them on the table and tossed them in the trash.

I returned to the Internet and found the address for a local numismatist. It was five-thirty. I called the number and a nasally voice answered.

"Paper Trail, Stanley Mann speaking."

"Hello. My name is Madison Night. I recently came into possession of a unique bill and I'd like to find out about it. How late are you open?"

"Let me check my schedule. Hold, please."

The line clicked into silence, and I wondered if the man on the other end had accidentally hung up on me. I watched the second hand sweep two laps around the face of my ball clock and considered hanging up and redialing just as Mr. Mann returned.

"I have an opening tomorrow at four."

"Can you see me any sooner?"

"Nope. I'm going to Plano to view a collection in the morning. You said you have one bill you want me to appraise?" He blew his nose like a foghorn. "Maybe I can give you some information over the phone. What is it?"

I hesitated for a second. "Mr. Mann, it's a James Madison five thousand dollar bill."

There was a slight pause. "How soon can you get here?"

I changed from my overalls into a pink polyester twin set with white piping, a pair of matching corduroys, and navy blue canvas sneakers. I left the five thousand dollar bill in the envelope and put the whole *Atomic Ranch* magazine in my handbag.

It was late in the afternoon. I drove my Alfa Romeo down Gaston to Garland Road, turned left, then right, then drove another half mile until I spotted the sign for Paper Trail. I followed the signs for parking in the rear, parked, and rounded the building to the front door on foot.

The door was wood, a flat rectangle, with a small square of glass in the middle. As a decorator myself, it always surprised me that people didn't consider the exterior of their business or house as part of their design philosophy. Stanley Mann had ignored the first impression his business would give to the people who approached his front door. I would have expected more grandeur from someone who studied valuable coins and bills. But maybe that was the thing. Maybe the nondescript front door, the small office attached to the house that sat off the road, maybe it was all part of flying under the radar, attracting the right kind of attention while avoiding the wrong.

I pressed the doorbell and was answered with sharp, staccato barking. I waited for the better part of a minute for a reply and rang the doorbell again. No one came to the door. The west-facing windows were protected from the hot Texas sun with thick, lined curtains on the inside. I couldn't see past them. I tapped on the glass and waited for an answer. Nothing.

With zero evidence the numismatist was there, I was tempted to go home, shower, change, and crawl into bed. I stepped away from the front door and looked around. A small silver bowl, half-filled with water, sat to the side of the door. A block of wood carved to look like a dollar bill read "In Dog We Trust." It hung from a piece of twine tied to two screws that protruded from either end.

I pressed my face up to the glass pane on the door and shut one eye, trying to make out the interior. Inside was a tidy living room. A mustard-yellow sofa was pushed up against the left-hand wall, facing a television on a small, metal TV cart. A collection of owl figurines sat on an end table next to the sofa. A worn, braided rug in shades of mustard, orange, and brown decorated the highly polished wood floor. A small rawhide bone, pockmarked with bite marks, protruded from halfway under the sofa.

To the right of the living room was a long, narrow kitchen. A stove, microwave, and refrigerator lined the left side. The right counter held a toaster, meat slicer, and ceramic containers labeled flour, tea, and coffee. I started to move away from the door when something inside moved. I pressed my face back up to the glass. A small furry brown face looked at me from a room beyond the kitchen.

I tapped on the glass. The dog took a few tentative steps toward me but stopped when he reached the rug and turned back. He looked into the darkness behind him, then back at me. He repeated the short, staccato barks I'd heard earlier.

I knew animal behavior. He was trying to tell me that something was wrong.

Next to him was a silver stockpot on its side. Something dark chugged from the pot onto the kitchen floor.

I hurried around to the back of the building. The barking grew more agitated. It pained me to think an animal was in trouble. I scanned the back windows and found one that was missing the screen. I checked the windows but they were locked. I looked by my feet for something heavy and settled on a rock about the size of a misshapen baseball. In my high school days, I'd played baseball and although it had been thirty years since I'd pitched a no-hitter, I hoped it was like riding a bike.

I stepped about fifteen feet away from the window, shrugged my shoulders front and back to loosen them up, took a deep breath, and threw a stinger. The rock crashed through the glass, making more noise than I anticipated. I used a second rock to knock away enough shards around the edge to allow me to feed a hand through the window and unlock it, then pushed it up and crawled through.

The small, dirty dog met me at the doorway to the house, tracking paw prints of marinara behind him.

"Shhhh, it's okay. I'm trying to help you," I said. I reached down, and he stepped away from me. He was scared. I took two steps into the room and held out a hand so he could sniff me. He turned away and scampered into a dark room that I hadn't been able to see earlier. I tiptoed into the room with him and tripped over something lying on the floor. I pushed myself into a sitting position and blinked a few times, forcing my eyes to adjust to the darkness.

The room smelled like spaghetti sauce. Something wet soaked through my pink corduroys and I shifted my legs, feeling around the floor through spilled tomato sauce to find out what I'd tripped over.

I screamed when my hand connected with a leg.

TWO

Furiously, I kicked my heels against the hardwood, trying to push myself away from the leg. The leg didn't kick back, didn't move. I reached out and felt an arm. I shook it. It was stiff, rigid. I felt up the arm, over the shoulders, to the neck, where I loosened a necktie and undid the top button on a white collared shirt.

The man's head rolled to one side. There was a bullet hole through his forehead. A trail of blood snaked from the hole toward his temple and pooled with the marinara that chugged from the pot on the floor. I felt for a pulse by his throat but I knew I wouldn't find it. I knew from the second I'd tripped over him he was dead.

My rubber soles skidded against the floor, denying me traction. After too many failed attempts I flipped myself onto all fours, fought the sickening sensation in my stomach, and pushed myself up to a standing position.

I tripped over my own feet, caught myself on the corner of the desk, and felt around until I found the phone. I dialed nine, then one, then stopped. I was alone in a house where I had no business being. I had broken a window to gain access. I was covered in marinara and blood and a man was dead. I had a strong feeling that his death had not been an accident.

I had a stronger feeling of being sick. This time I lost the battle against the nausea and threw up in a wastepaper basket in the corner.

I found the dog by the back door. I scooped him up and carried him to my car. Whether or not it was the right thing to do, I called the one person I knew in law enforcement: Lieutenant Tex Allen.

"Allen," he answered.

"Lieutenant Allen, this is Madison. Night. This is Madison Night." There was a pause. I squeezed my eyes shut, trying to block the scene inside Paper Trail. It didn't work.

"Madison Night," he said. "To what do I owe the honor?"

"I need to see you," I said. Before he had a chance for an inappropriate counterpoint, I kept talking. "There's a man at a shop called Paper Trail on Garland Road. He's been shot. I couldn't find a pulse. Whatever you're doing, stop it and get here. Now."

"Did you call 911?" he asked, the flirtation gone from his voice.

"I called you."

"Shit, Night."

Lieutenant Tex Allen was a local detective I'd met during a recent homicide investigation. He'd come on strong, grating on my every nerve with his playboy attitude. Circumstances threw us together; a difference of opinions kept us at odds. He had been with me the day I learned the truth about Brad. That was the last time I'd seen him. In the brief time our paths had crossed, he'd hit me over the head with bravado, pick-up lines, and the unexplained notion that, despite me being an independent woman in vintage apparel who had modeled her life after Doris Day, and he being a homicide detective with a revolving door by his bed, one day we'd date. Whether it was the calm after the storm of his investigation or the knowledge that my past was alive and kicking, we'd gone our separate ways. On more than one occasion, I almost missed him. That surprised me the most.

I hung up the phone, then wondered who exactly I thought I was, hiding five thousand dollar bills from my ex-boyfriend, throwing rocks through windows to rescue abandoned dogs, and commanding homicide detectives to react to my beck and call. The sick-to-my-stomach sensation returned, and I ran from the car to a patch of dry grass. My empty stomach responded only with heaves.

Tires on gravel sounded within minutes. I heard a door slam.

"Night?" Tex yelled.

I took a deep breath and called back, "Behind the building." The effort of yelling sapped what little energy I had, and I collapsed onto the concrete beam that marked the parking space next to mine.

Tex rounded the building with a purposeful stride. He had on a dark brown suit and tie. It was a more business-like appearance than I was used to from him, having mostly seen him in jeans. I thought about asking him what the occasion was, but didn't.

Before I could speak, he held up a hand.

"I ask, you answer. I don't want extraneous details. What happened?"

"I came here to meet with Stanley Mann to find out about a five thousand dollar bill I received in the mail." I searched Tex's expression to see if he wanted an explanation for the bill. I wasn't sure how I'd explain it if he did. His face was unreadable. "He didn't come to the door. I saw a dog inside. He acted funny. I broke a window and went in. I found a body."

He dropped his head and ran his thumb and forefinger over his eyes. "Then what?"

I glared at him, ready to defend my decisions. Instead, I calmed my voice. "I checked for a pulse. I threw up. I carried the dog out to my car. And then I called you."

He pushed his dirty blond hair away from his forehead and looked at the building. When he turned back to face me, his blue eyes were cold and sharp. "Stay here. I'm going inside."

He walked away. I sat back down on the concrete beam next to my car and ran my hands over the dog's fur. I didn't want to watch Tex go into the house. I didn't want to hear him feel his way through the dark rooms. I didn't want to watch him find the body I'd tripped over.

Out of some kind of respect for the awkward position I'd put Tex in, I waited for him to return. I didn't know how much time passed before he finally did. Could have been minutes or hours.

"Night, listen to me. Do you know that man's identity?"

"I think he's the man I came here to meet."

Tex held his hand palm-side up. "Give me your keys."

I reacted automatically and set my keys in Tex's palm.

He went behind my car and opened the trunk. Seconds later he slammed it shut and came back with a beach towel in his hand. He spread it over the driver's seat of my convertible. He handed my keys back and sat next to me on the concrete beam.

"I called it in. We have about ten minutes until the cavalry arrives and starts processing this as a crime scene. You have to stay because your presence spoiled the crime scene, and it's better for us if we know what you did than for you to lie. We'd waste time figuring it out anyway. Right now I want to know as much as you can tell me before anybody gets here. This time don't edit out details."

"I received a five thousand dollar bill in the mail."

"From who?"

"Brad Turlington—my ex, Brad. It had to be him. There was a phone number on the newspaper it was wrapped in. A Philadelphia phone number. I didn't call it. I wasn't going to do anything about it, but he showed up at my apartment. Here. In Dallas."

Our eyes connected and held. I wondered how clearly Tex remembered that day, nine months ago, when he sat next to me in a darkened theater as I learned the truth about Brad.

"Night, I know what you found out about him took you by surprise. It surprised me too. But you didn't have to walk out of the theater. I would have been there for you if you wanted to talk."

"It was my past, Tex. My issues. My baggage to deal with."

"Nobody said you had to deal with it alone." He paused. "Sorry. Maybe I'm jumping to conclusions. Maybe you didn't deal with it alone."

An eerie calm came over me at Tex's inference of Hudson James, the contractor I relied on for furniture repair and maintenance to the apartment building I secretly owned. After finding out the truth about Brad in that dark theater, I'd withdrawn from life. And then Hudson started coming over.

First, it was to check the smoke detectors in the building. When he said they were due for inspection, I didn't question him. A week later it was a tear in the carpet on the back steps. When he showed up the following week with a box of energy-efficient light bulbs for the hallway, I met him with two glasses and a bottle of merlot. From that point on, I created the projects, and we worked on them together. We never talked about the homicide. I never told him what I'd learned about Brad. We'd simply enjoyed each other's company. Slowly, in the months that followed, I'd started to deal with what I'd learned to be the truth about Brad.

Over two years ago, in the middle of a passionate relationship, Brad had surprised me with the news that he was a married man who wasn't going to leave his wife for me. We'd been on the top of a ski slope in the Poconos. I left him there, turned my back on him and skied down the slope, barely in control. My ski caught on a patch of ice. My tears clouded my vision. My reaction time failed. I fell. I blew out my knee and spent the rest of my vacation in a hospital room.

But that day, last May, in a darkened theater in Dallas, with Tex at my side and a government official in the wings, I learned that Brad's bombshell had been the real lie.

Brad had never been married. He lied because he was involved with bad people—that's what he called them—and he knew they'd come after me if I were a part of his life. He'd lied to drive me away—to protect me, not hurt me—but I didn't know what to do with the cauldron of emotions I felt as a result.

I'd established a new life when I moved to Dallas. I volunteered at a local movie theater and swam laps most mornings alongside senior citizens. I established a business and adopted a puppy. I got along just fine.

And then I met Tex. Despite the conclusions he'd jumped to, I set out to prove that I was an independent woman who could take care of herself. I saved Hudson's life, helped solve a cold case, and stared down a killer. But the vulnerability I felt after watching Brad's confession was an arrow through a chink in my armor. I had excused myself from the theater and left without saying good-bye. I hadn't returned to the theater. I hadn't returned to my morning swimming routine.

I hadn't seen Tex again. Until now.

"How did Turlington know you were here?" Tex prompted.

"I don't know. I haven't heard from him since—I don't know. The last time I heard from Brad was the message we watched in the theater."

"Keep going."

"I had to do something. I called the numismatist—"

"The who?"

"Stanley Mann. He specializes in collectible currency. He owns Paper Trail. I called him and asked if I could meet with him even though it was late. As soon as he heard about the five thousand dollar bill, he told me to come over. Nobody answered the doorbell when I got here, but I saw the dog inside. He was barking like something was wrong. I broke in because I thought he was hurt." I kept my hand on the dog's head. He was shaking.

I was barely making sense to myself, but I felt the pressure of the ticking clock and, like a contestant on the twenty-five thousand dollar pyramid, I babbled out every fact that had brought me to this spot in the hope Tex could process the oil spill of screwed-up logic.

"There's a bowl of water out front. There's a toy on the floor. So I looked through the glass on the front door when nobody answered the doorbell. The dog came out from the kitchen, tracking footprints of something. I saw the tipped silver stock and the sauce on the floor. I went around to the back and there was one window where the screen was missing so I used a rock to break the window and climbed in and the room was dark and I tripped over—" I halted abruptly before continuing. Sirens sang—*weeooo, weeooo*—filling my silence. More tires disturbed the lot out front. The whole time Tex kept his icy blue eyes trained on me. "—the body."

"That's it?"

"That's the highlights."

Tex stood up. He held out a hand and, after a moment of hesitation, I took it and stood next to him. He leaned close, his face inches from mine. "I'm not going to lecture you about what you did. I'm not going to question your motives."

He turned toward the small army of cops and EMTs who had arrived at Paper Trail. I turned the other direction and stared at the field behind the building.

"Right now, I'm going to go explain what happened here. Soon, I'm going to bring someone over here to take your statement. You are going to tell them what you told me. The truth. That was the truth, right?"

"Of course it was the truth," I said, turning to face him again.

"Okay." He started to walk away then stopped and turned back. "Listen to me, Night. Before any of that happens, I want you to do me one favor."

I stared into Tex's face, caring less about what his favor would be than the fact that I was in a position where I was required to grant it. "What is it?" I asked quietly.

"I want you to call your boyfriend."

THREE

Tex didn't wait for my reply. He crossed the parking lot and met the officers gathering at the back door.

I turned my back on them again and stared at the vacant lot in front of me. Soon enough, someone would need to take my statement, and they would easily find me when they did. Until then, I wanted no part of their investigation.

Still shaken by the sounds of the scene behind me, I reached into my car and pulled the magazine out of my handbag. Under the collectible bill was the phone number. I took my phone out of my handbag and stared at the keypad. I closed my eyes. It didn't matter that I'd tried to erase Brad from my memories. I might as well have tattooed his face on my thigh. He was that clear in my mind.

I punched the buttons and listened to a ring and a half before I thought about Tex's request that I make this call. Before I could analyze his motivation or question my willingness to comply, I heard Brad's voice. I had hoped for a recording; I was not so lucky.

"Brad?" I asked, even though I knew it was him. "It's Madison."

"Maddy?" There was a pause. "I was hoping you'd have a change of heart."

I closed my eyes and took a ragged breath.

"Are you okay?" he asked.

"I'm—no. I'm not okay." My voice quivered, and I fought to keep it calm. I was fairly certain I was unsuccessful. I looked at the house. Uniformed officers stood at varying degrees of proximity to the window. A few others were off to the side by my tire tracks.

Tex rounded the building with his hands on his hips. A female officer was behind him. Tex said something to her, and she came over to me and picked up the dog. Tex's eyes connected with mine. I looked away.

"You surprised me this afternoon," I said to Brad. "How long have you been in Dallas?" I asked.

"A few days."

"Where are you staying?"

"Mads, can we meet somewhere? There's so much I want to say to you, and I'd rather do it in person. Dinner? Can I take you to dinner?"

"Not Italian," I said, remembering the smell of marinara.

"I saw a Polynesian place by the highway when I drove in. Trader Josh's? Do you know where that is?"

"Yes. When?"

"Half an hour?"

"Fine. I might be a little late, but I'll be there."

We said goodbye, and I hung up quickly, preventing him from saying anything else. I had surprised myself by asking to see him, but something about tripping over a body had affected me. Brad wanted to talk to me, and I didn't want to be alone. Something about Tex's cold request that I make this phone call affected me too. I was an inconvenience to his crime scene. He was getting me out of the way. He was a cop, and he was there to do cop things.

Watching Tex work, I was reminded that his mind was not limited to only the most basic of male triggers. He was alert, constantly processing his surroundings, driven by a problem-solving obsession that made him an excellent detective. If I had been an anomaly in his landscape of women, he was the same to me. We were different but alike. An unanswered what-if hung between us, like a helium balloon at a party. But eventually the what-if lost its buoyancy and slowly descended, like a relic of a party that never happened.

"Yo, Night!" called Tex. He walked toward me. I stood and met him halfway.

"Did you make your phone call?" he asked.

"Yes."

"How'd it go?"

I didn't know how to tell Tex how I felt about seeing Brad again. I was barely able to answer that to myself. Questions assaulted me. The kind of questions a single woman in her late forties shouldn't have to answer.

"I don't want to talk about it." I waited for a couple of seconds. Tex didn't move. "I'm seeing him tonight. We're meeting at Trader Josh's."

I looked past him to the edge of the property where the gravel parking spaces gave way to grass that had turned a bland shade of brown. When I looked back at Tex to gauge his reaction, I got nothing.

A slight breeze swept past us, lifting the hair from his forehead. The door to my car knocked into the back of my legs and I fell forward. Tex put his hands out to catch me. I fell into his chest. His arms wrapped around my body as I pressed against him. Heat seared between our clothes. I pulled away and looked at his face. His pupils had dilated in the darkness, and his blue eyes went dark, smoky. He didn't move right away, and, selfishly, neither did I.

"You okay? He asked.

"I'm fine.

"Good."

"Fine."

I stepped back. He reached into the car and pulled out the towel, opened it up, and wrapped it around me. I pulled down the bottom of my sweater and looked up to find him staring at the gingham boat appliqué on the front of it. I took the ends of the towel from his hands and secured it around my waist to cover the stains on my pants and keep them from getting onto my car's interior. Another cop approached us and Tex made a brief introduction. Before he left me to make my statement, he leaned in and whispered, "I've missed you, Night."

*   *   *

I didn't remember driving back to the apartment. My mind was otherwise occupied and my internal auto-pilot got me to the building, through the back door, and into my apartment. Already I regretted making plans with Brad. I wanted to pick Rocky up from my neighbor's apartment and cradle him all night, but I knew if I didn't confront the issue, he'd show up on my doorstep a second time.

There was a note lying just inside the front door. *Madison, I took Rocky out to White Rock Lake. Can you pick him up tonight? Anytime after nine would be good. Thanks, Effie.*

Effie was a teenager who watched Rocky for me when he was a puppy. Now that he was trained, I knew I could leave him alone, but he'd traded his habit of knocking over lamps for chewing on shoes, and besides, Effie loved his company as much as he loved hers.

The note was time-dated seven thirty. I checked the clock on the wall. It was twenty after eight.

The first thing I did was take off the pink corduroys that were stained with marinara and blood. I balled them up, put them in a plastic grocery bag, knotted it shut, and set it by the front door. My left thigh held a six-inch-long scratch from the windowsill.

I hopped in the shower, and then changed into a vintage peony-printed, full-skirted dress, draped a whisper-pink cardigan over my shoulders, and slid my feet into pale pink ballerina flats. Before I left, I took the envelope from inside *Atomic Ranch* out, wrote Attn: Night Company on the front of the envelope, and left a note about a new paint job on the back. I dropped the envelope into the secure metal rent drop-off box in the front of the building. At least it was out of my apartment.

Brad was waiting for me by the bar inside the renovated Tiki restaurant. "I'm glad you called," he said. He brushed my blonde hair away from my face. "You're as beautiful as ever. Come here," he said gently.

He leaned forward and kissed me, and an electric shock snapped between us. I jerked away. I expected him to apologize for being forward. He didn't.

A thin gray-haired man in his sixties approached with two Mai Tais. He wore a Hawaiian shirt in shades of navy, orange, and yellow. A plastic nametag clipped to his collar had a piece of masking tape over it. Del had been written on it in black marker.

Brad was startled by the waiter's appearance. I took a glass and thanked him to cover for Brad's odd behavior.

"Don't thank me, thank the gentleman who ordered for you." He gestured to Brad and hovered by us for a moment. "We're clearing a table for you now. It'll just be a minute."

I thanked him again and took a sip of my drink.

"I thought you had second thoughts," Brad said.

"I almost didn't come," I said. I didn't know if I was going to tell him about the body at Paper Trail. I didn't want to think about it, let alone talk about it. If anyone asked, I could make the argument that the only reason I showed up was because this was the one thing that had the potential to distract me.

"So, Maddy, how are you? How have you been?"

"Nobody calls me Maddy, Brad."

"I call you Maddy. Don't you remember?"

"I've tried to forget."

"I made a mistake. I'm sorry. I'm sorry a hundred times over."

"Come on, Brad, you can do better than that, can't you?"

He pulled the tortoiseshell frames from his face and polished the glass between the thin cashmere of his sweater. After putting them on, he focused on me.

"If I were playing a game, I could. But this is for real, and I've missed you. More than I ever thought possible. Every single day I think about how I pushed you away, how I did it for your own safety. I've wondered if you knew that, or if you'd understand. Even when I took a job in Carmel, California, right after you left, I was still haunted by you. Didn't help that the job was in Doris Day's hotel. Hell, that's probably why I took the job to begin with."

I tipped my head down and looked at my drink. Brad didn't know that he *had* seen me while on that job in California. After getting out of the hospital, not sure where to go, I took a spontaneous getaway. The night he saw me, my hair had been stained to a temporary brown rinse and I'd worn a stranger's clothes. It had been paralyzing. We'd been face-to-face and he hadn't recognized me. That one fact had hurt as much as the break-up and the knee injury, and had been the tipping point between clinging to the emotional pain and shutting out the world and moving forward.

By the time I left Carmel by-the-Sea, I knew I had to start over. And I did. But I always wondered, if I really had been so important to him, why hadn't he recognized me when I was right in front of him? Was it me he really wanted, or the package: the vintage dresses, the poufy blond hair, the Doris Day-lookalike, fifties chick that seemed to fit so well with his hipster dude image?

"There are things about me you don't know, Maddy, things I wish weren't true. But you, you're pure. The blonde hair, the blue eyes, the way you look in those cute vintage dresses."

I cringed at how closely his words followed thoughts.

"The way your hair smells and how perfectly we fit together when we dance. I miss it all. How you used to watch the Doris Day show when you couldn't sleep. You know, after you vanished, I bought the entire series. I watched the episodes so many times I practically committed them to memory. It was the closest I could get to having you with me."

"But I wasn't with you. Not after you lied to me." I looked into my drink, swirling it around. The red plastic stirrer was stacked with pineapple cubes and a maraschino cherry. "I don't know if I can forgive that, Brad. No matter what you feel, no matter what I felt, once."

"Give me a chance, honey, and I'll spend the rest of my life making it up to you. Every day, every night. I'll be there. I'm on the straight and narrow from here on out. I won't risk losing you again."

The waiter returned. "Mr. and Mrs. Turlington? Your table is ready."

"We're not married," I said with a little too much force.

"Yet," said Brad, behind me.

Del smiled and asked us to follow him. We weaved through a couple of small tables, past the Moai, to a quiet spot in the back of the restaurant.

"Brad, that drink hit me harder than I thought it would. I need some air." My head was starting to swim. "I'll be right back."

I eased my way past the bar, through the narrow front hallway, past the hostess desk, and out the front door. The darkness of the interior matched the darkness of the night. Cool air hit my face. I walked to a wooden bench and propped my palms on the back, closing my eyes, breathing in, breathing out. I needed to relax. I needed to chill.

I opened my eyes, prepared to face whatever the night brought. Which was too bad, really, because as it turned out the night brought Tex, leaning against the back of my car, arms folded across his chest.

FOUR

"What are you doing here?" I asked.

"What do you think?" Tex smiled, softening the hard planes of his face and igniting the flirtatious glint in his eye. I hadn't seen that look for several months, and considering the crime scene we'd been at earlier, I was surprised to see it now.

"I think you're checking up on me."

"Maybe I wanted to see how your date was going," Tex said.

"It's not a date."

He scanned the fitted bodice of my dress. "Looks like a date dress," he said.

"I had to change. You saw the other outfit." I'd put this dress on because it was the counter-opposite to the blood-stained corduroys: innocent, feminine, sweet. "It had Stanley Mann's blood on it," I finished.

"Here's the thing. We don't think that was Stanley Mann. There was no wallet, no identification. We got a neighbor to come in and she said she didn't recognize the guy."

"But who else would it be?" I asked.

"That's the hundred thousand dollar question."

I shivered for a moment as an unexpected cool breeze blew past us. Tex reached forward and adjusted the cardigan around my shoulders.

"How's the dog?"

"Scared, but fine. One of the officers is going to look after him until we figure out what happened to his owner."

"Were there signs of a struggle? Any evidence that someone else was there?"

"The marinara was still warm. Whatever happened over there happened right before you showed up."

I shivered again, but not because of the temperature.

"Night, why would this Brad guy send you a collectible five thousand dollar bill?"

"I don't know. Maybe he's really, really sorry for what he did to me and is trying to buy a lot of forgiveness."

"Did it work?"

"Not even close."

We stared at each other for a couple of seconds. I didn't offer anything else about the conversation Brad and I had in the back room of Pierot's Studio when he first showed me the framed James Madison on the wall. I also didn't mention the promise I'd made Brad.

"I thought you'd like to know a little more about our victim," Tex said.

"Since when do you report in to me about your cases?"

"He was shot," he said, ignoring my question. "Five times."

"Sounds like someone didn't like him."

"One new one. You might have seen that one. And four old bullet wounds. Healed, mostly. Scattered over his thigh. Can't tell if they were from the same gun that killed him until I get a report from ballistics and that's going to take some time. He probably walked with a limp. Sound familiar?"

I misunderstood. "Tex, I have a torn ACL, not a series of gunshot wounds. Just because I occasionally walk with a limp doesn't mean I'm a card-carrying member of the 'injured below the waist' club."

One of Tex's eyebrows shot up for a second, and his eyes flicked to a place below my waist that was definitely not my knee. His gaze returned to my eyes. "He didn't have any identification, so for now he's a John Doe."

"But I talked to someone at Paper Trail not long before I got there. He said he was Stanley Mann. If the man I found wasn't Stanley, then where *is* Stanley?"

"We don't know. There's a chance you didn't talk to Stanley Mann but someone using his name. Based on what we know, our vic might have attracted attention because of his injury. Somebody might remember him, help us figure out who he is. Once we have an identity, we can start working on why he was at Paper Trail. We're putting out information to the public, trying to figure out if anybody knows anything."

"No wallet?"

"No wallet. No identification at all. Expensive suit, fancy shoes, Rolex. That's about it."

"Why would someone take his wallet but not his Rolex? Especially if it was valuable?"

Suddenly, Tex looked behind me. I turned around. Brad approached, walking casually.

"Maddy, I was worried about you."

He slid his arm around my waist. His fingers rested on my hip, above the pleats on my dress. He and Tex stared at each other for a few seconds.

Tex's face went rigid. Until this moment, the only knowledge he had of Brad Turlington was from the strip of film we'd watched together at the theater. I didn't want to make an introduction, but I wondered why neither of them were doing it for themselves.

"I told you, I needed fresh air," I said.

I felt Tex's eyes on me while I faced Brad. Brad tipped his head down and kissed my cheek. "You want to leave?"

"I'll be back inside in a second."

Tex uncrossed his arms and stood straight. "I need to be getting out of here anyway. You kids have fun tonight."

Without moving my head, my eyes bounced back and forth between the two of them. Brad's hand dropped from my waist, and his fingers closed around my hand. He stepped toward the restaurant and gently pulled me with him. I took two steps and then pulled away, back toward Tex.

He leaned close and whispered in my ear. "Call me tomorrow. I'd like to know your take on things."

I nodded, then returned to Brad's side and went back into the restaurant.

"Who was that?" Brad asked as we reseated ourselves at the table.

"Did I forget to introduce you two? I'm sorry."

"Forget about it. I have to understand that you have a life here, a life that I wasn't a part of. Is he one of your clients?"

"Not exactly." I stared at the windows that faced the parking lot, wondering about the real motivation behind Tex's appearance. The only reason he knew where to find me was because I'd told him. Was he there to check out Brad?

Brad put his elbows on the table and folded his hands in front of him. When he rested his chin on his knuckles, I saw the fine brown hair on his forearms, where his white shirt rode up at his wrists.

"You still have the watch," I said absentmindedly.

He sat up and put a hand on his wrist, then spun his watch around in a circle. The band was black crocodile, setting off a white face with black roman numerals, set in 22 karat gold. It was a classically elegant man's watch that I'd discovered in a pawn shop in Philadelphia one Saturday afternoon while on a break from a design expo.

"Of course I still have the watch. Until I found you here in Dallas, it was the only thing I had from you. I wasn't sure if you were going to be receptive to me showing back up in your life."

"How *did* you find me, Brad? It's not like I left a forwarding address."

"Mr. Pierot told me." He tipped his head down and smiled, then looked back at me. His face softened as he talked about the man who had trained him. "I went to see him a couple weeks ago. He turned eighty-eight. Turns out he read something in the papers about you. I didn't know what you'd been through. He gave me the article, and I tracked you down." He reached a hand across the table and rested it on top of mine. "When I heard about the pillow stalkings, I realized I might really have lost you forever."

"Brad, I have a life here. A life I'm used to, a life I like."

"Is there room for me in that life?"

"I don't think so." I knew it sounded harsh, but it was the truth. I needed Brad to hear it. "The way you showed up at my apartment, I can't handle that. Right now I come and go as I please. I'm still getting my business off the ground. I can't drop it all for you."

"I wouldn't ask you to do that. I'm here now. I'll be here until you're ready for me."

"That's not good enough, Brad. Where have you been? How long are you planning on staying in Dallas? Where are you staying?" My voice rose with every question and when I stopped, I looked around to see if anyone else had heard me. The waiter stood a few feet away getting drinks from the bar. He looked away and carried a tray of wine glasses to a table of college-age girls. "You can't expect me to not ask questions."

He leaned back in his chair. "I've moved around a lot in the past couple of years, but spent most of my time in Virginia. Right now I'm staying in The Brite House Apartments by White Rock Lake. It's a short-term lease and a bachelor apartment." He pulled the black plastic stirrer out of his glass and took a drink. "How long I stay in Dallas has a lot to do with you." He lifted my hand and I pulled it away.

Unlike Brad's sentimentality with the watch, I'd parted with everything he had ever given me. After the lie, I packed the things that I couldn't replace—mostly vintage items I'd collected from estate sales—filled out a change of address form, and left my life behind.

I hadn't been looking for the message from Brad when the police found it in my trunk. If I'd have known it was there, I probably would have thrown it away without watching it, never being the wiser.

What struck me now about that six minutes of film wasn't that Brad had bothered to hide it. It was that his confession had been interrupted by someone who never appeared on film. Six minutes in the camera tipped over. There were four gunshots and then the film went black.

Four gunshots.

Volunteering at that theater had been one of the highlights of my life after moving to Dallas. After viewing that film strip, I never returned. Like owning my building, establishing Mad for Mod as my mid-century modern decorating business, and swimming every morning at Crestwood pool with the elderly set, being involved with the theater had become part of my routine.

Brad's confession had tainted the theater for me. There was no way he would have known I was involved with the newly-renovated classic theater, or known I'd be watching his filmstrip confessional there. That's the way life had played out.

Until the moment Brad showed up at my apartment, I didn't know if he was dead or alive. I'd been going through the motions of my life, waiting for the other shoe to drop. And here he was, sitting across the table from me, telling me his troubles were behind him.

"I thought you were dead," I said.

"Not dead." His voice was low, intimate.

"And when I wasn't thinking you were dead, I thought you might have killed someone."

"I didn't kill anyone."

"How do you know it's over?"

"There was only one way out and I did what I had to do."

Four gunshots. My new five thousand dollar bill. Tex's John Doe with the four old gunshot wounds—and one fresh one to his head.

All of a sudden, I realized that I didn't know this new Brad. I didn't know him well enough to know if he was capable of shooting someone or coming back from the dead.

What I did know was this: the one thing Brad Turlington did not seem to need was a watch.

I became obsessed with the perpetual moving hands on the face of the gold timepiece. The lone crab Rangoon I'd eaten tossed in my stomach, and my face flushed. I pulled my hand away from

Brad's and touched cool fingers to my forehead. I was burning up. I had to get out of there, to process what I thought, acknowledge what I was starting to fear. It couldn't be, I told myself.

"Brad, I think it was a mistake to call you. Do you mind if we call it a night?" I asked.

"You want to leave already?" he asked.

"I want to go home. Alone." I stood up. Before he had a chance to follow, I hurried out of the restaurant to my car. My tires squealed against the asphalt as I peeled out of the lot, wondering if the former love of my life was a murderer. I was so lost in my thoughts that I was two miles into my drive before I realized I was being followed.

FIVE

The car behind me sped up and swerved across the stripe in the middle of the road. Just my luck to be followed by a drunk driver. I tightened my grip on the steering wheel and accelerated, trying to keep a cushion of space between us. I wasn't successful.

There were no other cars around, and the drive from the Polynesian restaurant back to my apartment included a couple of relatively familiar surface streets. I turned right on Turtle Creek Boulevard and snaked down the hill, did a practiced dogleg over the creek before approaching Greenville Avenue, and then made another right. When every pair of headlights eventually turned away except for one, I got nervous. The car behind me wasn't acting like a drunk driver anymore.

The dark sedan closed the gap between us and rammed my back bumper. My head bounced forward, then back. I tried to brake, but the car behind me pushed me forward. My handbag fell onto the floor and the contents spilled out. My phone slid under the passenger side seat. I looked into the rear view mirror but couldn't see the driver. The windows were tinted. All I saw was a dark blob behind the wheel. I hit the gas, speeding up again.

Semi-warm air from the open window, the closest I could get to a fall breeze in Dallas, pushed my hair away from my face and fought against the nervous sweat that had broken out on my forehead. I turned onto a narrow side street, double-backed on the last turn before hitting a cul-de-sac, and returned to Greenville. I slowed and looked in the rearview. The car was a brown sedan.

I sped up and turned into a neighborhood I knew well. The sedan followed. I turned right, then left, then right, then left, then two rights, then a left, then three rights. My Alfa Romeo swung wide on the turns. I fought to straighten it out when I hit a dark street. I checked the rear view mirror. He was still there. The traffic light ahead of me turned yellow. I was too far away to clear it, but I hit the gas and sped through the intersection after the light turned red, accelerating until I reached my apartment. The assigned parking spaces were in a lot behind the building. I pulled into the entrance on the east side of the building, swung the car around and cut the lights, and backed into my space. No other cars pulled in.

I glanced up at my bedroom windows. I lived in the back unit on the second floor. It overlooked the less-than-glamorous parking lot. Soft light filtered through the floor to ceiling pale pink curtains I'd installed in January. I must have forgotten to turn the light off in my haste to meet with Brad.

When I opened the car door and slowly stood up, a flash of pain shot through my left knee. I'd been tense through the drive home, and I felt it. I pulled an umbrella from behind the driver's seat and used it as a cane, distributing my weight off the injured joint while I hurried inside.

I climbed the back staircase and knocked on the door of Effie's apartment. I heard Rocky bark on the other side of the door.

"That was a short dinner," Effie said when she opened the door. She wore an oversized Batman sweatshirt and bright yellow leggings. Her feet were in fuzzy slippers shaped like bear paws.

"I wasn't feeling well and had to leave early. Was Rocky any trouble?"

"Nope. We spent a couple of hours at White Rock Lake. He made friends with a Chihuahua. We came back here and he played with my bear feet. He's pretty pooped right now." She looked over her right shoulder to where Rocky laid on his stomach with his feet thrust out behind him like a frog. He opened his eyes and lifted his head slightly. Effie picked up a leash from a white bookcase and clipped it onto his collar. Rocky stood up and padded over to me. She handed off the leash.

"Where are you two staying tonight?"

I felt my face tense. "Who two?"

"You and Rocky. You're not going to sleep in your apartment, are you? I don't think it would be a good idea with the paint fumes."

"What fumes? What paint?"

"You had the apartment painted, right? There was a guy in there earlier. I haven't noticed any fumes but it's probably not dry yet."

My hand closed tightly around my keys, the sharp, jagged edges cutting into my palm. Rocky pulled me toward the door, winding the leash around my left leg. My hands shook as I reached down the length of the leash to straighten it out.

"Effie, what did this man look like?"

"I couldn't tell. He was wearing a mask."

"What kind of mask?"

"Paint mask," she answered in the tone of a college student who thinks she's talking to an idiot. "But he had a black knit hat on, and safety glasses, so I guess I didn't see very much of him. Why?"

"When did he leave?"

"About half an hour ago. He hurried out of here pretty fast too."

I didn't like it. Half an hour ago I'd been at the restaurant with Brad. If someone had been in my apartment, they'd arrived after I left. My early return would have been unexpected. There was only one person who knew I would be out to dinner, the person who had surprised me with an invitation. Things were starting to add up, but I didn't like the sum.

"Thanks for watching him." I said goodnight, picked Rocky up, and walked to the front of the building to check my mail and the status of the rent box. Carlos, a retired mechanic who lived in the unit next to mine, stood in front of the building, smoking. The tip of his cigarette pierced the night like a fat firefly. He nodded when I approached and I nodded back. The rent box was still padlocked shut. I scanned the street in front of the building. Across the street, a car idled next to the curb. The only evidence that the engine was running was the soft cloud of exhaust that floated from behind the car. I couldn't be sure, but it looked like the same sedan that had followed me home.

I turned around, slowly climbed the stairs, and unlocked my unit. The scent of oil paint hit me. I choked back a cough and leaned in. The rug was pulled back from the far corner, exposing half of the unfinished hardwood floor. Paint trays and rollers were scattered around the room, as if the project had been abandoned unexpectedly.

I descended the back stairs, carrying Rocky under my arm. I ducked out the back door, crossed the parking lot, and let myself out the padlocked gate that served as too little deterrent to keeping our property secure.

I felt a little like I'd fallen down a rabbit hole. My entire reality had been flipped on its ear, and I didn't know what end was up. It was a five block walk from my apartment to my studio. Physical therapy had improved the condition of my knee after it had been reinjured, but this would test the limits of the newly-healed joint. Best case scenario, I'd do more damage to an already chronic injury, but would get to my studio undetected. Worst case, I'd be caught while walking down one of the dark residential streets that completed the maze-like path I took to get from here to there. I was willing to take my chances with my knee.

It was slow going at first. Every couple of steps I looked over my shoulder to see if we were being followed. Rocky pulled me forward. Once we were more than a block into the walk, I cut down a different street. I knew I'd have a variety of sofas on which to sleep and a freezer filled with ice packs for my knee, and right now, that was enough.

I didn't allow myself the luxury of mental distractions while I made my way. I coached myself to keep moving, keep moving, keep moving. The chant worked. I reached the alley that runs behind my studio and ducked into the opening next to the Dumpster. A stray cat scrambled out and triggered Rocky's barking. I shushed him and unlocked the door at the back of the building, locking it behind us once we were inside.

Afraid to turn on any lights, I felt my way along the wall to my office. Light from the street hit the furniture I had staged inside the studio and cast weird images around the walls of the room. I wished the windows had been blacked out, or that I'd installed shades to be drawn during off hours, but I hadn't, and tonight, I paid the price in privacy.

Inside my office was a custom desk, a white leather office chair, and a couple of Barcelona chairs for customers. Rocky went directly to his dog bed in the corner and curled into a ball. I wished I could do the same. But for me, it was either sleep on a sofa in the showroom, where anyone passing by could look inside and see me, or sleep on the floor of the office. Despite the guaranteed kink in my neck and promise of pains in various parts of my body, it didn't take a rocket scientist to figure out which was the better plan.

I found a crocheted blanket draped over the side of a raspberry-colored sofa. I grabbed the blanket and a pillow with an atom embroidered on the center of it and carried them back to the office, assembling a makeshift bed on the floor.

I spent the next four hours staring at the ceiling.

Someone had terrorized me on the way home from the restaurant. It could have been Brad. It could have been anyone. But while I was at the restaurant, someone had been in my apartment. It was entirely possible that Brad had orchestrated the opportunity for someone else to get inside while I was out.

The question was why? Why would someone want to get into my apartment when I wasn't there? With the exception of a closet filled with vintage dresses from the fifties and sixties, and a modest collection of furniture I'd cherry picked from the Mad for Mod inventory, I had little worth stealing.

Unless the thief was after the five thousand dollar bill.

Which made even more sense when I thought about where it had come from.

I was starting to think Brad's reasons for seeking me out in Dallas had less to do with the promise of a bright future and more to do with the deep, dark secrets in his past.

SIX

Two years ago I would have trusted Brad with my life. Today, he was a stranger. He'd been the genesis of my trust issues, and now I had a hard time getting past them.

The brass starburst clock that Hudson had rewired for me ticked off the seconds, the minutes, the hours. It wasn't the first thing Hudson had fixed for me, and I'd started to wonder if I should trust him with fixing more than just inanimate objects. Truth was, Hudson was more than a handyman; he was a friend. He could have been more if I was willing to drop the walls I'd put in place after my breakup with Brad.

When I left Philadelphia and moved to Dallas, I bought an apartment complex and hung out a shingle for my own mid-century modern interior decorating business. I busied myself with flea markets, estate sales, and other more creative ways to obtain inventory that included obituaries and the recently deceased. I pretended my past didn't exist. At the time, I thought it was the best way to function. Start over. Start fresh. Take care of myself. Move on.

I met Hudson six months after moving to Dallas. I was interviewing carpenters who could repair the damaged furniture I'd found in dumpsters and trash piles. He was the one who suggested I adopt a puppy. His artistic temperament and Johnny Cash good looks made a combination that, under normal circumstances, would have caught my interest, but a relationship would have complicated my life in ways I didn't want. And now, with Brad turning up in Dallas, the complications had complications.

I closed my eyes. Only an occasional siren, far in the distance, punctured the otherwise silent hours. I readjusted my position somewhere around four thirty. I finally fell into a tortured sleep somewhere after five.

The rattling of the studio door woke me up. I was disoriented, stiff, scared, and alone. Sometime during the night, Rocky left the comfort of his dog bed and joined me. The knocking woke him,too.

Sunlight flooded the studio. When I stood, several joints popped like a cheap package of explosives on the Fourth of July. I had slept in my dress, which had ridden up to my waist. I pulled it down, tried, unsuccessfully, to smooth out the creases that had developed overnight, and ran my fingers through my short hair. The knocking on the front door resumed. I peeked my head out of the office. A thin man with Mediterranean features stood in front of the door. He was dressed in a navy and white checked shirt, navy and white v-neck sweater, and navy blue trousers. A skinny navy tie was visible at his collar.

I balled up the pillow and blankets and tossed them in the powder room behind my desk. After pulling the door shut behind me, I walked to the front of the studio.

"Welcome to Mad for Mod," I said, as I unlocked the door from the inside. I held the door open. "Technically I'm not open, so you surprised me."

"I'm sorry. I drove past and saw your windows. The sign on the door says Open. I can come back if you'd prefer," he stammered.

I looked at the door. I didn't remember flipping the sign, but he was right.

"No, it's fine. I'd be opening in a few minutes anyway. I'm Madison Night," I said, and held out my hand.

"Archie Leach," said the man, returning my handshake.

Archibald Leach was the real name of actor Cary Grant. The nervous man in front of me couldn't have been further from his namesake.

"How can I help you, Mr. Leach?"

"I like your style. I mean, your decorating style." He blushed as though he'd said something inappropriate. "I recently moved into an apartment in Turtle Creek. For the past five years, it's been my wife and me, but now it's just me."

"I'm sorry," I said automatically, though I wasn't sure what I was apologizing for.

"Me too. Seems she wasn't so interested in me as a husband. Now, I'm back on my own."

"Once you get past the sting of it, you might find this is an exciting time."

He looked at me as though I were speaking another language. "How does this work? Do you want to see the apartment?" he asked.

I seriously doubted that Mr. Leach would come back to see me if I said it was as bad time. "Let's start with your contact information and address. We can get some of the paperwork out of the way."

We went to my office. Mr. Leach sat in one of the Barcelona chairs, while I pulled a New Client form from a drawer.

"The first page is contact information: name, address, phone number, email. The next two pages get into what room you'd like to have designed and any specifics you like. Designers, textures, textiles, et cetera."

He looked at the wall covered in paint chips, fabric swatches, pages from magazines, and stills from Doris Day movies. Thanks to a lifelong obsession with the actress, after discovering that we shared a birthday, I found inspiration in her vast body of work. From *Calamity Jane* to *With Six You Get Eggroll*, the precision and beauty of mid-century design was caught on the sets of her films, and, by studying it, I had perfected my eye.

I caught my reflection in the glass of a framed set of Eichler floor plans. I looked worse than I thought. The front door chimed and I excused myself. "I'll give you a couple of minutes." I stood from my desk and stepped out front.

A petite woman with jet black hair was bent over a Rat Pack-era portable bar that I used to house cleaning products.

"Connie? Is that you?" I asked.

She stood up straight and broke out in a smile. "I'm glad you opened early. I have news," she said dramatically.

Connie Duncan and her husband Ned were two of my newer clients. They'd recently bought a small house on Mockingbird Lane, a stretch of flat-roofed ranches that were among the cheaper properties in Dallas because of their unfortunate eighties remodel. The Duncans were interested in undoing the damage and reviving the original mid-century style. They claimed my method of using original pieces I'd amassed from estate sales, flea markets, and dumpsters had caught their attention. I suspected it had more to do with my new-client friendly rates and willingness to work with their shoestring budget.

"I wanted you to be the first to know. Well, not the first because Ned's the first, but the second, but really Ned's the second because I'm the first, not counting the insurance company—"

"Connie," I said and patted the air with my hand, prompting her to lower her voice. "I have a client in the office. Give me a second to finish up."

I left her wandering around the studio while I went back to see Mr. Leach. He was hunched over the application, the end of the pen in his mouth, deep in thought.

"How are you doing?"

"I'm having a hard time deciding."

"On what?" I asked. "Maybe I can help."

"You want me to list the room I want you to work on, but I want you to do the whole apartment. I can't decide where I want you to start."

"Why don't we decide that together after a walk through?"

He set the pen down and exhaled, as though I'd presented the solution to the biggest problem in his life. I had a feeling his divorce was taking more out of him than he would have liked to admit.

"Thank you, Mrs. Night."

"Call me Madison."

"Thank you Madison." He stood up and held out a hand. "When will you be in touch?"

"How's tomorrow?"

"Great."

I walked him to the door and watched him leave. He walked down the block and turned onto one of the narrow side streets, disappearing from sight.

"Connie?" I called. "I'll be out in a second."

She popped up from an orange ottoman. "No rush."

I went back to my office and picked up the receiver on the yellow donut phone that sat on the corner of my desk. I dialed Tex's number from memory.

"Lt. Allen," he answered.

"Lieutenant, it's Madison. I need to see you."

"One of these days I'm going think you mean that in a different way."

"Something happened after I saw you at Trader Josh's."

His voice took on an edge. "Where are you?"

"My studio."

"I'll be right there."

"Wait. I need a favor first." I paused. "Can you go to my apartment and bring me a couple of things?"

"Night, the citizens of Dallas don't pay me to be your personal assistant."

"Fine, I'll do it myself."

"Does the personal assistant gig come with perks? Because maybe I'll reconsider."

I slammed down the phone.

When I wandered out of the office into the studio, I found Connie studying a shelf of mid-fifties kitchen appliances in shades of yellow and aqua. She didn't hear me approach and jumped when she saw me.

"What's your big news?" I asked.

"I finally got reimbursed for a car accident two years ago. Totally not my fault, by the way, so don't let that affect your decision to let me drive your car some day. Anyway, Ned agreed that we should use the money for the kitchen. I've got one word for you: *atomic*! Can you fit me into your schedule?"

"Sure," I said. Immediately, I pictured Rod Taylor's kitchen in *The Glass Bottom Boat*. I hoped both Connie and Ned knew what they were in for.

Connie was the closest thing I had to a girlfriend in Dallas. The rest of my friends were either still in Pennsylvania or people I'd befriended over the Internet through decorating forums and volunteer work at the theater.

"Come to my office. I'm having a hard time getting started this morning." I ushered her in front of me and trailed behind her.

"No offense, but you don't look so good," Connie said when she reached my desk.

She wore a fitted baby doll T-shirt with a picture of a pin-up girl on the front, dark denim jeans with a two inch cuff, and black penny loafers. Her black hair was held back with a pair of cat eye sunglasses, and her bangs, trimmed to land above her eyebrows, hung perfectly straight across her forehead.

"I had a rough night," I said.

"I can tell." She handed me a Styrofoam cup of coffee that had come from one of the many 7-Elevens in Dallas. "I couldn't remember if you had a coffee maker here or not, and I don't really function until after I've had at least three of these."

"Thank you."

"It's black," she warned.

"That's fine." I sipped the bitter beverage out of necessity, not desire.

"You need something, I can tell. I'm good at reading people. What is it?"

"I need a change of clothes, but I don't want to go back to my apartment."

She leaned forward. "You spent the night here?"

"I'd rather not get into details, if you don't mind."

"I can bring you clothes. I have a whole closet full of them. Anything else?"

"Knock on the door when you're back. I'm going to lock up behind you."

"Madison, are you in some kind of trouble?"

I considered the truth, but I knew too little about my situation to know what the truth really was.

"I'm avoiding someone, that's all."

"Ex-boyfriend?"

"Something like that."

"I knew it had to be juicy. Listen. Stay put and I'll be back in a jiffy and you can tell me all about it."

That's what I was afraid of.

Connie returned with a change of clothes and an overnight kit. I freshened up in the powder room behind my office, changed from the wrinkled peony printed dress into a tight red pencil skirt and a short sleeved sweater with a scoop neck. A pair of red patent leather kitten heeled pumps was in the bottom of the bag. Connie didn't understand the reason I wore ballerina flats and canvas sneakers most of the time had as much to do with functionality as it did style. Judging the rockabilly style of both of the Duncans, I wasn't surprised by her taste.

"If I looked that good in a wiggle dress, I'd wear one all the time," she proclaimed when I returned to the room. "Here, tie this in your hair." She handed me a red and white polka-dotted chiffon scarf. I handed it back.

The door chimes sounded again. "Madison?" called Tex.

Connie put one hand palm-side out toward me and held the other in front of her mouth, motioning for me to be quiet. She stepped into the studio.

"You bastard!" she said.

I followed her into the studio just in time to see her slap Tex across the face.

SEVEN

Tex's hand flew to his cheek. The slap left a red mark. Connie stood in front of him with her hands on her hips. She was no more than five feet tall, but based solely from the look on her face, if they were to throw down, I'd put my money on her.

"What the hell was that for?" Tex asked. "Who are you?"

"I'm Connie. Aren't you the ex from Madison's past?"

"No," I said, stepping out of the doorway. "He's the *Tex* from Madison's past."

"What?" they said in unison.

"Connie Duncan, meet Lt. Allen. Lieutenant, meet my client, Connie Duncan."

"Lieutenant?" Connie said, her eyes wide. "I assaulted a police officer?"

"I don't think the lieutenant is going to press charges, are you?" I asked Tex.

"I haven't decided," he said.

I ducked into my office, pulled a cold glass bottle of Coke from the mini-fridge, and returned to the studio. I handed the bottle to Tex, and he held it against his cheek.

"Connie, can you give us a minute? Maybe take Rocky out for a walk?"

"Sure. I'm sorry, Lieutenant. I didn't know—"

"Forget about it."

Connie collected Rocky's leash and clipped it onto his collar while Tex and I stood by my office door. After she left, he opened my office and set the Coke bottle on the edge of my desk. His eyes lingered on my outfit.

"She thought you were Brad," I said.

His eyebrows went up.

"I told her I spent the night here and she brought me a change of clothes."

"You spent the night here to avoid your ex?"

"I don't want to talk about my ex."

Tex followed me to the front door. I looked up and down the street and spotted Connie about half a block away, across the street from one of Greenville Avenue's many Tex-Mex restaurants. Rocky trotted at a spirited pace, stopping occasionally to lift a leg and pee on a strip of crab grass that had sprouted up through one of the cracks on the sidewalk.

"I never noticed what a sweet walk you have, Night," Tex said.

"It's not me, it's the skirt. For the record, I would not have picked this outfit out for myself."

"Connie's responsible for this look? As far as I'm concerned, she's forgiven."

"I don't want to have to explain any of this to her. As far as she knows, I'm a successful interior decorator who may or may not be designing her new atomic kitchen."

"What's an atomic kitchen?"

"A colorful kitchen renovation re-imagined with the space-age, robotic influence of the fifties."

"Assuming that's even possible, someone actually wants that?"

"Mid-century decorating is a niche market, and I happen to be good at it."

He dropped his head and shook it from side to side. "Atomic kitchen. Crazy."

"Lieutenant, she doesn't know what happened yesterday. Can we keep it that way?"

"Sure. Why am I here again?"

"I called you. I told you I needed to see you. That was like twenty minutes ago. Remember?"

"Sorry. Once I saw you in that outfit, everything else went out the window."

"Maybe Connie was right to slap you."

"Maybe she was, but not because of this."

"So, how's life, Lieutenant? Are you still seeing Officer Nasty?"

"See, Madison, things were going perfectly fine until you brought her up." He rubbed his forehead. "Donna and I have gone out a couple of times. It's not like I asked her to wear my class ring."

I raised my eyebrows. He rubbed his hand over his eyes and forehead, then pushed his hair back and shrugged. "Feels like I'm driving Rizzo to Thunder Road with you sitting there looking like that." He shook his head. "Donna's fine. She's better than fine. Only, she's not like you."

Now there was an understatement.

My first run-in with Officer Donna Nast was during the homicide investigation. Her nickname, "Nasty," had been used by more than one officer, including Tex. She was a classic late-twenties bombshell, with long, chocolate brown hair, bottle-green eyes, and the kind of body that probably inspired a lot of wishful thinking. I'd bet that wishful thinking had more to do with her nickname than any behavior on her part. Tex was twenty years older than her, but in cop world, that didn't seem to matter.

I was the counter opposite of Nasty: blonde-haired, blue-eyed, forty-seven years old. I was a vintage-wearing, sunscreen-addicted Doris Day lookalike. It was the Doris Day lookalike part that put me at the center of a homicide investigation and had almost gotten me killed.

Tex had called me to the carpet on the emotional walls I'd put in place—ironic, since I was an interior decorator. I didn't like to admit that he'd gotten through. And despite the fact we'd kissed—a kiss we never acknowledged, but occasionally kept me awake at night—we moved on in separate directions. Tex and Nasty had fallen back into their on-again, off-again relationship.

I rebuilt my emotional walls faster than a bricklayer on a deadline and moved on with my life. And now, here I was. Sitting next to a playboy police lieutenant while my past reared its ugly head and threatened my way of life. Funny how life throws you the kind of curve ball where hanging out with a homicide detective is a pleasant escape from reality.

Tex and I stared at each other across my desk. The donut phone jingled its shrill ring that had become all too popular now that people could program it into their iPhones. I made no move to answer it. The machine clicked on after the fourth ring and Brad's voice filled the room.

"Hi Maddy. Just wanted to check in and see how you're feeling. I guess this is a lot, me showing up out of the blue. I didn't want to scare you off last night. I want to hear from you, to make sure you're okay. I'm still at The Brite House Apartments. I'll be here if you need me." He disconnected.

I focused on a pair of Holt salt and pepper shakers shaped like cats. They sat on either side of my computer screen. The wide, almond-shaped eyes of the cats looked suspicious, like they could read my thoughts.

"I left the restaurant shortly after you did. Someone followed me. No—not followed me. Someone tried to scare me. At first, I thought it was a drunk driver, so I took a lot of different roads until it was just me and a brown sedan behind me. The driver bumped into the back of my car a couple of times."

"Are you okay?"

"My neck is sore. I'm not sure if it's from being hit or sleeping on the floor."

"Night, that's not a joke."

"I know it's not a joke, Lieutenant. I was going to call you when I got home, but my neighbor said someone had been in my apartment. I went to leave and saw a car that might have been the one that followed me parked across the street. I left out the back door and walked here."

"You should have called me when you got here. I could have sent a car over to look for your friend in the brown sedan."

"Once I got here, I was fine. Besides, calling you feels like using a Get Out of Jail Free card."

I turned the salt shaker over in my hands while I talked. When Tex wasn't in lock down police mode, I could read his expressions fairly well. I didn't need to see *I told you so* written on his face.

"Did you go into your apartment?"

"No. Well, I looked inside. Effie was right. There's paint on the walls and a torn up carpet."

"You didn't want your apartment painted?"

"I started painting it yesterday. When Brad showed up, I tipped over the paint can. I didn't finish the job. Seems like someone is finishing it for me."

"What happened next?"

"I went out front, saw the car parked on a side street. At least it looked like the same car, and the engine was running. I ducked out the back and walked here."

"Does anybody know you spent the night here?"

"Only you and Connie."

His eyes dropped to my chest again. "I think you should consider bringing Connie on as your personal assistant. She shows good judgment."

The phone rang again. Again, I made no move to answer it. The machine clicked on, and I held my breath.

"Madison, it's Joanie from Joanie Loves Tchotchkes. I have a box of stuff here with your name on it. I'll be open until six." The message clicked off.

I grabbed a notepad and scribbled a message to myself. "Is there anything else, Tex?"

"Who was that?" he asked, his eyes trained on the phone.

I waved my hand to dismiss his interest. "That's a local thrift store owner. She calls me when she gets mid-century stuff. Ever since the *Dallas Morning News* ran that article about the pillow stalking, people know my routine. I used to fly under the radar and get first dibs on inventory but now everybody follows the obituaries."

Tex leaned back in his chair and studied my face.

"Say what you want, but that's my real life. Thrift stores, flea markets, Doris Day movies, dumpster diving. If you weren't standing here, I'd be on my way to her store."

"Night, is that how you want to live? Deny reality and build a world from a movie set?"

I stood up and slapped my hands palm-side down on the desk. "If I were interested in denying reality, I wouldn't have called you. I wouldn't be in the middle of this mess right now."

"What exactly do you want me to do?"

"Can you nose around Brad's background? See if you find any red flags?"

"The man lies to you about being married, to spare you from getting involved in something probably illegal. You freak out at the news and wind up hospitalized and still, he doesn't fess up. That was two years ago. Last May you got damn close to being killed by a murderer, and he doesn't show up until now? The fact that he showed up at all suggests to me he's known where you were the whole time. Want me to keep going?"

"There's a lot of history you don't know."

"And I don't want to know. That's in the past. Aside from your wardrobe, you haven't impressed me as someone who wants to live in the past."

"I'm not living in the past. I'm trying to live in the present. That's why I need you. Can you help me? Do a background check on him or something?"

"No, Madison, I can't. There are codes of conduct to being a cop. I know it took a lot for you to tell me about this, but he's a private citizen. U

nless he breaks the law, he's entitled to come and go as he wishes."

"So that's it. I'm on my own."

"Not exactly."

The chimes announced the return of Rocky and Connie. I tried to stand up, but the fabric of the sweater had gotten caught in my chair. I shifted my shoulders up and down, trying to free it. Tex came around the back of my chair, sliding his hand behind my neck. His fingers were like soft pads of fire burning through my skin. I didn't pull away. He freed the fabric and put his hands under my arms to help me stand. I stepped to the side of my chair and his hands slid down the sides of my body.

I turned to face him. His hands rested on my waist, our bodies almost touching. The kitten heels felt unfamiliar and I swayed forward, falling against him. He easily righted me and I stepped away.

Rocky bounded into the office. He yapped around Tex's feet, his caramel fur bouncing as he sniffed the lieutenant's leather shoes. He hopped up on his hind legs with his paws in the air. His back paws moved in tiny steps, like a ballerina in toe shoes for the first time. Connie came into the office as Tex withdrew a plastic bag filled with bone-shaped biscuits from the pocket of his windbreaker. He held one about six inches over Rocky's head; Rocky snatched it. Tex ruffled Rocky's fur and stood back up. Our eyes connected for a brief moment before I looked away, still flushed.

"Take care, Madison." He put on his silver aviator sunglasses and opened the door. Halfway through, he turned back and looked at Connie. "No hard feelings, Ms. Duncan." The door snapped shut behind him and he disappeared around the side of the building.

"Madison, is everything okay? What was a cop doing here?"

"He's a friend. That's all."

"Does he have a dog, too?"

"Not that I know of. Why?"

She shrugged. "I can't think of any other reason why some guy would be walking around with dog treats in the pocket of his coat, unless he was planning to run into a dog. Seems like maybe the lieutenant wanted to make an impression on you." She leaned backward and looked at the front door, then back at me. "Forget the ex. What about him? What's his story?"

"He has a girlfriend."

"Yeah, that's going to work."

*   *   *

I ushered Connie out the door with a stack of sketches for her kitchen. She was eager to share them with her husband and I was eager to find a way to lower my temperature. If ever there was a time to deny reality, this was it.

Joanie Higa was the owner of a small second-hand store called Joanie Loves Tchotchkes. She knew my style, my taste, and my budget. When she called, I responded. Besides, I was happy for the distraction.

I filed the notes on Archie Leach's apartment and changed out of the kitten heels and into a spare pair of white Keds that I kept in the office. I clipped Rocky's leash onto his collar and led him through the back parking lot to my car. Rocky hung his head out the passenger side window as I drove to Joanie's store. Twenty minutes later, I parked in front.

The doors to Joanie Loves Tchotchkes were propped open. Outside of the store, a selection of hodgepodge furniture sat under a Sale sign. I stepped past a Papasan chair and a small twin bed with a white wooden frame, gave the leash a tug so Rocky would ignore the patch of grass and went inside. Rocky sniffed everything within range.

A petite Japanese-American woman in her late fifties arranged a set of pink and copper canisters behind the register. She had jet black hair styled in a beehive and black liquid liner painted in a manner befitting a character in a Matt Helm movie.

"Check you out. Except for the sneakers, you look pretty hot. Are you going on a date? Is that what's been keeping you away from my store?"

"Not exactly."

"It's been so long I thought you found another source."

"I wish. My sources have all but dried up. I'm going to have to start taking road trips to the panhandle. Nobody's heard of me there."

"I wouldn't be too sure of that."

Years ago Joanie had retired from work in a corporate office, and now she owned a store that dealt in collectibles. Her uniform of choice was a white, zip-front beauty salon smock over skinny dark denim jeans. Joanie Loves Tchotchkes had been born when she cashed out her 401k and used her corporate training to write a business plan. Six months, a bank loan, and a series of strategic shopping trips to flea markets all over Texas was all she needed to open for business. I'd met her in Canton, where the First Monday Trade Days lured people in search of the treasures that came from attics and garages.

"Do you want me to carry your box to your car?"

"Not that I don't admire your hard-sell technique, but maybe I should see what you have before you assume I want to take it."

Her face scrunched up. "I'm not selling you anything today. Some guy dropped off a box and it had your name on it."

"I know that's what you said, but I don't understand."

"Maybe it'll make sense when you see it. Wait here."

Joanie disappeared into a doorway at the back of the store. My eyes glided over the assortment of knick knacks and *objet d'arts* that filled every nook and cranny of the interior. Joanie never met a tchotchke she didn't love, and her store shelves reflected it. Metal key stripping had been installed vertically on the walls, allowing for adjustable shelves to be placed where needed. She kept smaller items by the front of the store: salt and pepper shakers, Kokeshi dolls, and tiny frames. A glass case housed jewelry—nothing too valuable—including an assortment of brightly colored metal flower pins. I'd bought a few of these and pinned them onto the lapels of my vintage suits or dresses. On top of the glass case was her cash register, as old as most of her inventory.

And on the wall, above a mechanic's pin-up girl calendar from 1961, was a framed five thousand dollar bill I'd never seen in her store before.

Two five thousand dollar bills showing up in the Lakewood area in the same week? I didn't know what it meant, but whatever it was, I didn't like it.

I lifted the frame from the wall and turned it over. A small white price tag attached to a piece of string had been taped to the back of the wood. $100 was written in Joanie's sloppy cursive script. The frame had been glued together. I'd have to break the whole thing apart if I wanted to get at the bill inside.

Joanie returned from the back of the store, lugging a cardboard box. Rocky pulled his leash forward and hopped around her ankles. The flaps of the box were folded shut, and my name was written on top. Mad for Mod had been added below.

Joanie set the box on the glass case and patted the top of it twice. "Look familiar?"

I stepped forward to get a closer look and shook my head. "How'd you get it?"

"Some guy brought in a couple of boxes. This was only one of them. He was probably told to drop them off and got mixed up." She looked at the frame I held. "Funny you're looking at that. It came in from the same guy who dropped off this box."

EIGHT

"Who was he?" I asked.

"I don't really know. I mean, I saw the guy, but I've never seen him before. He said he was told to drop off a bunch of boxes. I almost felt guilty when I saw the stuff."

"Why?"

"It's right up your alley. If he came to you first, you probably would have made him an offer. But he came to me. You and I could probably make some kind of deal."

"I thought you said you felt guilty!"

"Your MO is to work with the dead. This guy was very much alive. Chances are, you would never have found each other."

Joanie was referring to my practice of reading the obituaries daily, identifying women of a seventy- to ninety-year old range who had passed, and making an offer on their estates to the next of kin. Brad was the one who taught me to do this back when he trained me at Pierot's. My first attempts at estate sale offers felt awkward and uncomfortable, but, with time and practice, I'd polished my approach. Reaching out to sons and daughters who had no interest in the never-renovated estates of their parents actually helped them. Most of the time they accepted my check and turned over the keys with gratitude. A few even sent thank you notes.

When I started Mad for Mod, I stocked my storage space and studio with pieces from these estate sales. My unorthodox business practice had been secret, until one particular estate turned out to be a crime scene. After the homicide was solved, the newspaper ran a profile on me and exposed my secret to the world, or at least, to the greater Dallas-Fort Worth area. Auction houses jumped on the bandwagon, outbidding me on estates but offering me a private viewing of the merchandise at their suggested prices. I'd had to come up with a different method for finding my inventory.

"Earth to Madison," Joanie prompted.

"What?"

"You spaced out. I thought for sure that 'working with the dead' crack would get a reaction."

"It's not how I'd put it, but if you keep talking up my old method like that, maybe the auction houses will decide it's too ick-factor for them, and I can go back to business as usual."

"You seem to be doing okay."

"So do you," I answered. "What else can you tell me about the guy who brought this stuff in?"

"Oh, no. You're not cutting off my supply. I have to make a living too."

Rocky sensed that Joanie was challenging me. He backed a few feet away from her legs, tipped his head back, and issued two short, sharp barks. We both looked at him. He looked at me, then back at her, and barked again.

It was evident Rocky misunderstood our standoff, and Joanie misunderstood my interest in the man who had sold her the box. I scooped Rocky up and rubbed his belly.

"Fine, be a businesswoman. Do you know if this guy is planning to bring in anything else?"

"He didn't say. Why?"

"If he had one box for me, then maybe he has something else I'd like. Do me a favor? If he brings in anything else, I want you to give me first right of refusal." While I was talking, I reached into my wallet and counted out five twenties. Her eyes dropped from my face to my hands.

"What's that for?"

"I'm buying this." I held up the framed currency. Rocky wriggled around in my arms, and I set him on top of the glass case of vintage jewelry. He sniffed a bowl of marbles.

"What do you want with that piece of crap? You could download the image from the Internet, print it, and buy a better frame at a craft store, all for a quarter of the price."

"Consider it a good faith investment in future purchases."

She peeled off her rubber gloves and squirted hand sanitizer into her palms. She pulled a box of surgical gloves from under the counter and held it out to me. "If you're taking that box, you might want to wear these."

"This is an odd business for a germophobe," I said.

"Since when do you know me to be a germophobe? This is precautionary. The guy who dropped that stuff off was covered with poison ivy. He warned me I might catch it from the cardboard and gave me the box of gloves. I don't know if he's full of BS or not, but I don't plan on taking any chances."

I wasn't sure if poison ivy was transferrable by cardboard but didn't want to insult Joanie, so I pulled on a pair of gloves.

"Poison ivy? He told you that?"

"He saw me looking at the rash on his hands. Small red spots popped up on his face, too, right by his hairline. The poor guy was trying his hardest not to scratch, I could tell, but he wasn't succeeding. I gave him a bottle of Calamine lotion before he left and I saw him dot it on in his car before he drove away." She laughed. "I sure hope he was heading home, because he didn't make a very nice picture, all spotted up like that."

She punched a couple of keys on the register and placed my twenties under the cash tray. She wrapped the frame in newsprint. I set it on top of the box, led Rocky back to the car, and drove home.

After parking the car and letting Rocky pee on the weeds behind my parking space, I unlocked the back door and climbed the stairs to my unit. There was a note from Hudson taped to my front door.

Once I had determined Hudson's vision and skills far surpassed other contractors I'd hired, he became my go-to contractor. He outdid himself on most projects, understanding the simplicity of mid-century design, often taking the extra step of fabricating a necessary element from scratch instead of relying on prefab parts available at home renovation stores.

It hadn't taken long for me to confide in him that I'd bought an apartment building. He was up to the task of taking on minor fixes—mostly electrical and paint jobs—but what really won me over was his agreement to spend a weekend with me, stripping all of the bathroom fixtures of the bland white paint the former owner had used to mask the original pink ceramic. When I started taking tenant applications, I knew only the right kind of people would appreciate the work we'd put in.

Because I preferred to keep my identity as landlord a secret, Hudson occasionally stepped in as the liaison to the Night Company. My neighbors didn't know me as Madison Night, they knew me as Madison and Rocky. New tenants received Hudson's contact information in their welcome packets and were encouraged to call him directly if they needed work done.

I often found invoices taped to the doorknob in the same manner I had him notify tenants of upcoming fire alarm inspections and water shut-off. I paid him immediately and constantly offered him partnership in either the business, the building, or both. He always thanked me and always refused.

I peeked inside the folded piece of paper before unlocking the door. Instead of an invoice, it was a note. *Madison, call me when you get a chance. –H.*

I folded the paper in half and in half again before going inside. Rocky ran ahead of me. I stopped, two feet in, and dropped my keys on the floor. They clattered against the newly exposed hardwood flooring. I stepped back two steps and checked the number on the outside of the door even though I knew I was home. I went back inside and shut the door behind me.

Soft yellow paint glowed in a satin finish from the walls. It was like stepping into a ray of sunshine. The apartment-grade carpet had been torn up and replaced with hardwood flooring, and the furniture had been repositioned. Vases of daisies peppered the room on tables, shelves, and window sills.

Above the sofa was a canvas, painted in vertical stripes of white, yellow, and ivory. It was about as wide as the sofa, six feet, and about two and a half feet tall. All in all, it was a beautifully designed room, and, being an interior designer myself, it surprised me that I didn't want to change a thing.

I unclipped Rocky's leash and he ran to the sofa and hopped up. His stuffed black panther had been carefully placed on top of a pink pillow, and he grabbed it with his teeth and shook his head rapidly, the legs flapping against the sides of his face.

A snaky tendril of anxiety crept up my back and chilled my shoulders. I turned around and looked at the room one more time.

Of course it was perfect.

Of course it was me.

Brad had done this.

But when? The only time I'd been away from the apartment was to go to dinner with him. He couldn't be in two places at the same time. The initial delight I'd felt at finding the room so suited to me now faded.

I wasn't ready to admit maybe Brad *did* know me better than anybody else in my life. I looked at the piece of paper in my hand—Hudson's note. I turned my back on the room and called him.

"Hudson?"

"Madison."

I smiled to myself. Hudson's deep voice made me feel cozy and protected. It wrapped around me like an electric blanket on a cold night, though cold nights in Dallas were few and far between. "You wanted me to call you?"

"Yes. Are you free tonight? Can you come over? There's something I want to talk to you about."

"Sure. What time?"

"Whenever you're ready. I'll be here."

"Give me half an hour."

"See you soon."

I half considered wearing Connie's clothes to Hudson's house for a reaction, but once presented with the option of changing, I did. I set the pencil skirt and sweater on the bed and stepped into a lavender-and-white checkered dress with a drop waist. The pleated skirt of the dress grazed my knees, revealing my ACE bandage. I kicked off the white sneakers, stepped into purple ballerina flats, and fluffed my hair with my fingers. After a quick kiss to Rocky, I slicked on lip gloss and left.

Hudson stood in front of his house by an easel. A card table next to him held an assortment of paints and brushes. He waved to me as I pulled into his driveway.

"That was fast," he said.

"I was happy to have an excuse to get out of my apartment. Besides, I didn't want to interrupt your dinner plans."

"Tonight, I'm planning on tossing a steak on the grill and enjoying this nice weather. I'd invite you to stay, but I only have the one steak." He smiled. "Care for a glass of wine?"

"Love one."

He wiped the bristles of the paintbrush off on a towel and set both on the card table. "Follow me." He headed to his garage.

I snuck a look at the canvas as I passed it. He had just started it, or so I assumed by the amount of white space still on the canvas. Squares of color in orange, yellow, and purple had been painted at random, outlined with a thin line of black. The purple and black would have suggested rage to me, but the orange and yellow softened it, giving it a lighter hand.

I was happy Hudson was painting again. His artistic passion infused most of his projects with a sense of purpose, but I knew furniture repair was far from a fulfilling creative outlet for him. I wondered why he never took me up on my offers of partnership. The offer came from a place of appreciation, as did the selfish satisfaction I got when he repeatedly said no.

He wiped the back of his hands on his jeans and turned his amber eyes on me. "Can I ask you a question?"

"Sure."

We stood next to the door that separated the garage from the house. Mortiboy, Hudson's black cat, slunk out of the narrow opening between the house and the garage, and glared at me. He walked to Hudson and brushed his whiskers against the legs of Hudson's jeans.

Mortiboy was an unfriendly sort, except when in the company of his owner. I'd had the pleasure of cat-sitting him briefly a few months ago, and as much as I'd tried to create a bond with the furry black devil, he never quite accepted me or Rocky. Rocky, however, had taken to Mortiboy like fish take to water and followed him around our apartment despite repeated swats to the nose. Hudson scooped up Mortiboy and held him against his chest, scratching the cat's ears until he emitted a rumble.

"Madison, I've been thinking about things differently now my past is cleared up. None of that would have happened if it wasn't for you."

"I never believed for a second you had anything to do with those murders."

"I know. And your belief in me kept me going. There's no way to thank you for what you did for me, but I'd like to try. Do you think we could go out some time?"

"Hudson," I started. "My life is—just got—it's complicated right now. I agreed to take on three new jobs, and the apartment needs repair, and—"

"Your complications don't have anything to do with your business, do they?"

Mortiboy wriggled out of Hudson's arms and jumped to the ground. I looked down at him. As much as I wanted to take Hudson up on his offer, my personal life was rooted in quicksand and until I found solid footing, I was in no place to start a relationship.

"My complications don't have anything to do with business," I confirmed. "You know how you had demons in your closet, demons that I learned of a couple months ago?"

"That's all behind me now, thanks to you."

"I know. One of my demons came knocking on my door yesterday. Can you understand what I mean?"

"I think so."

We stood together, the golden sunset bathing us in a rich glow that gilded the moment.

"Madison, if you need anything while you're sorting out that closet, don't hesitate to ask. For anything."

I thought about Hudson's artistic talents. "Well, there is one thing you could probably help me with," I said.

"Name it," he said.

"Well, you're an artist, and there's something I was wondering about." I looked up at him and took a deep breath. "Hypothetically speaking, how hard would it be to counterfeit a bill?"

NINE

Hudson put a hand on the doorknob, but turned back to face me. He leaned against the door with his hand behind him. For a moment, it felt like he was protecting me from whatever was on the other side of that door.

"Counterfeiting is a lot harder than the movies would make it seem. Impossible if you plan to pass it."

"What if you're selling to a collector? What if it's a denomination that's been out of print?"

"You don't sound like you're asking hypothetical questions anymore." Parts of the doorknob grated against each other as he turned it and pushed the door open. He stood back and let me through first.

I hadn't spent a lot of time in Hudson's house, but I knew the layout. Inside the door was a long hallway that ended in his living room. An orange tweed sofa sat along one wood-paneled wall, and a shag carpet the color of air-popped popcorn softened our footsteps.

This house had once belonged to his grandmother. She'd left it to him when she passed away. While the seventies interior seemed contradictory to Hudson's punk exterior, I knew he'd rather be surrounded by what felt familiar, what felt like family, than to gut it and start over. I liked that about him, that he had a quiet respect for who, and what, had made him the man he was, even if the rest of the world had renounced orange tweed and shag carpeting.

He pulled the cork out of a bottle of red wine and poured two glasses. He set one on top of the table in front of me. Mortiboy sat on the end of the sofa. He didn't move when I sat down, which demonstrated a new level of acceptance from the feline.

"What's this all about?" Hudson asked.

"I don't know."

"Madison, you're asking about counterfeit bills. That doesn't sound like a decorating project. If you know something about a crime in progress or a crime that's been committed, you'd do best to contact your friend on the police force and tell him what you know."

"He's partially aware of it. Besides, I don't really know anything. That's the problem."

Hudson sat down. Gently, he picked up my hand, flipped it over, and rubbed his thumb against my palm. Even though I was silently urging him to continue, he set it back down on my own knee. I took a deep breath and exhaled. I needed to talk and I knew Hudson would listen.

"Somebody sent me a five thousand dollar bill. I once said I could be bought for five thousand dollars, because it's the only bill with my name on it. It's the James Madison. It was a private joke." I looked down at my hands in my lap. "If it's real, it's worth a lot of money. If it's not real, well, I don't know what it means. It could mean somebody is in a lot of trouble."

"Do you know who this somebody is?"

"Somebody is the demon I was telling you about."

"How well do you trust him?"

"I used to trust him with my life."

Hudson picked up his wine glass and took a long sip. I could see him savoring the taste before he swallowed. He leaned back against the cushions of his chair and nodded at me. "But now?"

"The list of people I trust with my life got a lot shorter a couple of months ago."

Hudson was one of the people on that list. My being there, telling about my problem, should have tipped him off if he didn't already know it.

"There's more," I said. I leaned forward and swirled the wine around in my glass. "I was at Joanie Loves Tchotchkes earlier today. She had a framed five thousand dollar bill hanging behind the register. It seems like too much of a coincidence. I think at least one of them is fake. Maybe both. I don't know why someone would counterfeit a bill that's been out of circulation for half a century, but I guess I want to know what would be involved in the process."

"Madison, like you said, I just finished dealing with my own demons. I'm not itching to put myself back on the cops' radar."

I leaned forward and put a hand on his knee. "I would never ask you to do anything illegal. I hope you know that."

Quietly, after a long pause, he said, "It could be done."

"What would it take?"

"A powerful magnifying glass. Saturated inks, a very fine paintbrush. Rag paper, or the materials to make paper with the right fabric content. Maybe a piece of clothing from the era to provide the fibers, in case the paper gets tested."

"Like a forger painting a van Gogh who uses dirt from the original artist's neighborhood?"

"Same principles. How deeply are you involved in this?"

"I don't know yet. I still don't know exactly what it is I'm involved in."

I sipped at my wine but was too lost in my thoughts to enjoy it. Mortiboy curled up on his end of the sofa, his head on his front paw. One eye opened, looked at me, and closed again. Hudson's cat had a suspicious nature and I thought maybe I should take a page from his playbook.

"It's been a long day, and I better be getting home. Rocky finally stopped knocking over lamps, but now he's discovered a taste for vintage shoes. I don't remember if I closed the closet doors or not."

"I figured you'd learned that lesson already," Hudson joked. We both turned to look at Mortiboy, but this time he ignored us.

Hudson followed me out to the car. "That box in your back seat, that's from Joanie's, right?"

"Yes."

"Is the bill in there?"

I reached into the backseat and lifted the flat package. When I turned back around, I unfolded the butcher paper and exposed the rudimentary wooden frame.

"What do you think?"

"I can't say if it's real or not, but I can tell you one thing. Even if it is real, it couldn't come close to what you're worth."

I put a hand on his and his fingers curled around mine. There was something about Hudson's amber eyes that soothed me, made me feel like the rest of the world didn't exist. It wasn't a heated sexual urgency, but a cozy warmth, like being slow roasted over an open fire. He presented me with a cocoon of safety.

"Can I hold on to this for a couple of days?" he asked, lifting the package about an inch.

"Sure. Feel free to take it out of the frame if you want. For all I know, it's a color copy and the backside is blank."

"In the meantime, be careful, Madison," he said.

I didn't reply.

When I arrived at the apartment building, there was a minivan parked by the sidewalk. A redheaded woman stood next to the van and two boys tossed a Nerf football back and forth in the yard. I parked behind the moving van and approached as if I was a friendly person who lived in the building instead of the secret owner and landlord.

"Hi," I called out to the woman.

She held a cell phone to her head, but when she saw me she moved her hand away and set the phone inside the minivan on the passenger side seat.

"Is everything okay?"

She looked confused.

"I live here." I pointed to the building. "You're in a no parking zone, so I thought maybe something was wrong."

"Something is wrong. I've—we've been on the road for three days. I thought we had an apartment all lined up. I filled out paperwork, sent in a deposit, the works. The landlord just called. She said she didn't like the idea of renting to someone she hadn't met so she rented our apartment to someone else."

The older of the boys caught the football and ran over to us. "Mom, can we find a hotel soon? I'm hungry."

"Sure, Tommy. Stay with Billy."

She turned back to me. "I'm Mrs. Young. These are my boys."

"I'm Madison," I said. My eyes darted to the minivan. The back seat was packed with boxes and blankets. It reminded me of how I'd arrived in Dallas: with everything I thought I couldn't replace packed in the back of my car.

"Mrs. Young, I happen to know there's a vacancy in this building. I've lived here for a couple of years, and I like it."

"Is the landlord here? Can I talk to him?"

Inside, I smiled. Almost everyone assumed the landlord was a man, and I used that to my benefit to keep my role a secret. "No, not now. I can get you an application if you'd like."

"That would be great."

"Follow me."

We walked past the boys to the front door. I kept a clipboard filled with tenant applications by the mailboxes. I tore one off the pad and held it out to Mrs. Young. Before she took it I snatched it back and wrote Hudson's number across the bottom. "Call Hudson James."

"He's the landlord?"

"He works for the Night Company. I'll put in a good word for you."

Mrs. Young's face relaxed into a smile and I smiled back. "Thank you, Madison. This would be a nice break for us."

I gave her directions to the closest La Quinta hotel and walked her halfway down the sidewalk. She corralled her boys into the minivan and waved before getting inside and pulling out onto the street. I'd call Hudson about her early tomorrow.

I pulled my car around to the back of the building and backed into my space. After getting out, I came around the side of the car for the box from Joanie Loves Tchotchkes. I pulled the rubber gloves back on before grabbing it from the back seat.

For the second time that day, I entered a room I didn't know. Rocky ran out of the bedroom and danced around my feet. I set the box on the floor and joined Rocky on the carpet. Time to dig into the box.

On top of the box was a T-shirt with the smiling image of my favorite actress. Underneath was the caption, "Have a Doris Day." Under the T-shirt was a scrapbook filled with newspaper clippings about her movie openings. If I ever returned to my volunteer position at the theater, these would be a nice addition to the lobby.

Below the scrapbook were two lobby cards, one from *Midnight Lace*, one from *Julie*. A dog-eared paperback copy of *Day by Day*, her autobiography, was wedged into one of the corners. It was a good night for a bubble-bath and a couple of chapters. I pulled it out and set it in a separate pile from the scrap book and lobby cards. So far, no surprises. Someone who knew I'd modeled my life after Doris Day had arranged for me to receive a box of memorabilia that was worth more in warm, fuzzy, nostalgic feelings than cold, hard cash.

I plunged my hand into the bottom of the box and my fingers closed around a small bundle. I pulled it out with my right hand and transferred it to my left palm. It was wrapped in a white handkerchief monogrammed with the initials PS. I unwrapped the handkerchief and revealed a man's tri-fold, brown leather wallet. I flipped it open, and then flipped it open again. An unfamiliar face looked at me from a Pennsylvania driver's license: Philip Shayne.

I'd taken the box fair and square, so I ignored the unease that tickled the back of my neck. As I emptied the contents of the wallet on the floor, I wondered how this man's wallet had come to be trundled up inside of a box that had been dropped off at Joanie's store with my name on it. It wasn't until I peered inside the billfold that my heart skipped a beat.

Four bills were tucked inside: a twenty, two ones, and a five thousand dollar bill.

TEN

Coincidences like these were rarer than sightings of the Chupacabra. Slowly, I felt around on the floor for my handbag and fished around inside for my cell phone. I dialed Tex's home number, and a woman's voice answered.

"Could I please speak to Lt. Allen?"

"Is this Madison Night?" she said. I recognized the direct tone of Officer Donna Nast.

"Yes, it is. Donna?"

"Officer Nast."

"I'm sorry, Officer. May I speak to Tex? Is he there?"

"Is this your damsel in distress call of the day?" she demanded.

"I'm sorry to interrupt your evening, but this is important. I need to speak to him. It has to do with his case."

"He's off duty," she said and hung up.

I immediately called back. "Officer Nast, I'm serious. I need to speak to him."

"Like I said, he's off duty."

"It's important."

"If you need help, call the station." Her voice dropped to a whisper. "You're different, Madison, and I know how his mind works. Different to him is good. He sees you in those polyester outfits and thinks you're sexy. And I've seen how you two relate to each other."

"Then you know we spend more time arguing than agreeing on anything."

"To a cop, that's foreplay."

I took a quick, sharp breath and exhaled it in a huff. Officer Nasty was earning her nickname tonight.

"If you talk to Tex, let him know I'm on the verge of withholding evidence in his case." I hung up the phone and stuck my tongue out at it.

I called Tex's personal cell phone, and the call went to voicemail. I left a brief message. "I have something at my apartment I think you'll want to see. Come over when you get the message. I'll wait up."

As I waited for Tex's return call or possible arrival, I sorted the contents of the wallet into piles: business cards, credit cards, membership cards, and condoms. In truth, the wallet contained only one condom, but it warranted its own pile by sheer nature of "one of these things is not like the other."

I stacked the Doris Day memorabilia back into the box with the wallet at the bottom and poured a glass of wine. I dozed off in the armchair twice, until it seemed as though Tex would not be returning my call. After a brief shower, I searched the closet for a clean pair of pajamas.

I pulled a yellow chiffon nightgown out from a stack of peignoir sets that had been professionally laundered last year and dove into the sheer layers. Dozens of pleats heat-set in the polyester fabric cascaded over my trim body, like being inside a ray of sunlight. I blew kisses to Rocky, who stood up and followed me to the bed. Within minutes we were asleep.

An unfamiliar sound woke me hours later. An eerie glow from the parking lot behind the building illuminated the room through my curtains. My heart pounded like a drummer keeping time in a parade, but I lay still, listening for sounds of movement. A stillness hung in the air, until I heard it again. A single tap on my window.

My unit was on the second floor, facing the parking lot. Unless Spiderman had decided to pay me a visit, I doubted anyone was directly outside. I pushed the covers back and approached the window, peering between the floor-to-ceiling curtain panels. Tex stood in front of his Jeep. He wore a camel blazer over a white T-shirt and jeans and held a megawatt flashlight in one hand. He shined the light directly at me, and I backed away from the window. The light went out.

I glanced at the clock on the wall. It was close to three thirty. In my experience, nothing good happens at three thirty in the morning. I slid the window open and hissed through the screen.

"What are you doing here?"

"Unlock the back door. We need to talk."

"Can't this wait until the morning?"

"No."

"Fine."

I belted myself into a plush white terrycloth robe, slipped into matching slippers, and went downstairs. I turned the knob on the back door and pulled it open. One of my neighbors cracked their front door in the hall behind me, but no one appeared.

"Come in if you're coming in," I said in a low voice. I headed up the stairs to my apartment, and he followed.

"If anybody should ask, I was never here," he said once we were inside.

I shook my head. "My neighbors are going to think I made a booty call."

"It's a duty call, not a booty call. You said you have evidence?"

My eyes bugged out. "I called you hours ago! Why didn't you call me back?"

"I did. Your phone's off."

I looked around the apartment for my phone and located it on the corner of the Danish modern desk. The screen was black. I powered it on, the battery blinked twice, and it went black again. I walked away from Tex to the kitchen and plugged it in to the power cord. When I turned around, he was staring at the walls of the living room.

"If you couldn't respond in a reasonable amount of time, this should have waited until morning," I said.

"I had to get out of the house."

"In the middle of the night?"

"I knew it would be safe here."

"Safe from what?"

"I don't want to talk about it." He reached down and picked up one of the red kitten heeled shoes I'd worn earlier that day. It dangled there, rocking back and forth. They were a far cry from the stilettos I'd seen Officer Nast wear when she wasn't in uniform. I couldn't picture her and Tex as a couple. It seemed by his presence that he was having a hard time with the concept too.

"Tex, when people are in a relationship, they're supposed to want to spend time together. So why are you here?"

"I want to see this evidence," he said, and set the shoe on the table.

I moved back to the living room and waved a hand toward the box on the floor. "Have at it."

"What is it?"

"It's what Joanie Higa called me about today. Most people would call it junk. Somebody dropped it off at her store with my name on it. Mostly Doris Day memorabilia. Pictures, magazines, sheet music. A couple of lobby cards."

"If I didn't know any better, I'd agree with Donna that you made up an excuse to get me over to your apartment."

"It's a quarter to four in the morning. I was *asleep*. I didn't ask for you to come over here and interrupt my sleep, and I don't need to make up excuses to get you or any man to my apartment. Lately, it's been like Grand Central Station around here."

"Nice rant. Are you finished?" he asked.

I was vaguely aware that I wasn't making any sense, but I didn't care. "I'm tired and I want to go back to bed. Just take the box and leave. I hope poison ivy *is* contagious via cardboard and you get a rash all over your arms."

"What did you say?" he said, his head snapping up to look at me. His blue eyes drilled into me, and I tugged at the collar of my robe to make sure my privates were concealed.

I waved my hand toward the rubber gloves on the carpet next to the lobby card from *Midnight Lace*.

"Poison ivy. That's the reason for the gloves. The person who dropped the box off at the thrift store was covered in it, and I don't think I'd mind you catching it as punishment for coming here at this hour."

He stared at me.

"Take the box, don't take the box. If you insist on going through the contents here, please be quiet. And if all of this is an elaborate ruse to avoid your girlfriend, you can crash on my sofa. I don't care anymore. I just want to go back to sleep."

I stormed into the bedroom and shut the door behind me. I heard the front door open and close, heard footsteps on the stairs, and heard the back door to the building click into place.

I unbelted my robe and climbed between the covers. Rocky was fast asleep on the left-hand side of the mattress so I fit myself on the right and pulled the puffy comforter up to my chin. The apartment was quiet again. I rolled away from the window and closed my eyes, returning to sleep.

The rays from the sun filtering through my curtains woke me hours later. Rocky was upside down, paws in the air. I rubbed at his tummy. My stomach growled, and I realized neither Rocky nor I had eaten anything since yesterday morning. I pushed the covers back and got out of bed. Natural light flooded the living room. I padded in bare feet into the carpeted hallway before reaching the living room with the new hardwood floors.

Sunlight bounced off the yellow walls of the living room ahead of me. I wondered if I would ever become accustomed to the changes Brad had made to the room. As perfect as it had seemed initially, it felt unfamiliar now, something I didn't like feeling in my own apartment. The wood floors were cold, and I scampered through the room with my head down, not wanting to spend time thinking about it.

When I reached the kitchen, I lifted Rocky's water bowl from the floor, refilled it with fresh water from the tap, and replaced it next to his food bowl. I started a pot of coffee and leaned against the counter, waiting for it to brew.

As I waited, I thought about Tex's visit to my apartment in the middle of the night. There had been more to his arrival than avoiding Officer Nasty. He was interested in what I knew. But we hadn't gotten far enough for me to tell him what I found inside the box. He left before I ever told him about the wallet.

The clock on the microwave said six fifteen. I didn't know if Tex had returned to his apartment last night or not, but I had a better chance of reaching him now than if I waited. I picked up the now fully-charged phone and dialed his number. I listened to the rings. One. Two. Three—

And then I heard the ring in stereo, from the receiver I held to my left ear and from my living room.

If Tex had dropped his phone at my apartment, there were going to be issues, not the least of which was explaining to his surprisingly jealous girlfriend how it had come to be at my apartment in the first place. I rounded the corner from the kitchen and stopped short. Returning Tex's cell phone dropped a few notches down the priority list because his cell phone wasn't the only thing at my apartment.

Tex himself was stretched out on my sofa.

He lay on his back with his head turned toward the center of the room. His dark blond hair stood out in spikes against the pillow. I could make out his white T-shirt and the faded denim of his jeans under the loose weave of the white afghan that covered his midsection. A pair of boots sat next to the sofa, one upright, the other on its side. Rocky's head was inside the tipped one, his tail whipping from side to side. Tex looked at me, sleepy-eyed. He closed his eyes and then opened them again, blinking twice.

"Where did you come from?" I demanded.

"You said I could crash on your sofa." He stretched his arms over his head, then sat up and spun himself to a sitting position. "Damn, Night, is that what you always wear to bed?"

I looked down at the sheer yellow peignoir gown, all fluffy layers of pleats. I wasn't supposed to have to worry about decency in my own apartment, alone, sharing a bed with a Shih Tzu.

I stormed away from him to the bathroom and pulled my robe from the back of the door. I glanced at my reflection, started to leave, but turned back to the sink and put a few drops into my bloodshot eyes.

When I returned to the room, Tex held two cups of coffee. Rocky was draped over his foot swatting at the frayed edge of his jeans.

"I want to know why you're here," I said.

"You extended an invitation. I didn't know how long I'd have to wait to find you in that generous of a mood again."

"But you left! I heard you!"

"I'm going to have to teach you a thing or two about what you hear and what you think you hear. You heard your front door open and the back door shut. You might have even heard my car door. You didn't hear me pick up your keys and let myself back in. You never rescinded the offer, so I figured it was fine."

He raked his fingers through his bed head, but it fell forward against his forehead as soon as he let go.

"It is definitely not fine."

"You're kind of cranky for a morning person," he said.

"Don't try to make this about me. I want some answers."

He drank a good amount of coffee before answering. "You obviously are not a fan of being woken up in the middle of the night, but, after you mentioned the poison ivy, I wasn't about to leave."

"Why? What does the poison ivy have to do with anything?"

"For starters, our victim was covered with it."

ELEVEN

"You still don't know his identity?" I asked.

"Not yet."

"I think I can help you with that."

I made a great show of pulling on the gloves and rooted into the corner of the box for the wallet. At first, I flipped it open and held the driver's license for Tex to see. He leaned forward and made a grab for it, but I pulled it away, out of reach. Without speaking, I held up a gloved finger in a just-a-minute gesture. Using my thumbs to hold the billfold open, I waved the wallet closer to Tex's face to make sure he saw the five thousand dollar bill.

"Well? What do you think?" I asked.

"That's our vic."

"Don't you think it's suspicious that he has a five thousand dollar bill in his wallet?" I asked. "These bills are supposed to be rare, and they're springing up all over town like blue bonnets. It's like someone found a five thousand dollar bill printing press in their basement."

"Sit down, Night. Tell me everything you know. Tell me what you can about that box."

I lowered myself into the chair opposite Tex and adjusted the hem of the robe to cover my thighs. When I looked up, Tex was staring at my face, not my legs. His expression wasn't playful anymore.

"You heard Joanie's message. She runs a thrift store out by Lemmon and Inwood. When I got to her store, she brought this box out of the back. Apparently some guy covered in poison ivy dropped it off along with a bunch of other boxes. This one had my name on it. I guess she peeked inside, saw the Doris Day stuff, and figured somebody knew I was a fan."

His eyebrow twitched, and I shrugged. "So I'm predictable. Anyway, when I went to her store, I saw a framed James Madison on the wall behind the register. I asked her about it, and she said the same guy dropped off both things."

"Where is it?"

I held up a hand. "I'll get to that in a second. She told me to wear rubber gloves before handling the box, said the guy was covered in poison ivy. She felt so bad she gave him a bottle of Calamine lotion. She carried the box to the stockroom and probably called me right away. I don't think she even really went through the rest of the box."

"It doesn't make sense."

"There must be some kind of explanation that does make sense, but you're not seeing it."

"No, that's not what I mean. We have a victim covered in poison ivy. The guy who dropped off this box was covered in poison ivy. The contents of this box connect those two people. If we could find the guy who dropped this off, we'd have enough to bring him in for a nice long conversation in an interrogation room. So why would this guy risk it? Why not get lost and lay low until the rash is out of his system?"

"That takes more than a day or two. Poison ivy lasts about two weeks."

"You sound like you know from experience."

"Baseball camp, seventh grade. The whole team was down for the count. Well, except for the catcher. She was so suited up nothing could get to her."

"Baseball camp." Tex studied me for a second. "Every time I think I have you figured out, you throw me a curve."

"Here's what really doesn't make sense. You have to come into contact with the oil from the plant to get the rash. So, what, he rubbed the box down with the oil? Which he would only do if he wanted someone else to get the rash. And since it has my name on it, did he want me to get the rash? Why?"

Tex shrugged. "By this point, the rash would be mild enough it wouldn't do much damage. Maybe take you out of commission for a few days. Give somebody a chance to take care of you. You know anybody who would want to do that? Maybe somebody who recently came back into your life?"

I glared at him. "You recently came back into my life. Does that make you a suspect?"

"C'mon, Night. You have any other theories?"

I stared at the box for a few seconds when it hit me. "What if the guy who dropped off the box wasn't trying to protect Joanie from getting the rash as much as he was trying to protect whatever is in the box?"

"Saying the box is covered in poison ivy. That's a pretty good way to make sure people don't go snooping in your things." He lifted the flap with his index finger. "Did you unpack the box?"

"Yes, but I wore the gloves the whole time."

"So the guy who dropped off the box had everybody who touched it wear gloves. And inside the box is a wallet of the guy who was killed. You think—"

"That the whole point of the box was to get me the wallet?"

"I don't know. I'll have to spend more time thinking about it, but with the wallet, at least we can figure out if it's him. It's a start. Thanks, Night."

Being thanked came as a surprise. "You're welcome."

He looked around the apartment, taking in the changes. "This is the apartment makeover?"

"Yes."

"I'm surprised. I have to say, it looks like you. Do you like it?"

"Not really." I didn't know why that mattered to Tex, but I could tell that it did. "I'm probably going to redo the whole thing when I get a little free time. Let me know if you have any ideas. I'm open to suggestion."

As soon as I heard the words out loud, I braced myself for a sarcastic comment. None came.

Tex ruffled Rocky's fur, then stood up. "Was there anything valuable in there? Any of the Doris Day stuff?"

"Nothing I can't live without."

"I'm sorry, but you can't keep it."

"I know."

He hoisted the box up, balanced it on his knee and carried it to the door.

I turned the lock and opened the door.

"The framed bill, is it in here, too?"

"Um, no. I gave it away."

His face clouded. He slammed the box on the corner of my desk. "To who? Your long-lost boyfriend? I thought he was giving you space."

"I haven't seen him since dinner two nights ago. I didn't give it to him, I gave it to Hudson."

"Why?"

"I had a couple of questions about its artistic merits."

"Do me a favor, Night. Don't involve anybody who doesn't need to be involved in this. If something else happens, you call me. First." He stormed out of the apartment, down the stairs, and to his Jeep. This time when I heard his engine start, I looked out the window and watched as he drove away.

I showered and changed into a pink, gray, and yellow argyle pullover and a pair of gray trousers with a pink windowpane pattern. The ensemble was a favorite that got little wear thanks to the perpetual heat and humidity in Dallas, but the temperature had dropped somewhere around the holidays and today it was in the high sixties. I didn't know when the heat would return, so I wasn't going to waste the opportunity.

After spending yesterday morning in Connie's shoes, I was more than happy to push my feet into well-worn sneakers before leaving the house. I clipped a pink leather leash to Rocky's collar and off we went.

My physical therapist was located two blocks off Turtle Creek Boulevard in a tall building of medical offices. I spent the next two hours hooked up to electronic machines that sent a pulse through my knee, followed by limited range exercises and a soothing rubdown with menthol. Rocky spent the same amount of time with the receptionist. We were both in good spirits when we left.

Before I'd reinjured my knee, two miles of lap swimming had kept the joint limber. I missed the Zen connected with swimming at the early hours of the day but hadn't been able to bring myself to return to Crestwood, my regular spot, after what had happened there. Just like the theater, it was tainted with memories. The life I'd built was changing, whether I wanted it to or not.

I held the door open for Rocky, and he jumped in. He watched me walk around the front of the car and get into the driver's side, then padded over to me on his thick, furry paws and rested them on my right thigh. His dark brown eyes looked at me with concern. I ran my hand over his fur, scratching him behind his ears.

"What are we doing, Rocky? Are we inviting trouble into our lives?"

His tail thumped against the white leather and his pink tongue shot out and licked my palm. I kissed him on top of his head, and pulled out of the parking lot.

I wasn't far from the condominiums where Archie Leach lived, and even though I didn't have an appointment, I drove in his direction, half-tempted to drop in unannounced under the guise of measurement-taking.

Turtle Creek Luxury Apartments was one of the historic buildings in the Highland Park area of Dallas. It was designed by Howard Meyer and built in 1957. At one time it boasted the most luxurious apartments west of the Mississippi. Sixteen stories high, shaped like an octagon, with a pool on the roof and a fleet of valets, it had all of the amenities to woo the young nostalgia crowd, yet somehow it maintained its heritage rooted in tradition. There was something very old-Dallas about the condo; most of the units were owned by rich, elderly folks who had been there for fifty years. The staff stood on ceremony as they'd been trained to do, creating a stodgy time-warp effect.

I pulled my car up to the gate and rolled down the window. A man with shoe-polish-brown hair slicked away from his face took note of my license plate as I slowed by the valet stand. Rocky stood up and stepped on my lap, sniffing the man. A plastic nametag with the name Harry Delbert was clipped to the white collar of his shirt.

"Hello, I'm here to visit Mr. Archie Leach," I said.

"Is he expecting you?"

"Yes," I said.

"I'll let him know you're here. What's your name?"

"Oh, no!" I said, too quickly. He furrowed his brow and set his mouth in a firm line. It was obvious I needed a new approach to undo my reaction. I pulled a business card out and handed it to the man.

"I'm his decorator, Madison Night. He invited me over to take measurements, but I may have confused the time. Ten till two, or two till ten. It's possible that I'm either slightly early or woefully late. Maybe I should just turn around and reconfirm the time."

The man studied me for a couple of seconds. "Hold on a second and we can straighten this out."

He waved a hand to a thin man across the parking lot who wore the same uniform: white shirt, red vest, black tie, black trousers. I watched as he made a phone-to-the-ear gesture, then he turned around and picked up a receiver. Before I could hear what he said, he slid the glass partition closed, leaving me alone with my regret that I'd never learned to read lips.

I studied the building. I had first learned of Turtle Creek Luxury Apartments when I moved to Dallas. The most fascinating part of the building was the floor plan. Each floor contained three apartments with entrances in the middle of the building. Each unit had two exterior walls, allowing more natural light than if the floor had been divided into squares like most apartments. The Dallas sun being what it was, I imagined a hefty air conditioning bill went along with the natural light, but it was probably worth it. I would have loved to live there, but the price of rent had been my ultimate decision-maker. Two thousand a month was too steep for someone with a start-up business.

As I watched the building, the double glass doors by the entrance opened and an impeccably-dressed woman in a fur-trimmed, pink tweed coat and matching pencil skirt left the building. Her posture was stately, her head tipped up, helping to counter the weight she carried around her waist.

She walked to the end of the carpet runner that extended from inside the building and adjusted the pillbox hat on her frosted gray and white hair. Moments later Archie came out. He carried a small rust-colored Pomeranian. He set the dog down by the woman's feet and turned the leash over to her. He ignored the parking attendants and strode toward a small white Lexus. The dog led the woman down the side of the apartment building to the sidewalk, and the two of them disappeared past a neatly trimmed hedge that lined the street.

I looked at Harry to see if he'd noticed. He was still on the phone. I looked back at Archie. He started the engine and drove out of the lot in a cloud of exhaust. I craned my head to see the plates on his car, but he was too fast for me.

I waved to get Harry's attention. He slid the partition open.

"I must have had the time wrong. I'll just pull around and leave."

Harry hung up the phone. "Pull through and park in one of the first three spaces on the right marked 'Visitor Parking.'"

I pulled forward and parked in the spot next to a collection of potted plants in need of a week's worth of water. Rocky followed me out of the car. The thin man met me on the carpet.

"Did you speak to Mr. Leach?" I asked. The man didn't answer. "I think I understand. You're going to let me in to take measurements?"

"This way, Ms. Night."

He glanced at Rocky for a second and appeared to be thinking about something. I half-expected him to tell me to put Rocky in the car, and I prepared myself for the battle that would come when I said no. Instead, he stepped back and held out his left arm, ushering me away from the main glass doors of the building to a small enclosure that sat to the side of the valet lot. Harry stepped out of the valet booth and joined us. He stood behind me, his outstretched hand now poised by the small of my back. Something was wrong, but I didn't know what.

"Thank you for your help, but I think I'll come back when my client is here." I kept a tight grip on Rocky's leash while he moved between the different sets of feet, sniffing the toes of all of the shoes.

"What makes you think he isn't here?" The thin man asked.

"He just drove out of your parking lot."

The man looked at the parking lot, at Harry, and back to me. Two other men, in black T-shirts under gray jackets, approached from the front doors. They looked like they'd been hired for their solid build more than their sense of style.

"What is going on here?" I asked.

The two men came closer. I looked to my left and right. There was nobody else around.

"Ms. Night, what's the real reason you're here?" the thin man asked.

"I told you. Archie Leach hired me to be his decorator. I told him I wanted to come by to take measurements, but I forgot what time he expected me. He just drove out of your parking lot, so clearly I'm here at the wrong time. I'll schedule a proper appointment and come back later."

"Lady, Archie says he didn't hire a decorator," said one of the two beefy men.

"If I could talk to him, I'm sure we could straighten this all out."

The thin man in the red vest stepped directly in front of me. "Lady, I'm Archie Leach, and I've never seen you before in my life."

TWELVE

"You're not Archie Leach," I said instinctively.

"I think I know who I am."

"You're not the Archie Leach who came to my studio," I said, though my argument was losing steam.

"Ms. Night, we're condominium security, and we need you to answer a couple of questions for us," said one of the two men in black T-shirts.

I hadn't done anything wrong, but my desire for answers outweighed my desire to leave. Rocky and I followed them down a carpeted hallway. It was a slow procession with Rocky sniffing at the baseboards along the way. We ended in a break room with faux wood tables and folding chairs. A glowing Dr. Pepper machine stood along one wall, next to a flat screen TV, where a sportscaster reported on the potential of the Dallas Rangers.

The four of us took seats. I wasn't sure where we were going to start, so I took the first step. "I assure you, a man with your name came to my studio a couple of days ago and hired me to design his condo here."

I looked from one face to the next. Rocky stood on his hind legs and put his paws on the thin valet attendant's shins. The man pushed his hands deep into the pockets of his pants and stepped away.

"I thought he wanted me to design one room but it turned out he wanted me to decorate his whole apartment. Mr. Leach is going through a divorce—"

"Stop calling him that," said the thin valet attendant. His face was drawn together, his arms crossed over his chest.

I stopped mid-sentence and looked at the man who claimed to be the real Mr. Leach and apologized. "What would you like me to call him?"

"Call him Cary Grant," said one of the beefy security officers. When the other men turned to look at him he shrugged. "What? I watch TCM."

"Gentlemen, I don't understand why I'm sitting here in this office. Apparently I've been duped, and someone who said he wanted to hire me did not. I took no deposit, and, aside from the time I've spent on plans for his apartment and the time I'm wasting sitting here with you, I'm not out anything. I accept responsibility for the mix-up. Now, I'll be on my way."

I stood up, scanning the faces of the men in front of me. They didn't seem convinced of my innocence, and while it seemed inevitable that one of them would ask me to sit back down, I figured it would be up to them to say the words instead of up to me to interpret their implied command.

"Harry, you better get back out front and finish out your shift," said the thin man.

Harry scowled. "My shift ends in ten minutes. I think it can wait."

"C'mon, man, if the booth isn't covered, one of us is going to get reported. I'll take it from here."

"There is nothing to take from here," I said. "We're done. I have to leave."

"Lady, you're not going nowhere," the thin man said. He was starting to make me mad and not because of his grammar.

"Why don't you show me some identification so I know that you are the real Archie Leach?"

"Want to see my driver's license?" he asked. "Too bad. I was robbed a couple of weeks ago."

"So you can't prove you are who you say you are? How convenient."

"I didn't say that."

He pulled a nylon wallet out of his back pocket and extracted a wad of plastic cards. He maintained eye contact with me while he dealt them in front of me one by one.

I dropped my eyes to the display, just long enough to make out the name on every card, including his photo identification card for work, which showed a bit more hair than he had on his currently receding hairline. Of all of the things I could have commented on, that was the one I had to fight the most.

"Fine," I said, and stood up. "I'm sorry to doubt you, Archie."

"Art."

"What?"

"I go by Art, not Archie."

"Fine. I'm sorry, Art. Now, I'm going to be on my way."

"Ms. Night, sit back down."

"Why? I haven't done anything wrong."

With skills befitting a black jack dealer, Art slid his hand over the fanned-out credit cards, corralling them into a neat stack. He fit them back into his wallet and fit his wallet back into his pocket.

"Maybe you're telling the truth." Art folded his skinny arms across his chest. "Maybe not. I don't know yet."

"Maybe we can help each other," I said.

He made no move to speak.

"Okay, I'll go first. The man I met walked into my design studio two days ago. This is the address he gave me."

"Describe your guy."

"He's a well-dressed, thin man, sort of preppy. He has black hair slicked back from his face and bears a slight resemblance to Rudolf Valentino."

All eyes turned to the security guard who watched TCM. "What are you looking at me for?" he asked.

"Does he sound familiar?" I asked.

All three men shook their heads.

"Are you sure? Because I just watched him pull out of your parking lot in a white Lexus. Do you have cameras on the parking lot?"

"White Lexus? That's Mrs. Bonneville," said Art. "Her son Grant is visiting. I haven't seen the guy, but it must have been him."

"Where is he visiting from?"

"That's not really our business. Mrs. Bonneville is a long-term tenant. She's lived here since the sixties. You want to know what I know about her?" he asked.

"Sure." Whether intentional or not, they were getting my goat. I wasn't sure how to get information from these men, or how the fake divorcee-slash-client fit into the bigger picture, but I'd take what I could get and sort it out later.

"She has a Pomeranian she treats better than a lot of people treat their own children. She has fresh orchids delivered to her apartment in spring and poinsettias in the fall. White ones, until December, then she switches to red. She has her own driver, her own chef, and her own masseuse. And she tips every one of us a thousand dollars on December thirty-first. Other than that, her business is her business, and I'm sure she'd appreciate if we left it that way."

"Has her son visited before?"

"Not that I know of."

I leaned back in the small metal folding chair.

"Gentlemen, I've told you all I know. If the man who hired me isn't who he says he is, then I have no business taking up any more of your time."

I stood up and adjusted the hem of my argyle sweater. My keys fell from my pocket, and I scooped them up and headed for the exit.

"Where are you going?" Archie asked.

"I'm leaving. I've spent enough time here already."

I'd apologized enough. The fault of the mix-up lay squarely on the shoulders of Mrs. Bonneville's son, Grant. I didn't know why he'd lied about his name or identity. I didn't even know if he was a real client. The only thing I knew was that I would be bumping Connie's atomic kitchen up on the priority list.

"Ms. Night. Sit back down. The cops are going to be here any minute now, and I think it's best if you pass this story off to them."

"The cops? You called the cops?"

I stopped to think. Calling the cops was a good idea, regardless of their motivation. If Tex took the call, I could tell him what had happened.

"Fine. I have a feeling Lt. Allen will be happy to see me."

"Then it's a good thing I took the call instead of him," said a female voice behind me.

I turned to the doorway, where Officer Nast stood with a scowl on her face.

THIRTEEN

By the time Officer Nast escorted me from the small security office of Turtle Creek Luxury Apartments, hours later, I was convinced the only potential friend I'd made was the security guard with a penchant for old movies.

I repeated, for Officer Nast's benefit, how I had come to be at the condominium and how I had learned the name Archie Leach in the first place.

The last couple of days had shown me a different side of her that had nothing to do with police business and everything to do with possessive jealousy. I wasn't sure how the two different aspects of her coexisted on a daily basis, and it wasn't the right time to find out. So, for all of my forthcomings, there were a few things I kept to myself.

Officer Nast ushered Rocky and me back to my car, never more than a few inches from my left-hand side. It wasn't until my key was in the lock of the door that she spoke.

"I did you a favor in there, Madison. I'd rather not have to do you another."

"Officer Nast, this was a simple misunderstanding. Nothing more."

I opened the car door and lowered myself into the driver's seat. Nasty blocked the door so I couldn't close it.

"This boyfriend of yours, do I know him?" she asked.

"How do you know about him?" I asked instead.

"I hear things." She stood with one hand on my rear view mirror and the other on the hood of my car.

I didn't know how much Tex might have told her about Brad, but her question made me uncomfortable. "He's from out of town," I said.

"What's his name?"

"Brad Turlington."

"Are you seeing him tonight?"

"He's away on business."

"You sure he's not a figment of your imagination?"

I fought the urge to get out of the car and address her face to face. "You want proof? Maybe we should double date sometime." I grabbed the door and yanked it away from her. She jumped backward. I slammed the door shut and peeled out of the lot.

Although my blood was boiling, I kept myself calm until I was two blocks away from Turtle Creek apartments. I channeled all of my attention into the act of driving until I reached a shopping center off Mockingbird. I parked in a space at the end of the lot, cut the engine, leaned forward, and rested my forehead on the top of the steering wheel.

The more I thought about what had happened at the apartment building, the more angry I was over the hostility from Nasty. I'd done nothing to warrant her attitude—I'd done nothing, period. I'd been at the wrong place, wrong time. I was a victim of someone else playing a hoax.

The worst thing about it was that I was sure she was going to tell Tex. As I weighed the pros and cons of calling him first, my phone rang with an unfamiliar number.

"Ms. Night, this is Dennis O'Hara. I'm a real estate agent. Did I catch you at a bad time?"

"No, it's fine. What can I do for you?"

"It's what I can do for you, actually. I have a house that's been on the market for a couple of months, and there's no interest."

"I'm an interior decorator, Mr. O'Hara. I decorate houses. I don't buy them."

"Well, that's where this gets weird. The owner isn't interested in keeping up the taxes on the property, and he gave me your number. He wants you to have the house."

"I don't understand."

"The house belonged to a Thelma Johnson. Her son said you might want it?"

I couldn't believe my ears. Thelma Johnson was a deceased Dallas resident. My interest in her estate had started a snowball effect that brought a killer out of hiding. "Mr. O'Hara, people don't give people houses."

"Technically, you're right. Her son didn't give you the house. He gave you a tax bill. The house is paid off, and if you care to make up the back taxes, it's yours."

"Free and clear?"

"If four thousand is your definition of free and clear, more power to you."

I leaned back in the car and stared up at the crisp blue sky. I had a business. I had an apartment complex. I had a studio. What did I need with a modest split level house in the M streets?

"Why me?" I asked the real estate agent.

"He said you earned it. Something about you wanting his mom's stuff so badly you risked your life for it. I figured he was being. So, what do you think?"

"Can you hold for one moment?" I asked. When he agreed, I held the phone by my thigh and looked at Rocky. "What do you think, Rock? Do we want a secret hideaway?"

He cocked his head to the left like he was considering the question. It wasn't the first time I'd talked to my dog about major life events and it wouldn't be the last. Even though he couldn't answer, I knew what he'd say if he could.

"Mr. O'Hara? I think the answer is yes."

I made arrangements to meet the realtor to swap a rather large cashier's check and a couple of signatures for a rather small set of keys. He asked if he could transfer the utilities into my name. I wasn't sure what I would do with a 1954 house with a flat roof and a pink bathroom, but at least the next time I needed an emergency place to sleep, I had one.

I drove home, my thoughts a jumble of recent and distant memories. Effie was walking toward me in the apartment hallway. She carried her mail in one hand. Rocky strained his leash to greet her, and she dropped into a squat and ruffled his fur, then raised her hand and made him dance in a circle.

"I missed you, Rocky! Madison's been taking you everywhere!" she said to him.

"I can spare him for about half an hour if you want to get reacquainted. I'm in desperate need of a very long shower," I said.

"Did you hear that? Did you? Huh? Huh? Huh?" she said.

Rocky danced around on hind legs, trying to snatch an imaginary treat from her fingers. She stood up and took the leash from my hand.

"Thanks, Madison. I've been studying for finals all week and it'll be nice to have a break with Rocky."

"Thank you, Effie. You're always so sweet to him."

"How can I not be? He's such a good dog."

The three of us walked up the rear staircase to the building. I unlocked my door, and Effie and Rocky continued to hers, the middle unit on the opposite side of the hallway.

"I'll come get him in half an hour," I said.

"Take your time. I'd keep him all night if I thought you'd let me," she said.

I tossed my keys on the corner of the desk and took off my sweater. My pants followed, as did my lace bra and white cotton panties. I entered the bathroom and cranked up the hot water.

The hot spray massaged my shoulders, neck, and back, until finally I turned the water off. I stepped into a cloud of steam and dried off. When I opened the door to let in some fresh air, I heard a sound from my kitchen.

I pushed the door closed again, leaving it cracked a sliver, and pressed my ear against it. There was someone in my apartment.

That someone was singing *Que Sera Sera*.

The singing from the kitchen stopped. "Maddy? Don't be scared. It's me." Brad's voice carried from the kitchen.

It was dark outside. The apartment was dimly lit, with only a low wattage glow coming from the mismatched lamps placed around the living room.

I shrugged into my thick terrycloth robe and secured it with a square knot, making sure there was no chance that it would fall open. My bare feet carried me from the bathroom into the bedroom. I opened the bottom drawer of my dresser and pulled out a pair of blue flannel pajamas from my stash. I picked the yellow peignoir set up from the bed and shoved it into the back of the drawer. I wanted to be careful about signals that would trigger unwanted advancements.

I tapped my hand on the outside of the wall before I reached it. When I rounded the corner, Brad stood over the stove, stirring the contents of a large silver pot. He wore a gray and black checked sport coat over a white polo shirt with the collar up. On his head was a Hamburg that had been black once, but was now a varied shade of gray. A small pheasant feather stood out at a diagonal from the band above the brim.

"Chicken soup from scratch. I made it earlier today at my place and brought it over. Is it still your favorite?" he asked and held the spoon out for me to taste it.

"How did you get in here?"

"Your neighbor found me in the hallway. I told her I wanted to surprise you."

"Which neighbor?"

"The teenager across the hall, the one who's watching your dog."

"Effie let you in here?" Effie had a set of my keys in case of emergency, when I knew Rocky needed to go out and I couldn't get home in time. It surprised me to think that she'd let a stranger in.

Brad stepped closer to me. "She recognized me from the first day I came here. After you kicked me out." He dropped his head and looked sheepish. "She asked how I knew you and I told her I knew you from before you moved here. She liked that. I guess because she likes you."

"She shouldn't have let you in here."

"She said she was sad that you were going to pick Rocky up because she was having a good time with him. I asked her to keep him for the night so we could be alone." He watched my face for a couple of seconds and poured the contents of the spoon back into the pot. "It'll keep. Come here," he said, and opened his arms.

I stood in front of him, my emotions in a jumble. I needed something, just one thing, to signal which emotion to trust.

"Have you changed so much that you don't remember what it was like when we were together?"

Exhaustion hit me like a body slam from a professional wrestler and my knees buckled. Brad caught me and held me in his arms. With my head tipped against his chest, I exhaled a deep breath I didn't know I'd been holding. I inhaled the scent of his cologne, Old Spice. It was the same one he'd worn the night I first met him. The scent took me back to the room in Pierot's Interiors, when we were falling in love and our lives were less complicated.

"I know I said I'd give you space, but I couldn't stay away. I've missed you so much. This feels right, doesn't it?" he whispered into my hair.

"It feels familiar," I whispered back.

"Madison, let's pick up where we left off. It's not too late, is it?"

His hands moved up to my arms, and he gently pushed me away so he could see my face. The fingers of his right hand traced down the side of my cheekbone. I stood still, remembering what it used to feel like when Brad touched me.

Everything other than the touch of his fingertips melted away. For a second, it was like it had been when we first met, when I knew beyond the shadow of a doubt that if it were Brad and I against the world, we'd win. The impulse to go back in time trumped everything else in my world. I closed my eyes and leaned in, and his lips brushed against mine.

"Let's run away, Maddy. Let's start over. We both left Pennsylvania. I know things will never be like they were, but that doesn't mean we can't go someplace new and create something even better together."

I couldn't say that I wasn't the type to run away and start over because I was. Starting a new life had been the single best thing I'd done for myself. I'd never felt rooted. My family had passed away when I was in my thirties. Brad had been my family, until that one day when he wasn't.

I realized I'd run away from that life because it didn't fit me. This life did.

"I don't want to run away, Brad. This is me, this is my life. This is where I want to be. We can never go back to what we were."

"Then I'm sorry I tracked you down and I'm sorry I interrupted your life. Why don't you give me the James Madison? I can't leave until you give it back."

I stiffened. The five thousand dollar bill was sealed in an envelope in the rent box in the front of my lobby. I knew it was evidence—to something—and I couldn't risk Brad finding it. I couldn't risk anyone finding it.

I took a step backward, away from him. Did I still know this man? How much had I ever known him? What secrets did he hold that I didn't understand?

"That's all it'll take. Give me the bill and I'll leave." He put a finger under my chin. "Or let me stay and give me a second chance."

He stared at me, his smoldering gaze reminding me of the feelings I thought I'd buried. It had been years since I felt the touch of his hands, anybody's hands, for that matter, and after the way it had ended, I thought I'd turned that part of myself off forever.

I wasn't the same person I'd been when Brad and I had been together. I shut people out and discovered my independence. I got my affection from a Shih Tzu, and I let my business keep a barrier between myself and the most reliable men I'd met since moving to Dallas—Hudson and Tex. Even owning the apartment building in secret was a way for me to protect myself.

I didn't like facing how much Brad's betrayal had scarred me, and so I spent much of my time alone, not analyzing the person I'd become. But with Brad's return came self-analysis.

Tex had questions about his homicide. Nasty had questions about Tex. Hudson had questions about his future.

And I had questions about my past.

It was time my questions got answered.

"We need to talk." I set my spoon down and walked into the living room.

Brad followed me and sat in a chair opposite the sofa. He put his elbows on his knees and folded his hands in front of him. When he rested his chin on his knuckles, once again, I stared at his watch. He noticed.

"This watch tells me that time goes on. And now's the real test, just like the inscription says. 'Only time will tell.'" He dropped one hand to the face of the watch and traced the second hand as it swept in a circle.

"I wondered if this day would come," he continued. "I used to lie awake imagining what it would be like to have to answer to you. To explain what happened." He looked down at his Converse sneakers. "I stopped wondering after a year. I knew you hated me."

If he wanted me to say I didn't, I didn't. I couldn't. A part of me had hated him. A part of me still did. What he didn't realize was that I hated him for all the wrong reasons.

I hated him for lying to me, even if he said he lied to protect me.

I hated him for not coming to see me when I was hospitalized with my knee injury.

I hated him for driving us apart. If he hadn't lied to me, we might still be together, sharing that bed in the back of Pierot's. I might never have developed the life I had now.

And after the break, when I finally was on the verge of dropping my guard, when I was ready to move forward instead of fighting so hard to block the past, I hated him for the hidden message, the apology, and the explanation telling me everything I'd come to hate about him wasn't true.

I hated him the most for that.

As much of a release as it might have been to yell at him, to slap him ten times harder than Connie slapped Tex at my studio, to push him out of my life for good, I needed answers to questions that would otherwise haunt me. I also needed to tell Brad the truth.

"Brad, there's something you don't know. That first year, when you were waiting for some kind of response or reaction from me, I didn't know the truth. I didn't find the message you left for me until a couple of months ago."

"But—"

"I had no reason to think you were lying. When you told me you were married, you hurt me—badly. You damn near scarred me. I don't ever want to feel like that again."

"Your knee. Is that what happened in the skiing accident?"

"I'm not talking about my knee."

"Madison, I never wanted you to get hurt."

"But I did get hurt, Brad! You can't take that back. I don't care if your lie was a lie. I don't care if you claim you were trying to protect me. I'm a different person because of you. I'm not open anymore. I don't trust people. The damage is done."

"Then give me the bill, Madison. Give me the bill and I'll leave."

"No, Brad. No. Even if I could give you the bill, it wouldn't change anything. I need closure, and finding out the truth about that bill is the only way I'll get it."

"You don't have it?"

"It's not here."

He stood. "That's too bad, Madison. Without that bill, I'm a a dead man."

FOURTEEN

Our conversation was interrupted by a knock on the door. I was ready to tell whoever it was to go away until I looked through the peephole. It was Tex.

When I opened the door I kept one hand on the frame and the other on the knob, blocking him from entering.

"What are you doing here? I thought private citizens were entitled to come and go as they wished. Or maybe you wanted to drop by, see if I was dining alone?"

"Are you?"

"That's none of your business."

"Because if you're dining alone, I'd be happy to join you."

"No, thank you."

"So you're not dining alone. Anybody I know?"

"Shouldn't you be getting home to your girlfriend?" I asked abruptly. I stepped into the hallway and pulled the door shut behind me. Before I had it closed, Brad yanked it open.

"Maddy, is everything okay?"

"Everything's fine."

Brad and Tex looked at each other. I looked back and forth at the two of them.

"Brad, this is Tex. Tex, Brad."

Instinct kept me from introducing Tex by rank.

I turned to Brad. "It'll take just a second for me to finish up here, and I'll be back inside in a second." He nodded at Tex, and pulled the door shut behind him. A waft of chicken soup aroma followed me into the hallway.

"Does he know about what happened last year?"

"A little. He read the article from the paper."

"You didn't tell him anything else?"

"No."

"Interesting."

"What's so interesting? We have a lot of catching up to do. I'm sure it will come up in conversation."

"That's not what's interesting. I'm talking about the fact that you're keeping quiet about parts of your life."

"I'm not keeping quiet. I just haven't brought it up." I paused for a moment. "Does Donna know you're here helping me?"

"Yes."

"Interesting."

"Not really. She's on the force. Anything I do that's police business, she knows about."

"Does she know where you slept last night?"

He glared at me.

"I'm not going to keep you long, but I wanted you to know your Romeo checks out. He's got a couple of skeletons in his closet, but nothing you should be worried about."

"I thought you said you couldn't nose around in his background?"

"His name came up in the investigation." He stepped backward and winked. "I thought you'd like to know he's clean. If that's been keeping you from sleeping at night, well, there are better reasons not to sleep."

Five minutes ago, I'd been ready to say good-bye to Brad for good. There was a big difference between saying good-bye and signing his death sentence. I bit my lower lip and thought about what Brad had said to me.

"You know, Night, somebody once told me that when people are in a relationship, they're supposed to want to spend time together. You better be getting back inside before he misses you."

"Lieutenant, Brad didn't come to Dallas for me. He came for the James Madison."

"Did you give it to him?"

"I don't have it."

"Is it in there?" He pointed at my door.

"No." I reached out and grabbed Tex's forearm. "He says they're going to kill him. We might not have a future but I can't let him die over this."

Tex studied my face. "Can you keep him here tonight? I'll get a team together in the morning."

I felt an emotional tug toward Tex. We hadn't known each other long, but I felt like he could see straight through me.

"Thank you," I said.

I shut the door behind me and took a sip of my wine. Why had Tex really shown up on my doorstep? Was he was looking to crash on my sofa two nights in a row? I didn't think so. And worse, he said he wouldn't break the law to run a background check on Brad. The fact that he'd done so told me one thing: Tex didn't see Brad as an innocent private citizen any more. He knew more about Brad than he let on.

There was another tap on the door. I whipped it open.

"There isn't time for this—" I said to Tex, only it wasn't Tex in front of me. It was Mrs. Young, my newest tenant.

"I'm sorry. I thought you were someone else," I said.

"I hope it's not too late. I wanted to say thank you. My application was approved and my boys already love it here. Even the range hood. They say it sounds like a Pterodactyl. Why are kids so fascinated with dinosaurs?" She pushed her hair off her face with the back of her forearm. "I thought once we found a place it would be brownies and cupcakes, you know, bake lots of sweets and have them fall asleep early in a sugar coma. Not pterodactyls."

"You should call Hudson."

"I did." She looked confused. "I told you I got the apartment, right?"

"Right." I hesitated. Even though I'd said I'd put in a good word for her and I'd given her Hudson's number, I felt surprisingly un-centered. It had all gone so smoothly without any effort on my part. Little by little it felt like the life I'd established for myself in Dallas was slipping away.

"That's not what I meant. Hudson will fix your range hood."

"I thought I should notify the building owners and let them deal with it."

"Sure, you can do that too, but they'll just call Hudson."

"Maybe Hudson is the building owner. Have you ever suspected that?" she asked.

I smiled my most charming smile. "There are times I wish he was."

Mrs. Young looked past me into the room. Her hand was on the front door, and she pushed it open slightly, angling for a better look. "You have hardwood floors. Do other units have them too?"

"No. This is a mid-century building. The whole thing had hardwood floors when it was built. Only later, in the seventies and eighties, people covered them up with wall-to-wall carpet. The hardwood exists, it just needs to be exposed and refinished."

"You were allowed to do your own renovations?"

"I hired some people to paint the place. I'm not sure where the confusion happened but when I got home the carpet was gone. All I expected was to have yellow walls."

I didn't want her to get too curious or to attempt to contact the Night Company about renovations.

"Nice bonus," she said.

"Not really. The floors still need to be refinished and that's going to make a big mess."

Despite the fact that I was telling the truth, her eyes narrowed, and she stared at me. I felt scrutinized, as though she were measuring what she knew of me against what I told her to make a determination on whether or not she believed me. I didn't like that I knew nothing about her. I'd have to remember to get the application papers from Hudson the next time I saw him.

"Mrs. Young, thank you for stopping by. It's been a long day, and it's time for me to wind down."

I stepped back, away from the door, and pushed it half-way shut. She put a hand on the front of the door and for a moment we stood there, separated by a sliver of space. Again she rubbed at her hairline. I followed her hand and noticed a succession of small red dots by her temple.

"I changed cleansers and had a reaction." She smiled. "I should know better, at my age." She dropped her hand and stepped backward into the hallway.

I smiled and shut the door, locking the deadbolts immediately. I stayed there, waiting for her footsteps to retreat down the hallway. I didn't hear those footsteps until after I'd counted to seventeen.

I turned around and faced the dining room table, but it was empty. I went to the kitchen. Brad wasn't there either. The silver stock pot of chicken soup still sat on top of the stove, but the heat was off.

The light was on in the bathroom. I leaned back against the door and thought about Tex's request. I had a choice here. Move forward or hold on to my anger. I didn't want to be the kind of person who surrounded herself with anger. I was strong, independent, capable of taking care of myself. I'd proven that. Maybe now it was time to take care of someone else.

I crossed the apartment and tapped on the bathroom door. "Hey," I said softly.

The door cracked, and Brad looked down at me. "Hey," he said back.

"I was thinking. It's late, and I'm tired."

"Sure, I understand."

I held the door open for him, and he stepped into the hallway. The white afghan was folded on the end of the sofa and the pillow plumped in place. "You should stay here tonight."

"Maddy—" He stepped forward, and I put a hand out on his chest.

"The sofa, Brad. I'm offering you my sofa. Nothing more."

Brad went out to his car and returned with pajamas in one hand and a black plaid overnight kit in the other.

"Do you mind if I take a shower? Will that keep you awake?"

"I don't think anything can keep me awake tonight."

I stood by the end of the hallway, one hand on the wall to keep me standing. My left leg bent underneath me, the shin resting on the arm of the low sofa, my weight balanced on the right foot. From his vantage point, I expected that I looked like I had only one leg.

He set his pajamas and kit on the bathroom floor.

"Thank you, Madison."

He turned back and went into the bathroom, closing the door behind him. I went into the bedroom and leaned against the closed door. I didn't know how I would sleep knowing Brad was in the living room. Turns out my exhaustion made it a moot point.

When I woke, hours later, it was in pitch blackness, draped in a silence that choked me. I lay still. The clock read three forty-seven.

I have a theory about the hour between three and four o'clock in the morning. It is the dead of night. Too late to catch the remnants of the nightlife in Lakewood and too early to announce the morning people starting their routine. It is the hour when only the troubled are active: those whose thoughts are too filled with anxiety to wind down. Earlier hours might have been filled with a drug-induced sleep, but as drugs wear off, anxiety returns, circling through the brain in an endless loop of worry. I didn't like to admit it, but I knew anxiety well.

I hadn't known about the dead of night in the old days, the days filled with daisies, Doris Day movies, atomic kitchens, and refinished retro furniture. In those days, the dead of night might as well have been an exclusive club with an unmarked door and a password.

But somewhere in the past nine months, I had become a card carrying member.

The loneliness of being in my bed without a wriggling Rocky filled me with sadness. I missed him. I didn't know how early I could expect to hear from Effie, but it wouldn't be soon enough.

As the silence cloaked the night, I stood up and moved to the bedroom door. Brad's breathing was even. Silently, I crossed the room and drew back the curtains enough to see the moon casting a glow on Brad's black 1964 Mustang.

Brad was right. He knew me better than almost anybody. I had resentfully been denying the fact, while not acknowledging the obvious counterpoint to his statement. I knew him better than anybody else did too.

I knew he wouldn't wear a Hawaiian shirt past Labor day.

I knew he thought towels, soap, and underwear should always be white.

And I knew he never travelled for any length of time without a garment bag that held a formal suit, shirt, tie, and shoes.

I looked at the duffle bag sitting inside the floor of my bedroom. There was no garment bag in sight. His car keys were sitting on top of my dresser. Brad's even snoring sounded from the living room, and, as quietly as I could, I slid the key to his Mustang from the key ring.

I couldn't help thinking the story Brad told me had been edited to suit my needs. I needed to read the unabridged version. It was time to figure out exactly what kind of baggage Brad had brought with him to Dallas.

FIFTEEN

I devised a plan. It would be difficult, leaving the apartment while Brad slept. Difficult, but not impossible.

I'm not in the habit of going to my parking lot in the middle of the night in my pajamas, but this was a do-it-now opportunity. I knotted the terry cloth robe at the waist and slipped my feet into my slippers. I put my keys in one pocket, Brad's key in the other. I opened the bedroom and crept into the hallway.

As I tiptoed to the bathroom, Brad's snores grew louder, until a breath that caught at the back of his throat stopped his breathing altogether. I pressed myself against the wall and waited. A couple of seconds later he coughed twice and started breathing again. I slowly turned the deadbolt until the door was unlocked and slipped out of the narrowest opening I could.

A stiff knee and a need to be quiet made my descent on the staircase slow. When I reached the back door, I listened for a sign to tell me this was a good idea. The building was shrouded in silence so loud it was deafening. I looked out the glass pane on the door into the parking lot. A scraggly alley cat sat in the middle of the blacktop. I turned the door knob and pushed the door open and the cat turned around and ran underneath Brad's car. Good enough for me.

After easing the door shut behind me, I moved through the lot. Brad had backed into the visitor space, and the trunk of his Mustang butted up against the chain-link fence at the edge of the property. I looked up at my windows and saw nothing other than the lining of my curtains. With a deep breath of crisp night air, I went to the back of his car and plunged his key into the lock. The trunk popped open. A light illuminated the felted wool interior and exposed the contents. The expected garment bag. The expected roadside emergency kit.

And a very unexpected flat, brown leather briefcase monogrammed with the letters PS.

I recognized the initials. They matched the monogram on the handkerchief inside the box from Joanie Loves Tchotchkes.

The acrid odor of a skunk's spray caught my nostrils. I tucked my chin to my chest and pulled the collar of my robe up over my face. I looked around the lot for the culprit but saw nothing. It was difficult to take a deep breath with the smell hanging in the air, but I couldn't hold my breath forever. I grabbed the handle of the briefcase and pulled it toward me. I had to see what was inside.

A four-digit spinning lock kept two gold hinged plates in place. Without the code, I was at a standstill. The numbers stood sentry at one-two-three-four. I considered what that might mean.

When Brad and I worked at Pierot's, we changed the combination of the safe to our birthdays. Mine was April third. Four-three. Brad's was February first. Two-one. Together we were four-three-two-one. It was one of those silly things that felt special when we were first getting to know each other. Our own birthdays fit together as well as we thought we did. As a joke against the obvious, we kept the Pierot's lock at one-two-three-four, and shared a secret smile whenever Mr. Pierot commented on it.

I spun the dials to four-three-two-one. The night was so quiet, so still, that I heard the click of the lock popping even before I thumbed the release button.

Inside was an assortment of glass bottles, none bigger than a jar of craft paint. A collection of fine tipped brushes were rubber banded together and sat along the side. Nestled between the jars and the interior wall of the briefcase were stacks of hundred dollar bills rubber banded together. A lot of them. They were dog-eared, crinkled, and looked like they'd been in circulation for a while. And as much as I was spooked by the stacks of hundreds, they weren't the strangest thing in there.

No, the strangest thing was the sheaf of white paper with James Madison's image staring up at me from the center of a perfectly-rendered five thousand dollar bill.

Unlike the movies where sheets of uncut bills are confiscated as evidence to a counterfeiting scheme, these sheets each held one image. I picked one up and looked at the back. The reverse side was perfectly lined up with the front. The only thing missing was a very sharp paper cutter.

It didn't make sense. Five thousand dollar bills had been taken out of circulation in the late sixties. If the internet could be trusted, it was rumored that less than four hundred were in existence. Not only was the Federal Reserve not interested in producing them, but they destroyed them when they were discovered. It was one of the reasons the bill was worth so much to collectors.

But collectors required certification to establish authenticity. I could maybe see a person finding one in a suitcase of a relative's belongings that had been stashed in the attic, but how would someone go about passing a stack of them? What could possibly be the reason for copying a bill that's been out of circulation for so long? What did it have to do with the murder at Paper Trail and the missing numismatist, Stanley Mann? Where *was* the missing numismatist? And why did Brad care so much about the bill he sent me when he had a whole trunk of them?

I stood up straight, one hand on the lid to the trunk, and thought about the box from Joanie's. She said it had my name on it. Was it possible—could it be—that Brad was the one who put my name on the box and left it with her? That would be one way for him to be relatively certain he'd get the contents back—including the wallet that was hidden at the bottom. At least, if he was at my apartment, he could.

No, it couldn't be. It was too convoluted. The man who dropped off the box had a bad case of poison ivy.

Which might have cleared up in the time Brad claimed he was "giving me space."

Headlights bounced around the small driveway on the east side of the building that led to the parking lot.

I slammed the briefcase shut, but the paper I held stuck out between the hinges. An explosion of adrenaline shot through my chest, and I closed the trunk too. The latch caught, barely holding the trunk shut. I tried to free the key from the lock but it stuck. The scraggly cat shot past my foot. I stifled a scream and dropped onto all fours.

A dark brown sedan pulled into my lot and stopped in front of the line of parked cars. A door open and shut. A flashlight's beam danced across the gravel. I looked under the car at two shoes on the other side of the tire axel. Past them, under the next car, crouched a small animal. I assumed it was the cat, who would run away if either of us got too close. As the shoes walked around the right side of Brad's car, I slowly moved myself around the left, trying to stay quiet.

I reached the front of the car at the same time the trunk popped open. I was unused to having my bad knee bent for so long, and the pain was like a drill bit piercing the soft tissue under my knee cap. I had to stand up and flex it, or I wouldn't be able to move at all. I stretched my neck to the side and looked at the back of the car. The trunk lid blocked my view of the person. I turned around and looked at the car. It was the same brown sedan that had followed me home from the Polynesian restaurant. The front bumper was bent in two places from ramming the back of my car.

I slowly stood, bent at the waist. I was an obvious, open target in a white terry cloth robe and pink slippers, moving about a parking lot during the dead of night. I had to get back in the building.

Crouching low, I ran to the back door. My foot slipped on the loose gravel and I fought against tripping. I reached the back door and yanked on the doorknob. It was locked. I felt in my pocket for my keys, but they weren't there. I turned around and saw them lying in the gravel next to Brad's wheel.

The man from the brown sedan looked up from behind the trunk. His face—his whole head—was covered with a black knit ski mask that left distorted oval circles around his eyes and mouth. In the darkness, illuminated only by the full moon, I could make out little more than the whites of his eyes.

He pulled the briefcase from the trunk of the car and lowered the trunk lid until it snapped into place. His eyes followed mine to my keys, resting in the gravel. He came toward me.

I rattled the doorknob again, irrationally hoping it would jostle open. It didn't. I heard a hiss and the air filled with the stench of skunk again.

The man in the mask coughed twice. A furry black and white critter ran out from underneath and disappeared through the chain link fence. I pulled my robe up over my face. The man flung the briefcase onto the passenger seat of his car and drove out of the parking lot.

I gagged on the smell that hung in the air. I needed a deep breath but couldn't take one. I couldn't get into my car or into my building. I couldn't do anything without my keys. I had to go back for them.

I dropped to my hands and knees between Brad's Mustang and my neighbor's El Camino. My keys were within reach. The skunk spray must have hit the tire in front of me, because the proximity of the scent was sickening. I tucked my face into my robe again, inhaled through the fabric and held my breath as I reached under the car. By the time I succeeded, I was dirty, smelly, and nauseous.

The reasons I couldn't go back to my apartment were numerous. I unlocked the door to my car, pulled out of the lot, and drove into the darkness.

The roads of Lakewood were dark and lonely, the opposite of what I wanted. I had nothing with me, nothing but the pajamas on my back, the now-filthy terrycloth robe, and the fluffy pink slippers on my feet. I drove to my studio but didn't pull in. My car was too recognizable, like a yellow highlighter in the middle of a black and white page. I needed a different place to stay. One where nobody would think to look for me. I continued past my studio for about eight blocks and turned left on Monticello.

I was about to move in to Thelma Johnson's house.

Aside from the glow of an almost ripe moon, the M streets were dark. Thelma Johnson's house had a garage, and I remembered it to be empty. I used a key on my keychain to unlock and haul the door overhead, then returned to the car and pulled it in. One problem solved, temporarily, at least. After lowering the hinged door into place I threw the locking mechanism. I took off the skunk-scented robe and tossed it into the neighbor's trash bin, then scampered to the side entrance of the house.

Thelma Johnson had kept her house in the style to which she'd become accustomed sometime in the late fifties, I'd guess. Most of her belongings were in a storage facility behind my studio. Had I known that one day I'd seek refuge here, I would have left the furniture untouched, but it was too late to think about that now. It was too late to think about much other than a shower and sleep, both of which I desperately needed.

I found a half-empty bottle of liquid dish detergent by the sink and carried it upstairs. I stood under the hot spray of the shower far longer than usual and lathered twice. By the time I got out, my fingers and toes were wrinkled and I'd replaced the scent of skunk with lemons. The color of my normally pale skin was only slightly lighter than a third degree burn.

I wrapped a sheet around my torso like a toga and washed my pajamas and undies in the tub with the remainder of the dish detergent. The water bubbled up like a malfunctioning washing machine and seeped over the edge of the tub onto the floor. I hung my garments over the shower curtain rod and headed toward the bedroom.

From a hall closet that I'd yet to empty, I pulled a canary-colored blanket trimmed in satin along with a set of white sheets printed with faded flowers in pink, blue, and yellow. I carried them to the larger of the two bedrooms and set up camp in the middle of the floor where the four poster bed had once sat.

I was too keyed up to fall asleep, but there was nothing I could do until morning. The best thing for me to do was think. I stared at the ceiling for what felt like hours. My mind raced with implications and accusations based on the suitcase of questionable contents I'd seen in the trunk of Brad's car.

What did it mean? I didn't know. What I did know was that Brad's surprise visit to Dallas was a main course that came with a side dish of hidden agenda. Worse was the only thing I had for my snooping were more questions.

Which was the truth: the repentant former lover who wanted to pick up where we left off? Or this new Brad, who had secrets and a muddy past and was somehow connected to a counterfeiting plot I couldn't quite comprehend? Which version of the man I once knew was spending the night at my apartment?

Had Brad been watching me and my apartment since before he knocked on my door, bringing some unknown danger into my life? I'd invited him into my house. He was asleep on my sofa. Had he manipulated me into accepting his version of events, all the while vying for access to my apartment so he could search for the five thousand dollar bill?

The longer I lay there, the more I knew I had to do something. My mind raced a thousand different directions, and I couldn't begin to comprehend how Brad would react when he woke up and discovered I was missing.

I wasn't the only thing Brad would notice was missing. His key was missing from his key ring. If the masked man hadn't take it, then it was still in the trunk of his car.

I didn't know what Brad was up to, or whether he was one of the good guys or the bad.

By the time the sun came up, I'd dozed through fits of memories and nightmares. The sun filtered through yellow gingham curtains, painting the room with an innocent glow. And despite the idyllic colors of Thelma Johnson's bedroom, I was in a dark place.

I pushed myself into a sitting position, then stood up and flexed my joints. I was stiff in seven different places from sleeping on the floor again. The memory of the skunk's scent hung in my mind despite last night's shower. I moved to the bathroom and splashed water on my face. I wasn't sure what I was going to wear considering the only thing I had was a pair of not-quite-dry blue flannel pajamas.

I took another shower, this time using a squirt of pink liquid soap that sat on the edge of Thelma Johnson's bathtub. As the scalding spray massaged the kinks out of my muscles, I scrubbed my body like I wished I could scrub my life. I turned off the water and stepped into a room filled with steam.

Water was still running. I double checked the hot and cold nozzles, but that wasn't it. I dripped onto the yellow and white tile floor and moved to the window, looking for the source of the sound.

I found it in my front yard.

Tex stood in front of the flower beds with a hose in his hand, watering my garden.

I threw the lock on the window and pushed it open. "What do you think you're doing?" I yelled through the screen of the window. His head snapped up to look at me.

"Who is that?" He shielded his eyes. "Night?"

"Wait right there." I wrapped a towel around my otherwise naked body and descended the stairs. When I reached the front door, Tex had it open and was starting to come inside. I pushed him backward with my right hand and slammed the door with my left.

The towel dropped to the floor.

SIXTEEN

I whipped around and pressed my back against the door to keep it shut.

"Get out of here!" I yelled.

"Have you lost your mind?" he asked. "This is private property."

"Yes, it is private property. It's *my* private property. What about you? Who asked you to water my garden?"

"Your garden?"

"My garden."

"I knew there was a reason I wanted to water it."

"Go away, Lieutenant."

"I don't think so, Night."

"Then be a gentleman and get away from the front door so I can pick up my towel."

"Consider it done."

I turned my head to the side and watched Tex walk down the three concrete stairs out front. When I could no longer see him, I turned my head to the other side. He disappeared around the side of the house. I scooped up the faded towel from the floor and wrapped it around my torso, securing the end under my left arm. I went upstairs.

I put the damp pajamas on and looked out the bathroom window. Tex stood, hands on hips, assessing the condition of the flower beds. His apparent interest in gardening was unexpected.

"Wait there," I called out the window. "I have to talk to you about something." I went back downstairs and out the front door.

Tex hadn't moved. I felt about as naked in my pajamas as I had when I was naked.

"What are you doing here?" he asked.

"Terry Johnson left me this house. There were a couple thousand dollars in back taxes due, but I thought what the heck, so I paid them. Right now, nobody knows I own this place except me, you, and the real estate agent who made it all happen. I want to keep it that way."

"Where's your car?"

"In the garage."

"You're trying to lay low," he said. "Avoiding someone."

"Oh yeah, Mr. Detective?" I said, forgetting for a moment that Tex actually was a detective. "Care to elaborate on why you're here at the house once owned by the mother of your ex-girlfriend from twenty years ago? That wouldn't have anything to do with the fact that there's trouble in police paradise, would it? I'm guessing she wouldn't like knowing you're here tending my garden."

"Night, if you want me to take you seriously, you're going to have to stop talking about your untended garden." He smiled a half smile and turned around. "Okay, okay," he said, hands up like he was surrendering. "I'll leave."

"Wait—" I said, throwing a hand out to catch his arm. "I don't have anything here. Phone, wallet, clothes. I don't have Rocky."

"Where is he?"

"Effie's apartment. The center unit across the hall from mine."

"This is the second time you asked me to go to your apartment and pick up stuff for you."

I didn't answer at first. If Brad was up to something, it would be good for Tex to show up unannounced. See things for himself instead of taking my word for anything. I pulled my apartment keys from my key ring and handed them to him. "Meet me at my studio and we'll talk."

Tex looked up at the blue sky over the roof of Thelma Johnson's house and squinted at the sun. He rested one arm on the roof of his car and the other on the open car door.

"Let me give you some advice, Night. This thing with Turlington is a chance for you to get resolution. So get it and move on."

"You think I don't know that?"

"I'm just saying, don't ignore your garden so long that the weeds choke out whatever's trying to survive. If you do, you'll end up with nothing." He lowered himself into his car and pulled the door shut.

I was tired of double talk and of things not being what they seemed. I pounded on the driver's side window before he pulled away. He rolled it down halfway.

"What do you want from me?" I asked before he could say a word.

"I want you to acknowledge the truth."

"About what?"

"About your relationship with your boyfriend, for starters."

"What gives you the right to say that? Besides, you're in a relationship too. We are the same, Lieutenant."

He got out of the car and slammed the door. "You're right, we are the same. Only you won't see it." He moved toward me, and I stepped backward.

"I take it back, we're not the same. I asked you for a favor, but I never used you. You're using me now, just like you used me when you thought I could help you with the pillow stalkings. And as soon as it was over, after all of your attention, you dropped out of my life."

We were face to face. My eyes went from his eyes to his mouth. I closed the gap between us and kissed him.

His hands were like irons on my arms, searing through the flannel pajamas. I was shocked by my forwardness. As suddenly as I'd started the kiss, I stopped.

Tex's woodsy cologne mingled with the scent of the social garlic plant blooming by the foundation of the house.

"What do you want, Madison?" he asked in a husky voice.

"I want everybody to realize I'm an adult with a perfectly good life all by myself."

I could feel myself breathing deeply, could see the rise and fall of my own chest. I only partially knew what I was saying. Tex let go of my arms and stepped backward.

"Madison, my job is to protect the citizens of Dallas. You're a citizen of Dallas. But let me be clear. Ever since I saw you in that fluffy yellow nightgown, my thoughts about you are definitely of the adult variety."

I closed my eyes, afraid of the emotions I'd see in Tex's face. When I opened them, he wasn't looking at me anymore. He was looking at a Dallas Police patrol car that was driving past us.

I stepped back. I couldn't believe I'd kissed Tex in front of Thelma Johnson's house, or that we'd been spied by someone on the force. I was forty-seven years old, and I felt like I was fourteen.

I turned around and stormed back into the house. A part of me expected Tex to follow. He didn't.

I splashed cool water on my face and wrists and tried to ignore what just happened. Despite every single thing wrong with the way Tex and I interacted, there was a shred of attraction that I'd have to acknowledge, sooner rather than later.

What was it I'd said to Tex that he'd repeated to me? When people are in a relationship, they're supposed to want to spend time together.

So why was I spending more time with him than with Brad, or even with Hudson? And why was Tex spending time with me instead of Nasty?

I was not the type to juggle multiple men. I also wasn't the type to encourage cheating. Brad knew that. That's why, back when he was trying to get away from the people who he claimed were after him, he told me he was married. He knew it was the only way to get me to steer clear of him. But even before I had evidence that the reason for Brad's return was less than romantic, I hadn't been willing to open back up to him.

And there was Hudson, too. Why did I make excuses for not accepting his invitation or advances? Why did I go out of my way to only encourage our professional relationship?

And why, oh why, of all people in the world, did I end up kissing Lieutenant Tex Allen, the most annoying man this side of the Mississippi?

I gave Tex a fifteen minute head start before leaving for the studio. I didn't know if I could count on him to bring me anything, but I couldn't run about in my pajamas all day.

I drove to the studio and tried to read emails, but I was too tired to concentrate. I lay my head on top of folded arms and closed my eyes. It was the shrill ring of the donut phone that woke me up.

"Mad for Mod," I said into the receiver after knocking the base off the desk.

"Unlock your back door," commanded Tex through the phone. In the background I heard a small, excited yip.

I raced to the back in my wrinkled pajamas. I hadn't expected Tex to come through for me. When I opened the door, Rocky charged. Tex stood against his cop car with Rocky's leash in his hand. I ignored the leash and scooped up Rocky.

"I suppose I owe you a thank you," I said as Rocky licked the side of my face.

"Not now, Night," he answered.

Before I could think of a comeback, Officer Nast got out of the driver's side of the cruiser. Her eyes dropped to my pajamas and slippers, jumped to Tex for a moment, then settled on my face. Immediately, things changed.

"What's up, officers?" I asked.

"Donna has to use your restroom," Tex said.

I looked at his face, then hers, then back at his. She looked as annoyed with the situation as I felt. I didn't think for a second that they were there for a bathroom break, but I couldn't figure out anything else to say or do. I crossed the lot to the back door and unlocked it, then held it open for her to enter.

"My office is to the right. To the left of the cork wall is a small door. Inside is the powder room. Go crazy."

She pushed past me without saying thank you. I wasn't surprised.

As soon as I heard the sound of the door closing inside the office, Tex grabbed a bag from the back seat of his car and tossed it on the ground in front of me. He grabbed my upper arm and pulled me away from the building.

"We've got about three minutes. I did what you asked, now it's your turn."

"For what?"

"You know what I want, Night. You were holding out on me earlier, but I'm not a patient man."

"I don't think now is the time or place to talk about what that kiss meant." I looked past him at the back door. "Nasty is—Officer Nast is going to be back any second."

"Stop stalling, Night. You know what I'm talking about. Tell me what you know about the money."

SEVENTEEN

I searched Tex's face. His hand was still on my arm, biting into my flesh. I wasn't sure what he expected me to say or how I could possibly tell him my concerns in three minutes. Two and a half, really, since I had already wasted so much time thinking about our kiss.

"No," I said.

"There's no time for you to be stubborn."

"I'm not being stubborn. If you want to know what I know, you're going to have to figure out a way to be alone with me for more than three minutes."

His eyebrows shot up.

"That's not what I meant."

His crystal blue eyes bored into mine like drill bits piercing concrete, but I stood my ground. Despite what I'd said, I was being stubborn, but not for the reasons Tex thought.

He dropped his hand from my arm and tucked his thumbs into his front pockets, fingers dangling loosely.

"Fine. I'll figure out a way for us to be alone together."

The back door opened and Officer Nast walked out. The air smelled vaguely like the soap I keep on the sink. I couldn't tell if she had heard what Tex said or not, but the look on her face said she wasn't happy. I wondered, briefly, if I'd run out of toilet paper. As the two of them climbed into the car, Nasty behind the wheel, I picked up the handles of the duffle bag and backed away from the car. Nasty backed it around in a wide arc, then changed gears. Tex rolled down his window and pointed his index finger at me like a gun.

"I'll be in touch." The wheels spun across the gravel and they drove away.

I headed inside the studio and threw the bag on my desk. The scent of fried food wafted out from inside. I opened the industrial zipper and found a white Styrofoam takeout container nested on top of an ivory cashmere dress with tiny pearl buttons by the neckline. Onion rings and a knit dress? Tex's idea of thoughtful was to be questioned.

I wanted to focus on business, but I couldn't. Tex knew about the money. How? When? What had he discovered by going to my apartment? Something. His entire tone had changed in the span of an hour. I wanted to know what he knew, only I'd been down that path before. Tex was investigating a homicide. He might want to know what I knew, but that didn't mean he'd share anything with me.

The last few hours that I'd slept on the floor of Thelma Johnson's house had been a poor substitute for quality rest, and too many unfamiliar elements had crept into my life to allow me to be completely comfortable, even in my own home. My studio was more than simply a home away from home. I left the Closed sign on the front door, the lights off in the display area, and ducked into my office to try to figure things out.

The file on the fake Archie Leach sat open on the corner of my desk. I scanned everything I had on the man to try to figure out who he really was. Problem was, I ran an interior decorating business, not a crime lab. I couldn't dust his file for fingerprints or run it through a database of known criminals. There wasn't a whole lot I could do with the notes in the file. He filled out a questionnaire, let me know brief details about his living quarters, and given me an address I now knew not to be his.

Only, it was his address. Even the real Art had told me the white car that left the parking lot belonged to a long time tenant, Mrs. Bonneville, and that her son was staying with her. He did live there, even if he wasn't who he said he was. It would be easy enough to find him, if I enlisted the help of the valet attendant who had been robbed of his name. The only problem was the element of surprise.

The fake Archie Leach knew my car.

I rooted around on my desk for a different folder and the phone rang.

"Madison? You've been holding out on me!" said Connie.

"Good morning to you too," I said.

"That boyfriend of yours is a babe. You should have said something."

"What are you talking about?" I asked. "Connie, where are you?"

"The question is, where are you? I show up at your apartment with two cups of coffee and a file of ideas for my kitchen, and I'm greeted at your door by a tall, dark stranger with a serious case of bed head. Then he tells me he's your boyfriend. I thought you said you guys were on the outs?"

My concerns about Brad seemed fictional, like I'd fabricated a reason not to trust him. If I hadn't woken up in the middle of Thelma Johnson's bedroom floor, I might have believed I'd dreamt the rendezvous behind my building. But I hadn't.

"This is serious, Con. Where are you right now?" I repeated.

"I just told you I'm at your place."

"Get out of there. Now. Come to my studio. I'm here."

"I can't leave. Ned and Brad just went to the auto store. I said I'd wait here in case you got back."

"So you're alone?"

"Yes."

"And you brought a file of ideas for your kitchen?"

"Yes."

"And Brad and Ned are out somewhere?"

"Shopping for spark plugs, I think."

"Okay. Stay put. I'll be there before you can say 'Sputnik lamp.'"

I didn't comment on the fact that regular male bonding rituals transcended the cliques of hipsters. Ned and Brad probably did have a lot in common. The fact that Connie wasn't alone calmed me. In the cold light of day, I had to accept that I had nothing to back up my concerns.

I had no proof of what I'd seen in Brad's trunk. A briefcase filled with uncut James Madison five thousand dollar bills, lifted from the trunk of Brad's car by a man in a mask in the middle of the night? It was crazy, like a dream. Nobody would believe me.

I grabbed my copy of *The Glass Bottom Boat* and drove home. Maybe my life was a mess, but the least I could do was design Connie and Ned the kitchen of their dreams.

It took about ten minutes to get home. Connie was sitting out back. A purple bandana was tied over her head with the point jutting out in the back. Oversized white sunglasses hid half of her face. The two style elements made her look like a mod hillbilly. Not what she intended, I'd bet.

"You could have waited in the apartment," I said.

"I think I saw a cat out here. I was trying to make friends with it."

"You'd have better luck making friends with the resident skunk. Let's go inside."

I didn't tell her about my night or my morning. She didn't know me all that well outside of the decorating business. She didn't know me all that well inside of the decorating business either, I realized, and it hit me that here was my target client, a woman who had hired me legitimately. She didn't deserve to get caught up in my problems. What she deserved was a super-awesome atomic kitchen.

I popped the DVD into the player and cued up the kitchen scene. "I want you to see something," I said.

Connie sat transfixed while a small robot appeared on screen and cleaned up a mess that Doris Day's character had made. The six minute scene finished, and I paused the movie. I considered the possibility that I'd gone too far with the inspiration point and took a deep breath to start backpedaling. I'd play off the scene from the movie as a joke.

"Can you do that?" Connie asked in a quiet voice. The breath was still full in my lungs. My eyes flickered to the TV screen for a second before I looked back at her. "Is that something you'd be interested in?" I asked tentatively. She squealed with delight and clapped her hands twice. "Wait till I tell Ned. Oh, snap! That's so beyond anything I could have imagined! Do you mind if I call him now?" She pulled her phone out of her handbag and punched a couple of buttons.

Connie walked into the kitchen to make the call, and her voice trailed away. I grabbed a sketch pad from the desk and flipped to a blank page. I made a few quick notes. Computer programs for interior design abounded, but I'd always enjoyed the feeling of the pencil on the rough white paper.

I started a list of ideas down the right-hand side: remote control appliances, hidden trash cans, metal cabinets, magnets, Virden lighting, more remote control appliances, yellow CorningWare.

"Ned is stoked," Connie said. She set her phone on the coffee table and sat in the chair across from me. "They're planning a cookout, and he wants to know if you can bring the file over later."

"They—?"

"Ned and Brad. They're having a bromance. "

I didn't like that Brad was including Connie and Ned in his temporary Dallas circle. I stood from the desk and sat in the chair opposite Connie.

"Listen to me. I don't think it's a good idea for you or Ned to get too attached to him. We're not 100 percent a couple."

"He said that. But he said you're at about 85 percent, and I totally get 85 percent. That last 15 percent is what makes a relationship have sizzle."

"Connie, I need you to trust me on this."

"What did he do?" she asked.

Ignoring everything I'd learned or suspected about Brad since he arrived, I went with the truth.

"Connie, Brad lied to me about something pretty big. He wants me to forgive him, but a lot has happened since then."

"I don't know what happened, but he really cares about you, Madison. He told Ned that he came to Dallas to make big money, but I got the feeling that he dropped everything for you. When you weren't here this morning, he was worried."

"We've got some baggage."

"No offense Madison, but after twenty-five, everybody has baggage. Did I ever tell you about how I met Ned?"

I shook my head.

"It was at a lame karaoke bar where I worked. He was there with a whole crowd of people from work. I had never, ever sung at the bar even though my boss always wanted me to. Something about connecting with the customers. This girl Ned was with sang something stupid, some Joan Jett number. So I got up there and sang "The Ballad of Billie Jo." Knocked it out of the park too. I had five date requests by the end of the night but not one from him."

"So?"

"So instead of totaling his tab, I took a blank receipt and wrote 'Are you going to ask me out or what?' on it. He left enough money on the table to cover the tab and left. I couldn't believe it. I was on such a high and he squashed it."

"Nice story."

"He came to the bar four days later. He said he thought the right thing to do was to break up with his girlfriend first."

"So Ned's a stand-up guy."

"Ish. It wasn't until later that I found out that he hadn't even been dating the woman. It was all a story to keep me from feeling like I had that much control over him."

"Doesn't that make you mad? The fact that he basically lied and made up a story? That the foundation of your entire relationship was based on playing games?"

"No, I thought it was pretty cool. I love that story."

I'm the first to admit that I have not had the same romantic experiences as other women my age. There's a narrow pool of men who can justify the Doris Day appearance with the Gloria Steinem attitude. I've never been married, never been engaged. Most of my relationships bottomed out somewhere between six months and a year, thanks to the inevitable compatibility/control issues. Brad had been the one who changed all of that.

"You're coming to the cookout, right?" She turned toward the door.

"I don't know. I have a lot to do today." I bit my lower lip and thought for a second.

Connie's face fell. "Okay, sure. If you want to come, you should, but I'm not going to make you do something you don't want to do." She pulled the mod white sunglasses back down on her face and left out the back door.

I gave her a ten minute head start and called a cab. I had two hours to decide what to do about the cookout. The same two hours I had to go undercover. Half an hour later, driving a rented Ford Explorer, I was on my way to the Turtle Creek Luxury Apartments.

EIGHTEEN

I pulled up to the valet stand and rolled down the window. Art Leach scowled at me when recognition hit. "You again. What do you want now, Ms. Night? Or are you not Madison Night today?" he asked, glancing at the plates on the front of my car.

"I'm Madison Night as much as you are Art Leach. You're still Art Leach, aren't you?"

"What's your point?"

"I need to talk to you. Can you take a break?"

The thin man picked up the phone in his booth, said something, then hung up. "Put this on your rearview mirror," he said, handing me a hanging visitor tag. "Take any available space and meet me by the lanai."

I drove the Explorer past the valet stand and scanned the lot for the white Lexus. It wasn't there. I parked close to the building and cracked the windows for Rocky. Art stood under the canopy, shielding his eyes from the sun.

"Can we sit down somewhere?"

"No. I have about ten minutes until I have to be back in the booth. What do you want?"

"White Lexus. You told me one of the women who lives here drives a white Lexus, right? Mrs. Bonneville? And you said her son Grant was staying with her?"

"We don't spy on our tenants, Ms. Night. We're a little more formal. That's one of the reasons Mrs. Bonneville's been here for so long."

He checked his watch and looked at the valet stand. The white Lexus pulled in. I strained to make out the identity of the driver, but couldn't see through the tinted windows. Turns out it didn't matter. Harry came out of the valet stand and opened the driver's side door. A small orange Pomeranian hopped down to the side of the car and pranced around Harry's feet. The handsome woman with the gray frosted hair followed.

"That's her, isn't it? That's Mrs. Bonneville?"

"Don't get any ideas. My job is to make sure our tenants feel like they're at home here. If you tell her I told you who she is, she'll report me."

"With all due respect, Art, that woman's son hired me to do a job. It's not outside the realm of possibility that she knows something about it."

"No way." He crossed his arms and moved between us.

Harry waved his arms back and forth from the valet stand, trying to get our attention. Art looked at him. Harry pointed at his watch then held up two fingers.

"Okay, Ms. Night. You didn't come here to hang around, hoping to chat up one of our tenants, so why did you come here?"

"I know this is an inconvenience, but something is going on around Dallas that is connected to the break in at your apartment complex, and it's not good. I don't know the details, but anything you can tell me would help."

"You're not a cop. You're a decorator. Right?"

"Right."

"So why exactly am I supposed to tell you anything? What are you going to do with the information? Change my light bulbs?"

"I'm trying to piece together information. That's all. What did the police tell you when you reported the break-in?"

He rubbed his eyes for a sec, and then held his index finger at Harry. He turned back to me and dropped his voice.

"I didn't report the break-in. There was only one thing missing, and I didn't want anybody to know about it."

"What was it?"

"A wad of tip-money. I don't claim it on my taxes, so I thought it was better not to acknowledge it. Besides, I don't trust the cops. For all I know, they'd find the money and keep it for themselves."

It didn't surprise me that he hadn't bothered to report the theft, especially if it would possibly draw his high tippers into some kind of investigation. "If I might ask, how much are we talking about?" I needed to establish a frame of reference.

"Eleven thousand dollars."

I leaned forward and tipped my head slightly. Just last night I'd seen a wad of hundred dollar bills in Brad's trunk along with the counterfeiting supplies.

"Did you say eleven thousand dollars?" I asked, making sure I hadn't been imagining things.

He nodded.

"That's a lot of cash to have sitting around your apartment."

"That's a lot of cash to *not* have sitting around my apartment."

He had a point.

I didn't know what else to ask Art, and I sensed our chat was almost over. In the background, Mrs. Bonneville walked her Pomeranian out of the building toward the sidewalk that lined the street, much like she had done the last time I saw her. I waited until she rounded the corner before I spoke.

"I know you have to run. Thank you for taking time to talk to me. Is it okay for me to leave my car parked for a second while I take my dog for a quick walk?" I gestured to the Explorer, where Rocky's head was peeking out of the opening.

"Sure, just don't take too long."

I opened the door and Rocky bounded out. I clipped his leash onto his collar and whispered details about our plan to him. Rocky, I have found, makes an excellent undercover operative.

We headed to the sidewalk. I held my head high and acted like everything was fine. Twice Rocky pulled over to sniff the colorful impatiens that filled the garden beds by the door, but I tugged him forward. We had to hurry. I couldn't afford to waste a perfectly good pee on flowers outside of Mrs. Bonneville's range.

As soon as we rounded the corner by the hedge, I scanned the sidewalk for Mrs. Bonneville, surprised she'd gotten away. And then, as if she'd been hiding, she straightened up from behind a wrought-iron bench that faced the street. I imagined I knew what she'd been doing, and I was impressed a woman of her apparent means was responsible enough to pick up her Pomeranian's poo.

"Let's go." Rocky led the way. Mrs. Bonneville was heading back toward us and, as we grew closer, Rocky pulled me to the side while he lifted a leg on the landscaping. When he finished, he trotted back to the sidewalk and stretched his leash so he and the Pomeranian could sniff each other.

"Your Shih Tzu is charming! What's his name?" she asked.

"Rock. After Rock Hudson," I added.

"Now there was a looker. And you looking so much like Doris Day, it's perfect!" she smiled.

"That's what I like to think. He does make an excellent companion, that's for sure. And who do we have here?" I asked. I started to bend down to pet her Pom and pain shot through my knee at the deep bend. I felt my face contort with the pain.

"My dear, are you okay?" she asked. She put a hand out onto my arm and touched it ever so lightly.

"I'm sorry. I recently had an operation on my knee and occasionally the pain flares up. I wasn't expecting it."

"Sit, sit, sit. Let's let Rock and Giuseppe get to know each other while you rest."

We moved to the bench and sat next to each other, staring at the perfectly manicured grounds opposite the apartment complex. The green grass sloped down into a small creek. A white footbridge connected the yard to the other side. Mrs. Bonneville caught me staring at the scene.

"Pretty, isn't it?"

"It is."

"I've seen a lot of people get married on that bridge. It looks so peaceful, doesn't it?" When I agreed, she laughed. "But what people don't know is there's a secret hidden below that bridge."

"What kind of secret?"

"Most of the boys from the neighborhood can probably tell you. The slope is lined with poison ivy."

I sucked in a breath. "Where, exactly?"

"Oh, don't fret. It doesn't spread and I've never seen it on this side of the street. My son took Giuseppe for a walk last week and, Lord help me, I don't know why he decided to stray down to the water, but he did. His arms were covered with a rash for a few days. Giuseppe is lucky that he didn't catch it, aren't you?" She scooped up her dog and nestled him to her chest in an affectionate hug. His pointy nose lifted up to her face and he sniffed her check.

My heart was racing with this new information and I couldn't wait to share it with Tex. Before I could think of what to say next, Rocky jumped onto my lap and put his paws on my chest. He sniffed me, sniffed Mrs. Bonneville, and licked her pearls.

"Rocky!"

She broke out in a charming laugh. "Young lady, puppy kisses are to be cherished. When life gets to the point when you can't appreciate the spontaneous affection of a dog, then you need to reassess your priorities. And now I can tell my friends I've been kissed by Rock Hudson." She laughed again. "We must be getting back home, but you sit here for a few more minutes and give that knee a chance to rest." She set Giuseppe onto the sidewalk and he pulled her away in the direction of Turtle Creek Luxury Highrise.

Our spontaneous trip had netted me enough information to be worthwhile, but I knew Mrs. Bonneville would become suspicious if I followed her back to the apartment complex. I ran my hand over Rocky's fur and kissed the top of his head while we waited. A crisp breeze swept over the grass in front of us, tipping the blades. I closed my eyes and breathed in the scent of the vibrant purple flowers behind us.

After waiting ten minutes that felt like an hour, I stood up. Rocky hopped onto the sidewalk and we walked back to the building. I hesitated by the corner, peeking around the hedge for signs of Mrs. Bonneville or her dog. They weren't there. I led Rocky to the Explorer and clicked the locks open. Rocky jumped into the passenger side door. After I shut it behind him, I felt a tap on my shoulder. It was Harry.

"Sorry to scare you, ma'am, but Art says you wanted to talk about Mrs. Bonneville's son?"

"Yes, I do, but he won't cooperate."

"I can tell you a couple of things."

I felt my forehead scrunch up in confusion.

"Art's on probation for getting caught talking about the guests. He's not going to risk his job by talking to you."

"That's too bad, but I have to respect his decision." I walked around to the driver's side of the car and opened the door. Harry stood back while I put the car in reverse and backed out of the space.

There was one car in front of me by the exit. Harry walked alongside of the Explorer. He put his hand on the door by my window. I got the feeling he didn't want me to leave, so I gently depressed the brake a second time.

"You're going to have to let go of the car if you want me to leave, Harry."

"It's just—Ms. Night, I keep thinking, maybe Mrs. Bonneville's son had something to do with the robbery."

I hit the brakes more forcefully this time. "Why? Did you see something suspicious?"

"I didn't see anything. I wasn't working here that night. But I didn't trust that son of Mrs. Bonneville when he arrived and I still don't. She's a nice lady, and she takes care of us. All of us. I don't know where her money comes from, but I don't want to see it go away too quickly, if you catch my drift. Art might not want to help you out, but I will. The son showed up uninvited and she's too polite to tell him to leave."

"What makes you say that? Anything specific?"

"Right now it's just a feeling. Something about that guy stinks, only I don't know what it is."

A horn sounded behind me and I realized I was holding up the exit lane. "Here's my card." I slid a Mad for Mod card out from my silver business card case and held it out to Harry. "Do me a favor. Keep an eye on him. If you see any patterns in when he comes and goes, let me know. You can call either of the numbers on that card and leave a message."

He stared at the card for a few seconds, and then flipped it back and forth against his fingertips. Another car got into the lane to exit the parking lot. I couldn't tie up the valet station any longer.

"Harry, I have to go."

"Not yet. Park over there," he said, pointing to the five minute loading space in front of the building. I followed his instructions and waited for him to come over to the car.

"I've seen this card before."

"I gave one to you the other day. Art too."

"No, before that. It doesn't make any sense. Two days after the son showed up, he asked if I'd heard of your business. No offense, but I didn't. I looked you up and printed out the directions for him. A couple of days later I asked if he found you okay. He looked at me like I was nuts and said he didn't know what I was talking about. Got so angry I thought he was going to lodge a complaint against me, so I apologized and forgot about it. A week later Mrs. Bonneville asked me to have her car cleaned. I drove it to the car wash and found your business card under one of the floor mats. I had my proof that I wasn't nuts, but for some reason the guy didn't want me to remember he asked about you."

"When was this?" I asked.

"Last month."

"That can't be. I only just met him at my studio two days ago."

"Seems like the guy takes his time making a decision, then. It was definitely last month because it was my girlfriend's birthday. Mrs. B. gave me a nice tip, and I tried to spend it all on dinner."

"Tried?"

"That's the weird part. The restaurant wouldn't take my money. Said I was trying to pass a counterfeit bill."

NINETEEN

"Counterfeit?" I repeated.

Harry nodded. "It had to be some kind of a mix-up. My girlfriend was embarrassed, and I wanted to get her out of there. I charged the meal, and we left."

"Do you have the bill?"

"No. I took it to the bank the next day and deposited it."

"But—"

"That's why I said it had to be a mix-up. There was no problem at the bank."

The horn sounded a second time, and Art waved me forward. Harry tapped the roof of the car twice, and I pulled out of the parking lot, sure of nothing.

I drove to Thelma Johnson's house only because I needed a safe place to sit and think. I parked out front next to the hedges that lined the property. They looked as if they'd been maintained. More of Tex's handiwork? Exactly how much time did he spend here?

I shook thoughts of him from my head. There wasn't time to think about Tex now. I had to try to figure out Brad's true motivation for being in Dallas. Had Brad and Mrs. Bonneville's son ever been in the same place at the same time? I didn't think so. Which maybe meant they were working together. Or ... maybe not.

I was at a loss.

If Brad knew someone was after him, that someone had tracked him to Dallas, maybe he had been looking for a place to crash. Whether it was because he wanted a reconciliation or not, my apartment building would suit his needs. But he wasn't staying at my apartment. He said he kept a room at the Brite House. I wasn't familiar with that apartment complex, but Dallas was filled with temporary living quarters that were constantly bought, renovated, and renamed. It was almost impossible to keep up with them all.

There was no avoiding Brad, not tonight. Connie's invitation rang in my ears. I couldn't leave her or Ned alone with Brad. Not when I wasn't sure what he was up to. When I saw him tonight, I'd ask about the Brite House.

I was surprised Connie hadn't called to see what was keeping me, and I made a preemptive call to let her know I was running late. I got her voice mail and left a brief message of apology.

Next, I called Joanie. She answered on the first ring.

"Joanie, it's Madison. Do you still have that white twin bed in your store?"

"Sure. I had to move it to the back room because of space. Why?"

"If you can deliver it for me, I'll take it."

"Twin bed? Sure. It fits in the pick-up truck."

I made arrangements to buy the bed and negotiated delivery in exchange for dinner at the Japanese Kobe Steakhouse. I offered an extra hundred if she picked up sheets, blankets, pillows, and dog food. After giving her directions to Thelma Johnson's house and telling her where to find the spare key, I added, "I'm not going to make it there until late tonight."

"Why are you setting up camp at this place and not sleeping at home?"

"It's complicated," I said, just like I'd told Connie.

"Does 'complicated' mean you're going to be buying more stuff from me?"

"Possibly."

"Then I'm all for complicated," she said. "I'll deliver the bed after I close at six. That okay?"

I thought about my afternoon plans and the cookout at Ned and Connie's place. Brad would be with me, and we'd be nowhere near Thelma Johnson's house.

"After six sounds perfect. Thanks, Joanie."

I was so late that I thought for sure Connie would have called me back by now. That or she was so angry at me that I was no longer welcome at her house. Kiss a fat commission and a friend good-bye.

I flipped through the recently dialed numbers on my phone until I found her cell and called it again. Again, the call went to voicemail.

"Connie, it's Madison. I'm sorry it's taking me this long. I'm on my way. Promise. Call me back if you want me to pick up anything."

As much as I wasn't in the mood to go to the cookout, I had to, to protect my friends. I didn't want to accept that Tex was right; life was like a garden. At the rate I was going, every friendship, every relationship worth keeping would dry up and die because of my refusal to tend to them. If I wanted everything to come up roses, I was going to have to get dirty.

I drove the rented Explorer to the Duncan's house. Brad's Mustang was parked in the driveway. Had he found his key in the trunk of his car, or did he have an extra one?

Brad was sitting on the front step with his head in his hands. I got out of the car and fumbled with Rocky's leash. Brad rushed over and threw his arms around me, pegging my own arms to my side.

"Maddy! You're okay!" He held me in a bear hug that allowed little reciprocity. "When I didn't hear from you, I got worried."

"I got up early and went to the studio."

"But your car was at the apartment—"

"I had to pick up some furniture so I rented an Explorer." I looked over his head at the house. "Where are Connie and Ned? I've been trying to call her to tell her I was running late, but she's not answering the phone. Did they cancel the cookout?"

Brad eased his embrace and stared at me as if something was wrong.

"Brad, what's going on?"

"Connie's in the hospital."

"The hospital? Why? I just saw her this morning. What happened?"

"I thought you were with her."

Brad's curly black hair was more wild than usual. I could tell he'd been running his fingers through it. His styling product had long since lost the battle against his natural curls. A breeze pushed the top of it around and he reached up and pushed it back and held it down.

When he realized I was staring at him, he dropped his hand and hugged me a second time.

"Brad, why is Connie in the hospital?" I asked again, pulling away from him.

"She was in a car accident. It's all my fault."

"I don't understand."

"She said she wanted to drive your car. Your spare keys were in a drawer in your kitchen. I didn't see the harm in it, so I told her to take it for a spin."

"What happened?" I asked. A numbness radiated from my chest to my arms and legs.

"I don't know."

Concern for Connie kept my other emotions in check. Anger, that Brad thought he could offer up the use of my car to Connie. Fear, that Connie's accident was a message. Suspicion, that Brad had been going through my drawers, looking for something. I was going to have to act like nothing had changed.

"Take me to the hospital, Brad." I picked up Rocky.

"You can't take Rocky to the hospital. Leave him here."

"He's coming with me. This house is unfamiliar to him and I don't want him to think I'm abandoning him."

"He's a dog, Maddy."

Something inside me snapped. My fists balled up and I stepped away from him. "Will you stop calling me that? My name is Madison! And this is Rocky! And he's not just a dog!"

"Hey, hey, calm down. I'm sorry. I thought you liked it when I called you Maddy. I didn't realize—I'm sorry. Come here," Brad said.

He held his arms open again. I stayed where I was. Inside I was freaking out. My life was being divvied up amongst everyone I knew and I was losing myself in the process.

"I can't leave Rocky," I said. "He has to come with me."

"Anything you say, Mad-Madison. We'll figure it out."

We walked to his Mustang. He unlocked my door and held it open while I got inside, even though I'd told him more than once I could open my own doors. I buckled into the seat without saying a word.

We made it to the hospital quickly. Brad parked in a visitor spot by emergency. A terror had come over me, a dread that something was far more wrong than I imagined. I didn't want Brad to know how scared I was to walk into that emergency room.

Brad got out of the car first. I hugged Rocky and set him on the driver's side seat. I leaned in close and whispered, "Sometimes we have to pretend we trust people we don't. This is one of those times. I'm going to go with that man, but I'll be back. Okay?"

Rocky looked up at me and tipped his head. Another person might feel foolish confiding in a Shih Tzu, but in the middle of all of the lies and secrets, it felt good to talk to Rocky. I talked to him all the time before Brad had showed up. For the first time in days, I had my confidant back and I could tell him how I really felt.

I cracked the windows and locked the doors. Ned rushed across the lobby to us as soon as we entered the waiting room.

"They haven't told me much, but she's going to be okay. I still don't know what happened. I got a call that she was here, and the doctors came out to ask about allergies and her medical history. They had to operate. Somebody came out and said things went well and now she's resting. I keep asking when I can see her and they keep saying soon. I don't know what soon means, man, I don't know what any of it means."

"Wait here," I said.

I approached the desk. My knee was throbbing and I took full advantage of the limp. A woman wearing pink leopard-printed scrubs looked up at me.

"Hi, I'm Madison Night. My friend was brought in earlier. Her name is Connie Duncan. Do you have any information on her condition? Do you know when we can see her? Her husband's been here for a while and he's in bad shape. Is there anything you can tell me?"

A voice behind me said, "You're Madison? Madison Night?"

I turned around and faced a young male doctor in standard blue scrubs. He held a clipboard by his side. A white face mask hung around his neck, the top strings untied.

"Yes, I'm Madison Night."

"She's been asking for you."

Ned stepped forward. "Can I see her? I'm her husband."

"Madison first. She's been asking for Madison since she came in."

I crossed the lobby and squeezed Ned's hand. "I'll be fast."

Before anybody could argue that Connie and I weren't close enough for me to get first visitation privileges, I followed the doctor down the hallway.

Connie's room was not unlike the room I recovered in after my operation. White gauze curtains allowed sunlight to offset the grim reality of the machines by the head of her bed. Instead of a knee held in a stirrup like mine had been, her head was wound with gauze. A steady beep monitored her heart rate. When she saw me, she tried to sit up. The doctor told her to relax.

"Keep your visit short, Ms. Night. With all due respect, her husband should be the one in here, not you."

I nodded. When he left the room, I moved closer to the bed. Connie spoke before I could.

"I'm sorry, Madison. I'm so sorry," she choked out. Her face turned red and her eyes filled with tears that spilled over the side of her face and dampened the pillow. "Your car. It's destroyed." Sobs took over, shaking her.

"Hey, hey. It's just a car. It's you I'm worried about. I can get another car, but Ned can't get another wife. Not one who can sing the 'Ballad of Billie Joe,' " I said, trying to cheer her up.

"I should have listened to you."

"Is this about Brad?"

"It's about your car. I told Brad I wanted to drive it and he gave me your keys and told me to take it for a joyride."

I tensed up, my hand going numb. "How did the accident happen?"

"I don't know. I was driving along fine and all of a sudden I slammed into the back of a semi. It was like—" She stopped crying for a second while she searched her thoughts. "It was like something snapped under my foot and the brakes stopped working."

TWENTY

My knees, the good one and the bad one, went weak, and I reached behind me for something to sit on. My hand connected with a small stool on wheels and I dropped into it.

"The brakes stopped working?"

She wiped the tears from her eyes. "I don't know how else to describe it. I wasn't going fast. I saw the red light well before I got to the intersection, even from behind the truck. I stepped on the brakes and nothing happened. I stepped again and again, and the last thing I saw was the back of the truck coming at me." She started crying again. "I don't remember getting here. I don't remember being operated on. I don't remember anything."

I pressed the call button on her nightstand and a nurse showed up and pushed me out of the way. "Please go back to the waiting room."

I stumbled out of the room and back to the men. I was too stunned to speak, afraid that whatever came out of my mouth wouldn't make sense. Ned rushed past me to the doctor, who led him into Connie's room.

"I want to go home. Take me home, Brad. Please."

"What happened in there?" he asked.

"I don't want to talk about it."

"You have to talk about it, Madison. I don't know what's going on, but you can't shut down. First you're gone when I wake up, then you're two hours late to a party, and now your friend is in the hospital and you're acting like it's you, not her. You have to tell me what's going on."

"Just get me out of here now. We'll talk when we get to my apartment."

I clutched Rocky to my chest on the ride home, staring out the window at the trees whizzing by. Brad parked in the back in my space, expertly backing into it in one attempt. The three of us walked to the door.

I slowly ascended the stairs and entered my apartment. I looked at the yellow walls, the daisy curtains, the newly exposed hardwood floors and back at Brad. We were always talking about how well he knew me. It was time for me to find out a little more about him.

"Sit down, Brad, we need to talk."

"Maddy—"

"I'll get us a drink." I went to the kitchen and fixed a small pitcher of martinis. I carried it, along with two glasses, to the living room. Brad sat on the sofa and Rocky was in front of him, growling.

"Rocky, go to your bed," I commanded. He looked at me, and I repeated myself. He dropped his head and tail and padded into the bedroom. I handed Brad a glass and lowered myself into a chair opposite the sofa. Brad poured the drinks and handed me one. I stared at the olive, speared by a plastic red sword, resting in the bottom of the glass, like it was a crystal ball that would give me answers. I knew the answers would have to come from Brad instead.

"This thing between us, you being here, back in my life, it's overwhelming."

I don't know how I expected him to react. I hadn't said that the brakes of my car were tampered with or that it could just as easily have been me driving, but judging by the way his face went white, he got the picture. I was glad. I didn't want to spell it out.

"Baby, it doesn't have to feel that way. I keep trying to tell you that I'm here for you, like I wish I had been all along."

"I hear you, and I want to believe you, but everything started happening when you sent me that five thousand dollar bill. I have questions. I need answers."

"Ask me anything, Mads."

I looked at his face. He was the picture of openness, of honesty. He leaned forward, watching me. Inviting me to confront the questions I'd been wrestling with since I found out the truth about his lie.

"Tell me about the night you recorded the message to me."

Brad leaned forward and held his head in his hands. His fingers buried deep in his hair. When he looked up, I noticed dark circles under his eyes. I didn't know how I'd missed them earlier.

"A couple of men came to Pierot's studio one night. They bought a pair of Eames lounge chairs. The originals. Remember them? They were beautiful. Rosewood, mint condition. Mr. Pierot was out of the country—Paris, I think—and he left me in charge. You were out with some friends so I stayed late remerchandising the store, rotating the inventory. I'd always wanted to change things up, but Mr. Pierot had very specific ideas. Why that night, I don't know. I had free time and extra energy. I knew if business picked up he'd be okay with whatever I did, so I took a chance."

"Which friends?"

"A couple of women from the decorator's guild. You left early that day. I'll never forget that. We spent the morning on the four poster bed in the back room, but that day you said you couldn't stay with me. You had plans—I think *Lover Come Back* was playing at a theater in New York and a bunch of you took the train."

"I remember that day too." I thought back for a brief moment to those unwanted memories of my time in Pennsylvania. There had been spontaneity to my life then. A movie plays in a different state, and I rally some friends and hop a train to go see it in on the big screen.

"These two men came in to the store and looked around. They saw the Eames chairs I was bringing up front and made an offer. Cash. Fifteen grand."

"You didn't think it was strange that they gave you cash?"

"It happened every now and then. Remember how Mr. Pierot said cash customers were some of the most loyal? When someone walks in with that amount of cash they have a reason for not using a credit card. It wasn't the most common thing, but I thought maybe these were some of his regular clients. I didn't want to screw up the sale while he was out of town."

"When did you realize something was wrong?"

"We finished the transaction, and I locked the money in the safe. The banks weren't open for a couple of days. I figured it would be fine. Only, it wasn't. When I went to deposit the money, I found out it was counterfeit. I'd given away fifteen thousand dollars of merchandise because I was too stupid to look closely at the phony bills."

"Why didn't you say anything?"

"What was I going to say? That I'd made a fifteen thousand dollar mistake because I was bent on impressing Mr. Pierot? No. I had an address for the men, where they wanted the chairs and ottomans to be delivered. I didn't know what I was getting into, so I took Mr. Pierot's pistol, the one he kept in the case in the office, and went to see them."

"Brad, that's crazy."

"Madison, I created a problem. I wanted to solve it. Anyway, when I knocked on the door, two guys asked me inside. They'd been expecting me."

"Do you know who they were?"

"Philip Shayne and Grant Bonneville."

I sucked in my breath but hoped Brad didn't notice.

"What happened?"

"The money was a test. They wanted to see if I could tell the money was fake and how I'd react. They wrote me a cashier's check for the furniture and made me an offer I couldn't refuse."

He went silent. I waited a couple of seconds for him to continue. Rocky carried his stuffed panther into the living room and dropped it by my feet. I reached down for the stuffed animal and tossed it into the hallway.

"That's not good enough, Brad."

He looked up at me. "They said if I helped them with their operation, they'd let me live. I started working for them the next week."

I leaned back in my chair. Rocky ran back to me with the Beanie Baby in his mouth. I pulled it from him and tossed it again. He ran after it, and I turned back to face Brad.

"That was in summer. That was six months before we went skiing in the Poconos."

He nodded.

"You were trying to get out, weren't you? You lied to me to keep me out of it."

He nodded again.

"How do you know it's over?" I asked suddenly. He looked confused. "You act like you're sure it's over. How can you be? How can I be—how can you be—sure?"

He stood up from the sofa and came over to my chair, kneeling on the floor in front of me.

"Come on, Mads, don't you remember that first night together in the back of Pierot's? You fell asleep in my arms. When you woke up, we opened that bottle of Perrier Jouet Mr. Pierot was saving for a special occasion. It was three thirty in the morning, and you walked to the window wrapped only in a sheet."

I turned my face away from him. I wouldn't let him pull at my heartstrings.

"You looked luminous, with your skin glowing like alabaster. You held a radiance that I wanted so desperately to believe I had something to do with. That's the night you told me you had a price: five thousand dollars. You said you couldn't argue with a denomination with your name on it."

Brad's hands were on my knee, and his voice was pleading. He wanted me to acknowledge that I remembered that night, but I couldn't.

From the moment he lied to me and let me ski away from him, down the black diamond slope at the Poconos ski resort, snap my knee the first time and end up in the first of a string of hospital rooms, I had done my best to block out all evidence that Brad Turlington existed. I'd done such a good job that his return had stunned me into emotional amnesia. It was time to rely on that shock, to keep me calm, keep me strong.

"Brad, you say it's over, but it's not. Grant Bonneville is here in Dallas. He's going by a different name, but it's him. He came to my studio and posed as a client."

"What about Philip Shayne?"

"He was found dead a few nights ago."

"That means Bonneville found a new partner."

"Brad, if you're involved in something illegal you need to go to the police. I'll give them the bill. You tell them what you know. They'll find these guys."

I stood up and reached for my phone. "I have friends on the force. They'll help you."

He chuckled. "Your friends aren't my friends, Maddy."

"They can be."

"I don't think so. Your cop friend tried to scare me away. Said something about not playing games with you, even though nothing could be further from my mind."

I got angry. Tex hadn't said anything about warning Brad.

"I can't believe Lt. Allen said that to you. When did this conversation take place?"

"Her name wasn't Allen, it was Nast. Officer Nast."

I froze. Nasty had been the one to warn Brad about me? I hadn't expected that of her. It didn't sit well, but I didn't want Brad to know that.

My body tensed up and immediately I fought to relax so he wouldn't notice.

Days ago, I thought the five thousand dollar bill was at the center of everything. Now I didn't know what I thought, except that the five thousand dollar bill had been in the rent drop off box in my apartment building, where I'd put it the day it arrived. It was about a week past the date that rent was due. That box was probably overflowing, and someone might start to get curious about the

Night Company and whether or not they were taking care of business. I had to do something about that envelope. Slowly, I stepped away from Brad.

"It's been a long day. Why don't you take a shower first? We can talk about this in the morning."

As soon as I heard the shower running, I left the apartment and headed to the rent drop off box. I stopped two feet shy of the lobby.

The drop off box was unlocked and the checks—and the original five thousand dollar bill—were missing.

TWENTY-ONE

Mrs. Young was next to the rent drop off box on her cell phone. "One of my neighbors said I should call you about it. Are you sure the landlord won't mind?" she said.

She tossed a grocery store circular into the recycling bin and said, "Yes, I can hold." Her hand hovered over the receiver and she mouthed "Does the Night Company usually leave the box unlocked?" She nodded at the wall.

"Not usually." I reached up and flipped the brass lid shut.

"You don't think something happened, do you?"

"Like what?" I asked.

"I don't know. Maybe the mysterious Night Company met with some foul play." Her eyes grew wide, and she smiled. "I have a bit of a dark side. Read too many mysteries, I imagine. Probably just a mistake."

"Probably." I hesitated a moment, flipping through the keys on my key ring. "Are you talking to Hudson?" I asked.

"I'm holding for Hudson," she said to me. "Yes? I'm still here," she said into the phone.

"May I talk to him?"

"Now it's your turn to hold on," she said into the phone and held it toward me.

"Hudson, it's Madison."

"Hey, lady," he said.

"Hi," I said. My hands were shaking, and I could hear the waver in my voice.

"You okay?" he asked.

I forced a smile at Mrs. Young, "I'm—it's been a long night." I turned my back on my new tenant and looked out the front door. There were no signs of life on the street. "Hudson, I'm the one who told Mrs. Young to call you. I don't think the Night Company will mind, do you?"

"I think it'll be fine." The low, singsong gravelly sound of his voice sent a tremor down my spine. "Listen, Madison, I need to talk to you. Can you come by tomorrow? In the afternoon?"

"I'll try."

"Good. See you then." he said.

"See you tomorrow, Hudson," I said and handed the phone back to Mrs. Young. I said good night and was halfway down the hallway when she called out to me.

"Have you ever met anyone from the Night Company?"

I turned back around. "When I first moved in, yes. We did a walk through. Didn't you?"

She shook her head.

"Then I guess my referral did some good." I smiled.

"You really don't think it's odd that Hudson has keys to the apartments?"

"No, I don't."

"I guess I'm not so used to trusting people. I'm in a new city, in a new building, and I find out a stranger has the key." She scratched the back of her hand. "But you seem to trust him, and he's obviously sweet on you."

"Mrs. Young!"

"Two years with that man coming to your apartment and neither one of you has made a move?"

"That's just the way Hudson is." I turned away from her and continued down the hallway.

"Does he know how you feel about him?" Mrs. Young asked, trailing me through the hallway.

I stopped again and turned around. "I don't know what you're talking about."

"Suit yourself. But if he doesn't know, let's hope you do a better job tomorrow than you did tonight, or I'll never get my range hood."

She continued past me to her apartment but stopped by her front door and fussed with her keys.

"Good night, Mrs. Young," I said, and hurried back to the apartment.

The shower was still running when I came back. I went to the bedroom and saw a camouflage duffle bag that had tipped over and partially spilled onto the carpet. I recognized it as Brad's. I bent down to set it upright, bumping into the dresser in the process. I reached down to the pile of clothes on the floor and used my hand to corral the spilled wardrobe back into the bag. My hand connected with something solid.

I readjusted my position to take the stress off my knee, and patted my hands over the pile of clothes. My hand landed on a cube-like object wrapped in a white Philadelphia Phillies T-shirt. I grabbed the hem of the T-shirt and peeked inside the folded cotton. It was the wooden box that Brad's Rolex Watch had come in.

I pulled the box from the T-shirt and ran my fingertips over the highly polished wood grain. I flipped the box upside down and read the inscription. *Only time will tell. Love, Madison.* The words, originally intended as a sweet message that hinted at our future, carried a very different message now. I flipped the box back over and started to rewrap it in the T-shirt, but it wasn't properly closed. I flipped the lid up and stared inside. It wasn't empty, but it didn't hold a watch.

Inside was a small, black pistol.

TWENTY-TWO

I don't know guns. I haven't shot one, haven't held one, don't endorse the ownership of one. I favor gun control and believe that more damage can be done by keeping a loaded gun in a house than not. As I stared at the gun from Brad's bag, with Rocky on my left side and a pile of Brad's clothes on my right, I couldn't define why I had to look at it, or what I thought I would discover once I held it in my hand. I only knew it seemed like a good idea to know something.

My body went numb. My legs, my arms, my breathing, my ability to move, all stopped. As I stared at the box, I knew my reaction spoke volumes of my true feelings. I had to get out of the apartment and talk to Tex.

I stuck the gun between the mattress and box spring of my bed and shoved the box back into Brad's duffle bag. For the second time in two days I had to sneak out during the night.

The water was still running in the bathroom, and I needed Brad's shower to continue indefinitely. I had to get out of the apartment and I had to ensure he wouldn't follow me.

I carried the martini pitcher into the kitchen. Another drink. I'd make him another drink.

"Rocky, stand guard," I commanded. He stared at me, his brown eyes wide with judgment. The water shut off in the bathroom. I pulled the jar of olives from the refrigerator and used the tip of a red plastic sword to extract the pimento from the center. I pulled a spoon from the dishwasher and took my prescription pain killers from a drawer.

Swiftly, I pulled a pill from the small amber vial, cracked the plastic capsule, and poured the contents into the middle of the olive. I capped both ends with slivers from the pimento. Next I crushed two melatonin pills with the back of a soup spoon and dumped the powder into the pitcher. I stirred it with a glass swizzle until it dissolved to clear. Brad rounded the corner, dressed only in a towel wrapped low on his waist. His torso was lean and muscular. I looked away.

"I was going to surprise you," I said. I refilled his glass and held the drink out to him.

I picked my glass up from the counter.

"To the truth," Brad said, holding his glass out for a toast. "No more secrets."

"To the truth," I repeated and clinked my glass against his. I faked a sip and watched him.

He lifted the red plastic sword to his mouth and pulled the olive off with his teeth. He rolled it around in his mouth and poured the contents of the glass down his throat.

"Come with me," Brad said. He took my hand and led me to the bedroom. I couldn't do this. I couldn't pretend to go to bed with a man I didn't trust. As we entered the bedroom, I paused by the vintage record player that I kept in the corner and placed the needle on the beginning of the first song. Doris Day's voice, crisp and clear, surrounded us.

When I turned around, Brad held out a pair of white cotton pajamas to me. He folded down the thin duvet that covered the bed. I picked the duvet up by the corner and put it back.

Brad ran a hand over my hair. "I don't know what I would do if I lost you a second time. Every day I regret what happened with us. If you give me the chance, I'll spend every day making it up to you, but I'm not going to rush you. I'll be on the sofa." He leaned over and kissed my forehead.

Rocky jumped on the bed and nuzzled my hand. I looked away. Was it possible I was so screwed up in the relationship department that I had fabricated a reason to drug an innocent man? No. The reason was as plain as the gun sandwiched between the layers of my bed.

"If you need me, I'll be right outside." He stifled a yawn. "I'm pretty tired, so I hope we get through the night with no new emergencies."

"Goodnight, Brad."

He left the room. The music drowned out any sounds he made from the living room. The only thing left for me to do was wait. Wait for the album to end. Wait for Brad to fall asleep. Wait for a chance to get out of there.

I went into the bathroom. I turned on the shower but didn't get under the spray. Condensation appeared on the mirror as I changed into my pajamas. After several minutes I cracked the door and listened. Brad's snores sounded from the sofa.

I turned off the shower and crept into my bedroom. Rocky was on the bed. I slid the gun out from under the mattress. I zipped it into a turquoise cosmetic bag I'd gotten as a gift with the purchase of a large tube of sunscreen and placed it at the bottom of the green canvas tote bag I used when I went to the pool. I threw in a self-belted green tunic and matching pants and a pair of brown loafers. I tiptoed out to the living room and stood by the end of the sofa.

Brad lay on his side, facing the opposite wall. There was probably a 10 percent chance that he would wake up when I opened the door, but I was willing to take those odds. I scribbled out a note: *Went to Physical Therapy. Didn't want to wake you. –M.* I clipped Rocky's leash on his collar and closed my fist around the building keys that sat on the desk.

Slowly, I turned the first deadbolt. When the tumbler fell out of place, I turned around and looked at Brad. He didn't move. I opened the second lock and twisted the doorknob. Time to go. I set my tote bag in the hallway, set the note on the desk by the computer monitor, and then moved into the hallway and pulled the door shut behind me.

We tiptoed down the hallway. Faint light from the front of the building cast enough of a glow to guide us. Rocky led the way to the stairs and down to the front door. The Explorer was still parked by Connie and Ned's house, so I called for a taxi and arranged for a pick-up.

The taxi driver was waiting by the gas station at the corner of Gaston and Glasgow, just like I'd requested. Rocky and I climbed into the back seat, and I gave him directions to Thelma Johnson's house. I wondered if I'd ever think of it as mine.

I paid the driver in small bills and let myself in the back door. With a small flashlight, I highlighted my path so I wouldn't bump into anything. I unclipped Rocky from his leash and he bounded inside. I wanted to be more tired than I was.

I looked out the front window for signs of life but there were none. Thelma Johnson had lived in a neighborhood that went to bed by ten o'clock every night. Far be it from me to be the new resident who interrupted the peace.

Rocky danced around my ankles. I picked him up and he lapped my cheek. This was the kind of affection I craved. The kind that didn't come with strings attached or secret agendas.

I found two bowls in the cabinet over the sink. I filled one with water from the tap and shook a small amount of dog food into the other. I set them up along the wall under the window and put Rocky next to them. He buried his head in his food while I headed upstairs to assemble the bed Joanie had delivered.

It surprised me to find it was already put together and made up with a set of floral sheets. A light blue blanket trimmed in a border of satin covered the bed. I fluffed the pillows and headed back downstairs to the kitchen, hoping she'd put something in the fridge for me to eat. I tipped my head back then rolled it from side to side. I'd spent too many nights sleeping on floors. It was taking its toll on me.

There was a carton of milk in the door of the refrigerator. I checked the expiration date. It was new. I pulled the plastic tab from under the screw cap and drank directly from the spout.

"She looks like Doris Day, but she drinks her milk from the carton. Do the surprises never stop with you, Night?"

I dropped the carton and spun around. A flood of milk chugged out of the open nozzle and saturated my canvas sneakers.

Tex crossed the kitchen and picked up the container. He set it on the counter and looked at me. I slapped him across the face.

"What?" he said, immediately covering the sting with his palm.

"What—where—how did you get in here?" I demanded.

He leaned against the blue and white floral wallpaper and crossed his arms over his chest. "I'm having a hard time figuring you out, Night."

"Must you call me by my last name?"

"You were telling the truth. You really do own the place." He rubbed his cheek a bit more. "I didn't see that coming."

"I'm waiting for answers."

He opened the cabinet under the sink and pulled out a roll of paper towels. I watched him unwind a healthy amount from the roll and sop up the milk on the floor. When he was done, he stood back up and tossed the wad over my head into a small trash bin nestled in the corner of the kitchen, easily making the shot.

"You know, I could have you arrested for trespassing," I said.

"And I could have you arrested for assaulting a cop."

"You wouldn't do that."

"You're right, I wouldn't. But you tried to have me arrested for Grand Theft Auto nine months ago, remember? You're so desperate for me to be locked up that I'm starting to wonder if you don't trust yourself around me."

"I trust myself around you just fine."

"You sure? Because those aren't the signals you're sending."

I blushed, remembering our kiss in front of the house earlier. "I'm not messing around here, Tex."

"Considering you had a twin bed delivered to your secret hideaway, it's pretty obvious you're not messing around here. I would place money on the fact that you're not messing around anywhere."

"How do you know about the bed?"

"Who do you think put it together?" He opened up a cabinet and pulled two stemmed glasses down, then opened another cabinet and pulled out a bottle of wine.

I leaned forward and looked into the cabinet that, earlier today, had been empty. Tex pulled a corkscrew from a drawer and opened the wine.

"You haven't stocked the place up yet. That tells me your residence here is temporary. I took a few liberties earlier today."

He poured the wine and held a glass out toward me. I crossed my arms over my pajamas and waited for an explanation.

"Thelma Johnson kept a spare key hidden," he said.

"I know. It's under the flower pot behind the back door. I asked a friend to bring me some stuff. She was supposed to take the key back with her."

"I convinced her to leave it with me."

"Why would Joanie trust you?"

"I may have shown her my badge. I don't remember."

"How did you even know about that key? You haven't spent time in this house for twenty years."

He shrugged. "Earlier today when I was watering your untended gardens," he paused for a moment, "I happily discovered that some things don't change." He hooked his wrist through the handles on my duffle bag and picked up the two glasses of wine. "Hey little fella," he said to Rocky. "Lead the way."

Rocky yipped, and the two of them left the room. Seconds later footsteps sounded on the stairs.

I followed them up the stairs into the bedroom. Tex unrolled a sleeping bag next to the bed. He lowered himself onto the bag and set the two glasses on the floor. He ran his open hand over Rocky's head.

"So here we are, Night," he said softly. "Time to let your guard down."

I didn't expect tears to fill my eyes and run down my cheeks. My chest ignited like a fiber optic lamp with glowing filaments that tickled from the inside. I swiped the tears off my cheek and inhaled sharply. The following exhale happened slowly, through pursed lips, as though I were blowing a hot breath through cold air.

As I sat on the floor, with Rocky curled up on the twin bed and Tex two feet away from me, I knew I was at the right place at the right time. There was a reason Tex was sitting in front of me. There was something I had to do, and he was the only person who could make it happen.

A collection of clouds passed in front of the moon, darkening the room temporarily. I leaned forward and swept my blonde hair behind my shoulder. Tex's eyes held mine. Being alone with him in the middle of the night gave me a new perspective.

"Lieutenant, there's this thing between us, and I'm pretty sure it's been there since we met. It's time for you to act on your impulses. I won't fight you."

He didn't move, didn't say a word.

"You're not going to make this easy for me, are you?" I said softly.

"No, I'm not. I need you to spell it out."

I took a deep breath and looked up at the ceiling. I arched my back slightly and gently shook my head side to side. I lowered my chin and let my hair fall forward to better frame my face. I'd never asked a man to do this before in my life, but there was a first time for everything. I exhaled and leaned closer to him, dropped my eyes to the floor, and slowly let them move up Tex's body until they reached his eyes. It was go time.

"Lt. Allen, I need you to take me into custody."

TWENTY-THREE

Tex reached across the sleeping bag to my pajama top and adjusted it slightly. For a second, I thought he misunderstood me. I swatted his hand away.

"Did you hear what I said?"

"Oh, I heard you alright."

"So?"

"That was quite an act. Is that what you think I want?"

"I think the thought has crossed your mind."

He shook his head and leaned back on his hands. "Exactly what is it you've done that would motivate me to arrest you?"

"For starters, I've been withholding evidence."

A subtle squint at his eyes brought out creases that belied his age. His jaw line went rigid, too, and his temples moved ever so slightly, a sign that he was clenching and unclenching his teeth. Gone was the smoldering darkness I'd played to moments before.

"What kind of evidence?" he asked.

I leaned to the side and snagged one of the handles of my tote bag. I pulled it toward me until I could put both hands on the bottom and flip it over. The contents spilled out in a pile of vintage clothes, loafers, an overnight kit, and an embarrassingly lacy bra and panty set. The last thing that fell out of the bag was the turquoise makeup bag. I handed it to Tex still zipped.

"Look inside."

He did as he was told. I didn't know what kind of a reaction I expected, but no reaction was worse than anything I could have imagined. The room was dark, but my eyes had adjusted to the minimal light coming from the moon.

"Where did you get this?"

"I found it with Brad's things earlier tonight." I waited for another question, but Tex was silent. "It could be completely legit. He could have a permit to carry it. He's been nothing but nice since he showed back up. He redid my living room for me, and he's been giving me my space. He even explained what happened back in Pennsylvania."

Tex stared at me. "When did you ask him about Pennsylvania?"

"Tonight, after the car accident."

Tex ran his hand over his hair twice. "What car accident? Damn it, Night, I left you alone for twelve hours. Could you not stay out of my investigation for half a day?"

"This isn't about your investigation, it's about my life." We stared at each other for a few seconds. "Okay, it might be about your investigation too. I'll let you be the judge."

"Start with what happened after I left you at your studio."

"First let me tell you about what Brad told me. He admitted that he knows Grant Bonneville and Philip Shayne from Philadelphia. Grant Bonneville is kind of my client. He's staying at Turtle Creek Luxury Apartments, and I found out there's a bed of poison ivy across the street from the apartment complex under the foot bridge. Is that enough to bring him in?"

"Night, I have a homicide at Paper Trail. Nothing about that crime connects back to anything you're talking about except for the name Philip Shayne. Turlington's arrival in Dallas puts him closer than anybody else we've found."

"You think he cut the brakes on my car?"

Tex looked confused.

"Connie Duncan, my client. You met her the other day, remember?" He nodded. "She borrowed my car and was in an accident. The brakes went out and she slammed into the back of a semi. She's at Baylor Hospital right now." I didn't realize my voice had risen, but it had. I actively dropped the volume. "It was my car, Tex. I should have been driving, not her. She could have been killed. If I were driving, I could have been killed. Someone tampered with my car to send a message. I know Brad's involved in something bad, but I don't think he would have cut the brakes on my car. I don't see it."

His eyes drilled into me. I almost wished the moon would drop behind a set of clouds and blacken the room again, but it didn't.

"You don't think he could have done it?"

"No, I don't."

"What happened next?"

"Brad took me home. I couldn't take it anymore, so I told him I needed to know what happened in Pennsylvania before he lied to me."

"And?"

"There's something else I have to tell you before we get to that."

"What else, Night? What else haven't you told me?"

I knew I needed to tell Tex that the original five thousand dollar bill was missing. I knew it, but I was afraid to say it.

"I'm a responsible person. I own a business and an apartment building. I pay my taxes and have good credit. So how come, all of a sudden, every person around me seems like they have motives that I can't see? Even you, here. Why are you really here, Tex? You could avoid your girlfriend by going to a hotel or a strip club. You didn't do either. You came to me. Why? What could possibly have been going through your mind to make you show up here in the middle of the night? What were you thinking?"

"You want to know what I'm thinking? Here it is." He leaned in close. "I think your judgment is clouded because you were in love with this guy once, but he hurt you, badly, and you're afraid to trust him. Brad Turlington represents a part of yourself you thought was gone, but the Madison I know, this woman in front of me, was born the day you put him out of your life and your mind. I think you are a strong, smart, and sexy woman, but you're the absolute worst person to determine if Turlington's on the level or not. I think you are searching for something to anchor yourself to and you can't tell if this is it, if this relationship with Turlington is the last thing you'll have a chance to grab."

I stared at Rocky, the mainstay in my life post-Brad. He twitched in his sleep, like he was chasing phantoms in his dreams. How well I knew the feeling. How unprepared I was to hear Tex spell it all out to me.

"You're on the brink of not being able to trust anybody, Night. You have to work out your issues on your own time, but this isn't about you anymore. Your personal choices are yours, but right now, your choices are putting innocent people in danger."

I couldn't make eye contact for fear Tex would see too much, but I knew the only way to break any kind of spell—the only way to clear the clouded judgment—was to calmly, rationally, acknowledge the truth. Tex was as good a person as any to help me sort through the trash in my mind. In a voice so quiet I could barely hear it myself, I started to talk.

"Last night, I found a leather briefcase in the trunk of Brad's car. It had the letters PS on it."

"Philip Shayne?" Tex interjected.

"I think so."

"Do you know so?"

"There was a four number lock on the valet. The numbers were at one-two-three-four."

"Not exactly a difficult combination to guess."

"That wasn't the combination. The combination was four-three-two-one." I waited a couple of seconds for Tex to comment again. When he didn't, I continued.

"I share a birthday with Doris Day. April third. When Brad and I first started dating, we discovered our birthdays were four-three-two-one. April third, Feb first." I spared Tex the notion that the dates seemed significant at the time. "When I saw the spinners on the lock turned to the numbers one-two-three-four, I had a hunch. Turned out I was right."

Tex shook his head. "Coincidence is well and good, but in police work, we like our clues a little more concrete."

"Think about this, Tex. Someone dropped off a box of stuff to Joanie's store. It had my name on it. Philip Shayne's wallet was in the box along with a bunch of other Doris Day memorabilia. Maybe Brad dropped off the stuff. Maybe he set that combination because he was thinking back to those days at Pierot's Interior."

"Or, he put your name on the box, stashed a couple of lobby cards inside to throw anybody off and made sure you'd end up with it. If he's the one who killed Shayne, then—"

"He's not a killer," I said instinctively.

"Are you sure of that?" Tex countered. He moved his hand to the outside of the turquoise satin cosmetic bag that held the gun.

I pulled my knees up to my chest and wrapped my arms around my legs. "Something changed with him. I don't know what it is. He's afraid of something. He's scared, and he's trying to hide it, but he came to me. He needs my help. If he's trying to move on, if he's telling the truth, I can't just ignore him. My biggest problem is that I can't trust him."

"Do you trust me, Night?"

I nodded. "Don't let this go to your head, but the only reason I keep pushing aside my doubts about Brad is because you said to trust him."

"I didn't tell you that."

"Yes, you did. When you came to my apartment, you said he checked out. You don't remember?"

He sat up. "Shit."

"What?"

"When his name came up in connection to the investigation I asked Donna to check him out and let me know if she found anything. She's the one who said he was clean."

TWENTY-FOUR

"So I'm basing my entire assessment of him being trustworthy on your jealous girlfriend's words that he's on the up and up? How do you know she even checked him out? She doesn't like me. She's made that obvious on more than one occasion."

"I told you he was a person of interest. Has been since we found the five thou in Philip Shayne's wallet. Donna's been on me about not being professional. Said she would make sure I didn't cross the line."

"She seems to be very concerned with people crossing lines and not crossing lines."

"What do you mean by that?"

"She warned Brad not to play games with me."

"When?"

"I don't know. He told me about it before I—" I stopped.

"Before you what?"

"Before I came over here."

"Turlington's at your place and you're here? Again?"

"He was worried about me after the accident. He said he didn't feel good about leaving me alone."

"You're alone now."

"He doesn't know I left. I waited until he fell asleep and put a note on the coffee table."

"What kind of a guy doesn't wake up when someone comes and goes?"

I stared at the floor. "The kind of guy who had a pain killer and a couple of tablets of melatonin dissolved in a slightly strong martini."

"You drugged him?" Tex's mouth curled up slightly on one side. Even in the dark room, I could see the glint in his blue eyes. "Do you do this often?"

"Am I going to get a lecture for this?" I asked.

"No, but you're coming close to getting your wish about being taken into custody. Are we just about done here?"

"No, we're not. I'm just getting warmed up."

"Damn it, Night, what else could you possibly have left to tell me?"

"The contents of the briefcase." This time I looked Tex directly in the eyes. I needed to see his reaction. "There were little glass jars and detail paint brushes. And a stack of paper with the image of a five thousand dollar bill in the middle of it."

"Did you take one?"

"I didn't have a chance. Someone in a black ski mask pulled into the parking lot and took the briefcase with him." I paused, then continued. "I think it was the same guy who followed me from the restaurant the night we found the body. At least it was the same car. I saw dents in the front bumper."

"Did he see you?"

"Yes. And if he wanted to hurt me, he could have. I was an open target. The only reason I didn't tell you sooner is because I didn't get hurt. I don't have any proof except for what I saw. I didn't think you'd believe me."

"The only reason I'm leaning toward believing you is that I can't imagine what kind of person would make up a story like this. Maybe custody isn't the place for you. Maybe I should call ahead to the loony bin and reserve a padded cell."

"Do you think I can't see this is nuts? Why do you think I haven't told anybody about it? Right now, it's all in my head." I tapped my temple twice with two fingers. "Only it's not. It sounds crazy to you, but to me, it's real."

"What did he do when he saw you?"

"Who?" I asked.

"The guy in the mask."

"Nothing. He kicked my keys under a car and took off with the briefcase."

"When was this?"

"Two nights ago."

Tex ran his hand over his hair several times then turned and punched a fist into my twin bed mattress. The springs bounced more than I expected, considering it was new.

"Damn it, Madison, I was here the morning after that happened. Why didn't you tell me?"

Why hadn't I told Tex? Because I'd been confused by the meaning of his kiss. I'd yelled at him and stormed away. The next time I'd seen him, he'd been with Donna at my studio.

"I told you I needed more than a couple of minutes with you to tell you what I knew."

"What else do you have to tell me? Anything? Because if my captain finds out you've been hindering my investigation of Turlington all this time, I'll get pulled from the case."

"What do you mean your investigation of Turlington all this time? You just said he's been a person of interest since you found the five thousand dollar bill in Philip Shayne's wallet. You didn't know Brad was involved in anything until that night, right?"

Tex didn't move.

"That's not right, is it? When you said you couldn't look into Brad's background, you were lying. You've been watching him all along. You suspected him of murder since we found the body at Paper Trail. And what about Stanley Mann? Is anyone looking for him? Or have you added kidnapping to Brad's suspected crimes?"

"Night, calm down."

I ignored him. "I don't know what Brad's involved in, but he was at my apartment the same day I found the body. I don't think there was time for him to leave, get to Paper Trail, murder someone, move a kidnap victim, take me out to dinner, and redecorate my living room."

A floodgate of thoughts, mental snapshots of the past several days, clicked through my mind like a malfunctioning slide show.

Tex showing up at the Polynesian restaurant. Tex watering the gardens at Thelma Johnson's house. Tex coming to my apartment the night I introduced him to Brad in the hallway. He suspected Brad all along, from the minute he asked me to call Brad from the crime scene. He used me to get leads.

Tex leaned forward and put a hand on my upper arm. "Night, you've never been in danger. I've had someone watching you the whole time. If anything had happened, you would have been safe."

"You what?" I flung his hand off my arm. "You have a guy watching me? Who?"

"I'm not going to tell you."

"Then we are done here."

He stood up and pointed a finger at me. "I hope you mean that, because you are done here. You're done with this whole thing. You got me?"

I stood up too, but not as fast as Tex.

"How exactly do you want me to be done with it? My car has been totaled. The man at my house is your chief suspect. One of my clients is in the hospital, and the other one is using a fake identity. And if you remember, all of this started when Brad sent me a James Madison bill in the mail. Remember that? The original five thousand dollar bill?"

"Calm down, Night."

I jabbed Tex in the chest, and he stepped backward. "I will not calm down. This isn't about counterfeiting money and passing it off at the mall. Why would there be three five thousand dollar bills floating around Dallas?"

I ticked them off on my fingers. "One mailed to me. One dropped off at Joanie Loves Tchotchkes, and one in the wallet of Philip Shayne. And a piece of one some kids found at the Dallas Arboretum. I saw that on the news. And then there's a whole trunk filled with uncut sheets of paper with the image of James Madison in the middle. You want me to stay out of your investigation? Maybe you need to figure out what your investigation is about, first."

"I'm going to need you to give me that bill, Night. The original five thou. You have to trust me."

"But I can't trust you, Lieutenant, and you know it. My judgment is clouded and I'm on the brink of not being able to trust anybody. You just said so yourself."

We had a stare-off for a few seconds, until Tex turned around and left my bedroom. It wasn't until after I heard his car drive away that I started to cry.

When I woke up the next morning, Rocky was on my pillow. On a queen sized bed, we could have functioned. On a twin, it was a challenge. Sunlight flooded the room and tore through my swollen eyes. I scooped him up, got out of the bed, and let him take up the middle of the mattress while I went to the bathroom. After several splashes of cold water and possibly more eye drops than were recommended, my eyes returned to something close to normal. I dug a compact from my handbag and swept the fluffy terrycloth puff over my face, and then slicked on a peachy lip-gloss that I'd forgotten was in the bottom of my overnight bag. My phone rang from the bedroom, but I ignored it. I pulled my hair into a low ponytail, stepped into the green pants and matching tunic that I'd packed, and headed downstairs. Rocky followed.

Tex had surprised me with the bottle of wine last night. This morning, I discovered a package of English muffins and a jar of cheap instant coffee in the cupboard. I didn't know if this meant Tex had anticipated staying over with me or not. I didn't care. I was hungry and this was food and to ignore it out of spite would have demonstrated poor judgment.

I poured fresh water into the bowl on the floor and leaned against the kitchen window by a row of neglected African violets that lined the sill. In the clear light of day, I knew I had to find the original five thousand dollar bill. It was at the center of everything. The only problem was I didn't know who had it.

I cleared the kitchen of dirty dishes and went upstairs to retrieve my handbag and my phone. The missed call was Tex. I turned the ringer off and put the phone at the bottom of my orange handbag. I wanted to hear neither lecture nor apology from him. Whatever he had to say, he could say to my voicemail.

I moved Rocky's food, water, and a couple of plush toys to the closed in porch. "I'll be back soon, Rocky." After a kiss on the top of his furry head, I was off.

Hudson's house was about a mile from Thelma Johnson's, and it was a relatively peaceful walk along the dusty road. Dallas weather in February was a tolerable sixty-five degrees. Even though I was underdressed in my tunic and pants, the crisp air kept me moving. About twenty minutes later, I saw Hudson's blue pickup truck parked along the edge of his lawn. It had a few new spots of primer on it and a bobble head of Flo, the Progressive Insurance woman, on the dashboard.

The bed of the truck was filled with cardboard boxes labeled with magic marker. It was a familiar system to anybody who found themselves moving to a new house. The idea that Hudson was moving from the house that had been in his family for generations was unsettling.

I hadn't thought much about Hudson in the past couple of days. The last time I'd seen him was the day I'd told him about Brad. It was the same day I'd asked him about counterfeiting. My self-awareness forced me to confront the fact that the only time I called on Hudson was when I needed something. I didn't want to acknowledge that I was becoming that kind of person, particularly toward someone I cared about.

"This is a nice surprise," said a deep, velvety voice from the garage. "I wasn't expecting you until later."

"What's all this?" I waved at the bed of the truck and fought to keep my tone light. "You're moving?"

"Not moving. Taking a long-overdue vacation. Getting my head together. I should have done it before, but the timing never seemed right."

"What am I going to do without you?" I half-joked.

"Seems like you're in good hands now. I think you'll manage."

I wouldn't be so sure of that, I thought to myself.

"I stopped by the apartment building a couple of days ago. Showed your new tenant around. That's what you wanted me to do, right?"

"Sure. Thank you." I hesitated. "Sorry about the surprise visit. I would have called first, but I didn't think you'd mind."

"No, I don't mind the visit." Hudson leaned back against the open bed of his truck. His black T-shirt fit his lean body closely, showing off broad shoulders, muscular arms, and a flat stomach: the build of a man who earns his physique through labor and not exercise. His black hair blew around his forehead. It was longer than he used to wear it, but it suited him. A torn, paint-stained rag hung out of his back pocket. "If I had my way, you'd be here all the time."

My face grew warm. Hudson reached a hand out to my cheek and flipped a lock of blonde hair that had escaped my ponytail with his fingers. When he reached the ends, he turned his hand over and cupped the side of my neck. "You okay?" he asked in a low voice.

I thought about confiding in Hudson. He would listen. Only, my problems weren't his problems. His problems, ones that had haunted him for decades, were over, and he was ready to move on. I'd selfishly believed he would be waiting for me if I ever felt I was ready, but for all the things I didn't know, the one thing I did was that for Hudson and I, the timing wasn't right.

"I'm fine. Just working through some personal stuff, that's all."

"Madison, can I tell you something? I think you're amazing. I think if I'd met you twenty years ago, my whole life might have been different. I think you know how I feel, but I can't wait around here, hoping for something that might never happen. Do you understand that?"

"I am not asking you for anything, Hudson."

"I know. You never asked me for anything, and you could have, a thousand times. The fact that you never did helped me make my decision."

I fought the urge to ask Hudson to reconsider. I wasn't where he was, emotionally. I couldn't offer him anything other than the occasional job at the apartment building or Mad for Mod, and unlike one of the other men in my life, I was pretty sure money was the one thing he wasn't after.

"Wait here," he said. He jogged to the house and returned a few moments later, carrying a cardboard box stuffed with unopened envelopes.

"You picked up the rent checks?" I asked. Of course Hudson had picked them up. It made perfect sense. He was acting like the owner of the building. No wonder Mrs. Young suspected him of being more than the handyman.

"I noticed you hadn't picked them up for a while. Figured you might need some help with that. Mrs. Young's application is in there too. Her background check came back clean as a whistle, but I'm sure you want it for your files."

It wasn't the first time Hudson had read my mind and with almost stifling desperation, I hoped it wouldn't be the last. I thumbed the ends of the envelopes that jutted out of the box.

"Looks like I'm heading to the bank. People are going to wonder why their checks aren't getting cashed."

I looked at his face. The sun had etched lines by the corners of his eyes and the sides of his mouth, leaving him looking older than I was despite the fact that I had eight years on him. I reached a hand up to his face and ran my fingers over his mouth. He kissed my fingertips.

"You got room for one more in the truck?" I whispered.

He stood up, away from the bed of the truck, and tipped my head down, pressing his soft lips to my forehead.

"I'm afraid this time there's just room for Mortiboy and me."

As if on cue, Mortiboy approached and rubbed his back against

Hudson's shin. "Besides, I think you have unfinished business in Dallas."

"Unfinished business," I repeated. That's what I'd felt when I learned the truth about Brad. That I had unfinished business. And now I had loose ends all over the place and it was time to tie a few of them up.

Hudson twisted his torso and pulled a small brown shopping bag from the inside of the truck's bed. "This is for you. Consider it a parting gift, something to remember me by." He handed me the bag.

"I should be giving you a parting gift, not the other way around."

"You gave me a gift already, Madison. You gave me back my life."

Mortiboy meowed, and Hudson scooped him up and stroked his head. "Don't open it until you get home. Okay?"

"Okay."

He reached into the front pocket on his jeans and pulled out a small key ring with two keys on it. He took my hand and set the keys in my open palm, then closed my fingers around it.

"Those are the keys to the house. If your past gets to be too much to handle, you're welcome to stay here."

I thought about telling Hudson about my secret hideaway. But the truth was, I didn't want him to rescind his offer. It wasn't so much as wanting a place to get away from Brad—I already had that—as it was knowing that Hudson still wanted me in his life.

"Saying goodbye to you was the last thing on my agenda. Guess we can get an early start, right Mortiboy? Stay as long as you like."

"Thanks, but I better get going. I'm on foot today."

His forehead creased with concern. "Where's your car?"

I could have told him about the accident, but instead of causing unnecessary worry, I lied. "Fender bender. It's in the shop."

"You need a ride?"

I held up the bag of checks. "The bank is practically in your back yard. If I can't make that walk, then my physical therapist should lose her license."

"Physical therapy. What about swimming?"

"Soon," I said. "I'm not ready yet, but soon."

Hudson walked me to the edge of his property. "One last thing. The five thou you gave me was junk. Color copy, printed on one side."

"Is it in here?"

"No, I tossed it. But there are a couple of referrals in there. Nobody who can replace me, just some leads in case you need something done while I'm gone."

"That implies that you'll be back."

"I'll be back." He smiled. "Take care of yourself, Madison."

"You, too."

We hugged tighter than I would have hugged anyone other than Hudson. When we pulled apart, I took a step backward and looked down. I glanced at his face quickly, waved, and walked away. Someday, maybe. But despite what might have been, somewhere along the line, right now, there was nothing more to say.

I took a scenic route past White Rock Lake to Buckner to get to the bank. A branch sat across the street from Paper Trail. Halfway through the walk I transferred the rent checks from the box Hudson gave me to my handbag and left the empty carton in a public trash can.

I went inside the bank and stood by the center island, sorting through rent checks. When I got to the one I'd addressed myself, I opened it and slid the James Madison from the envelope into the zippered pocket on the inside of my handbag, taking care not to bend it. I waited for an available teller to make the rent deposit.

The line moved slowly. I juggled Hudson's gift from one hand to the other and inched forward like the other bank customers. As I neared the window, one of the tellers, a young woman in a black and white polka dot blouse, set a sign in front of her window indicating that she was closed.

She pointed to the window to her right, where a man fiddled with the keyboard of a computer behind the window. He looked up, directly at me, and I froze.

The only available teller was Grant Bonneville. The fake Archie Leach.

TWENTY-FIVE

"It's your turn, lady," said a voice behind me. An elbow jabbed into my arm, and I stumbled forward. "Window 5."

I looked at the imposter, and he looked back at me. He showed no sign of recognition. I was more scared by that than if he'd smiled and waved and said something about the coincidence of random interactions.

"I forgot to fill out my deposit slip," I said and got out of line. The man behind me shook his head, as if I was one more example of a bubble-headed blonde in Dallas.

I moved slowly past the waiting line, stopping for a moment by the island of deposit slips. My back was to the teller's windows. I didn't know if Grant was watching me or not. I didn't know how he had gotten a job at the bank or how this figured in to the murder at Paper Trail right across the street. All I knew was that I wanted to get out of there. Despite my anger at Tex, I needed to tell him what was going on.

I dug around inside my handbag and found my phone. 47 missed calls. Forty-seven?

I sent a text message. *Fake archie leach at bank on buckner. Across street from paper trail. Check out.*

I sent the text and buried the phone back into my bag. Now what? I had close to eight thousand dollars' worth of endorsed checks in my hand and a five thousand dollar bill hidden in the lining of my bag. A bank was the one place I should have felt safe.

I didn't.

An ATM sat to the left of the tellers' windows. Despite the retro nature of my business, I was a fan of technological advances. I liked the self-service machine at the post office. I paid my bills online. I used the GPS on my phone when I needed directions. I'd never trusted the ATM with the rent money, but there was a first time for everything. I stepped up to the machine and looked behind the wall of glass for Grant. He wasn't there.

I looked to my right and my left. Where did he go? Had he seen me as a threat, someone who would question how he got a job working at the bank? Had he made his way out of the lobby before I could point a finger and yell fink?

"Having trouble with the machine, ma'am?" asked a male voice from directly behind me. It was him.

My body went rigid. Nobody else was near us. Nobody else would hear what he said. And his mere proximity told me he was confident there was nothing I could do. He leaned closer and his voice dropped to a hiss. "Act normal and everything will be fine."

I didn't turn around. "I don't know what you're doing here or how you got behind that window, but whatever you think you're going to get away with, you're not. The police are going to be here any minute now."

I pulled my ATM card from my wallet and fed it into the machine. The screen prompted me for my pin number. I got an idea. I keyed in the wrong pin once, twice, a third time. The screen flashed a warning that I'd exceeded the allotted number of attempts to login.

"Your machine ate my card," I said, loud enough for the other patrons to hear. "What do I do now? I need to talk to the manager."

Grant's olive skin reddened and his mouth pulled together into a tight line. "That was a stupid move," he growled.

A man in the line behind him let out an annoyed sigh and craned his neck to see what the holdup was.

"I'm sorry, sir. I think the machine's broken." I turned to Grant. "If you can't help me, can you find your manager? Thank you."

Grant stood up straighter. "Ma'am, why don't you have a seat? I'll send our manager to help you with a replacement card."

I moved past him to a gray tweed chair and pretended to choose a magazine from a pile of *Time*, *Newsweek*, and *People*. Grant consulted with the next person in line while I waited. It was three thirty-eight. The bank closed at four. Where was Tex?

I pulled my phone from my handbag and checked the screen a second time. The missed calls were up to sixty-two. That was beyond crazy. No sane person would call me sixty-two times.

No sane person.

I punched a couple of buttons and cued up a list of missed calls. Tex was among the early listings. He'd stopped calling hours ago. He was only five of the missed calls. One was from Joanie Chen. Two were from Connie.

And fifty-four were from Brad.

I clutched my phone in my palm. A man with a youthful face and a fringe of salt and pepper hair around his head approached me. He wore an olive green suit and a necktie printed with dollar signs.

"I hear our machine ate your card. Come with me and we'll get a new one ordered for you."

I followed him to a desk in a small office with glass walls. I picked a business card from his desk and dropped it into my handbag.

"Are you the bank manager?" I asked.

"Yes."

"The man—the teller who was trying to help me—he's not who he says he is."

The bank manager continued to type on his keypad. "Who did he say he was?"

"He's—he's not Archie Leach."

"I know he's not Archie Leach. Who said he was?"

"Archie Leach."

The bank manager stopped typing. "Ms. Night, are you okay?"

"He pretended to help me, but he really wants to get my money."

"We're a bank, Ms. Night. It's his job to try to get your money." He chuckled.

"No, not that money. This money," I said, and pulled the five thousand dollar bill from my handbag. His eyes opened wide when he saw it. He reached across the desk, but I pulled it away. "No. This is mine."

"Would you excuse me for a moment?" He stood up. He looked over my head at the row of teller windows, then scanned the interior of the bank. "I'll be right back."

I sat against the chair and ran my palm back and forth over the worn wooden arms. The clock on the wall was closing in on four and the line had dwindled. Five of the six teller windows had This Window Closed signs in front of them.

The bank manager stood in front of the sixth window. Grant was talking to him through the glass and the manager was listening intently. They stopped talking, and both turned to me.

I slipped the James Madison bill back into the interior zippered pocket of my handbag. I had to get out of there. I dug my phone out of my bag for the third time since I'd arrived and sent Tex another text. *Need you. Bank on buckner across from paper trail. SOS*

My palm sweated. I squeezed the phone like I was juicing a lemon. I stood up on shaky legs and flexed my knee a few times. I wasn't close to the door, but I was closer than either of the two men.

The possibility existed that I was acting irrationally, that there was a perfectly normal explanation for everything. I wanted a sign, an indication that running out the door of the bank, screaming that they were after my money, was a bad idea. My phone vibrated, startling me. I didn't recognize the number, but whoever was on the other end of that call might be the only person to help me.

"Hello?"

"Is this Madison Night?" said a vaguely familiar male voice.

"Yes. Who is this?"

"Harry from Turtle Creek Luxury Apartments. You asked me to call you if anything happened with Mrs. Bonneville's son?"

"What happened?" The connection was quiet, and I pressed the phone against my head and looked at the carpet, concentrating on the valet attendant's voice.

"I thought you'd want to know that a couple of cops came into his apartment earlier today. Art let them in. I'm not sure what they wanted, but it seems your suspicions were right."

I looked up at the window. Grant was no longer there. The bank manager was on the phone at a different desk. A door, between where I stood and the exit, opened toward me and Grant stepped out. In two steps, he'd be standing between me and the only exit I had.

The phone beeped, and I looked at the screen. *Come to parking lot. Now.*

I grabbed the handles of my bag and stepped away from the chair. With the explosion of a sprinter who hears the shot of a starting pistol, I ran past Grant, past the bank manager, past the ATM machine, to the glass doors that led to the parking lot. I ran to the second row of vacant spaces and looked around for Tex. Where was he? What parking lot was he hiding in?

This was no time for games. An alarm blared behind me from the bank. The now-familiar brown sedan swung into the parking lot and pulled in front of me. The passenger side door swung open.

Brad was behind the wheel of the car.

TWENTY-SIX

I stepped back. "Where did you get this car?" I asked. "What are you involved in?"

"Get in the car, Maddy," he said. "I'm not involved in anything—I'm trying to get out. Buckle your seatbelt. Let's go." He peeled out of the parking lot and jerked a hard right onto Garland Road.

I braced myself with hands on the dashboard as he sped down the street. Something fell against my foot. I looked at the floorboards. The box for Brad's watch lay open. Loose hundreds were scattered around my feet.

Brad turned off Garland onto the dirt road that wound around White Rock Lake and pulled the car under an overhang of trees. He threw the car into park and got out. I jumped out of my side and slammed the door behind me. Brad ran his hands through his hair and turned to face me, the brown sedan between us.

"You're acting crazy, Mads. You're going to get us killed."

"What about you, Brad? You have a gun. I saw it. Since when do you carry a gun?"

"It's for protection. That's why I'm here. I'm trying to protect you, just like I tried to keep you from getting involved years ago."

"But you didn't! Whatever is going on, you brought it to my back door." My vision was distorted with the kind of extreme emotional agitation that removes everything from sight except the other person in an argument. "Why did you send me the original five thousand dollar bill? What did you want from me? Why are you really here?"

Brad took a step backward from the car and dropped his arms to his sides. He moved around the car and walked toward me. I stumbled away from him.

"I never wanted to hurt you, Madison. You have to believe me. But you were the one person no one would have suspected."

"Brad, where did you get this car?" I asked again.

"I borrowed it."

"From who?"

"Forget about the car, Maddy."

"This car tried to run me off the road once, so I'm not going to forget about it."

He grabbed my forearm. I yanked away from his hand and he let go, his eyes wide, as if he couldn't believe I thought he was going to hurt me.

"That wasn't me. C'mon, Mads, you know me."

"I used to think so, but not anymore."

"Listen to me. Philip Shayne was after me. He's the man from the film strip. He had a gun and was going to kill me. The only way I got away was because I shot him first. Four times in the leg. It gave me the time I needed to get lost. I've been running ever since, looking for you. I had to tell you it was all a lie, that I never stopped loving you. For two years. He followed me from Pennsylvania. I thought I'd lost him. I never expected to see him again. You have to believe me, Maddy."

"I don't have to believe anything you say." I spun on a patch of dirt and spotty brown grass and headed back toward Garland Road.

"Madison," Brad called from behind me. "He found me four months ago. He told me he was going to get to me through you."

I stopped walking. Brad's words sank into my brain slowly, but loops of information, of lies and truths, of circumstances beyond my control kept me from understanding a chronological timing of events. Brad caught up to me and put his hand on my shoulder. This time I didn't pull away.

"Madison, I couldn't let that happen. After everything, I couldn't let any harm come to you because of my mistakes."

I turned to face him. "How did he connect us?"

"The article about you in the newspaper. Something about murders related to Doris Day and a mid-century modern interior decorator living in Dallas. The story was picked up and run in the *Philadelphia Inquirer*. There was a sidebar about your past, working for Pierot's Interiors, and how you had successfully relocated and started Mad for Mod. I don't think it was hard for him to put it all together."

"Is that why you sent me the bill?"

"I needed a way to let you know something was wrong. I had to give you a warning, in case I wasn't around to tell you what was going on."

"Tell me the truth, Brad. What happened at Paper Trail?"

Brad ran his hand over his hair. It seemed there was more gray than there'd been a week ago. Sweat and desperation had caused it to fall from its usual style. The front hung across his forehead. When he let go, he reached out for my hand and pulled me a couple of yards away from the dirt road. The car was hidden, thanks to the cloaking of the trees.

"You know the numismatist you went to see? Stanley Mann?"

I nodded.

"Philip Shayne was holding him prisoner in his own home. He starved him, beat him, until he agreed to authenticate fake James Madison bills to sell on the collector's circuit. It was the same scheme he'd run in Philly. But Stanley had morals. He refused to cooperate until Philip threatened his dog."

I thought about what Brad said he'd done to protect me, and what I'd do to protect Rocky.

"They didn't hurt the dog, did they?"

"No. Stanley agreed to do what they wanted. I went to Paper Trail after I left your apartment. I wanted to get him and his dog out of there. But then you called. I heard you say you were coming over, and I knew I had to get lost. Stanley wasn't the person who took the call. Philip Shayne was. He wanted to get the bill I sent you. You were going to walk into a trap."

"I found Philip's body when I went to Paper Trail. He'd been shot. The dog was there but Stanley wasn't. Who killed Philip?"

"Philip had a partner. I never saw his face but I think he's Grant Bonneville. Same build, same height. He was always in a black knit ski mask. Philip found me hiding in Paper Trail. We fought in the field out back. He wasn't in good shape when I left, but he was alive."

"What do you mean he wasn't in good shape?"

"Let's just say I won the fight."

"What about Stanley? Where is he now?"

"I've been trying to find him. The guy in the mask dragged Stanley with him and left Philip behind. I took his wallet and arranged for you to get it."

"Why?" I asked.

"Because I know how your mind works. You have a need to figure things out. I put other stuff in the box that anybody else would ignore but would get your attention. I knew you'd obsess over that wallet until you had answers."

"But the bill—why did you send me the bill?"

"Mr. Pierot trained us both to consult with a professional if we ever questioned a piece's authenticity. I knew you'd go to a numismatist when you got that bill. That might have tipped off the professionals that this ring from Philly was here. I only wished you'd gotten there sooner."

"A man died that night. If I'd gotten there sooner I might have—"

Brad cut me off. "You might have gotten killed too." He hung his head. "That's why I wanted you to meet me for dinner. I knew if you were with me, I could protect you."

"Do you know where the numismatist is? Is he's okay?"

"I don't know. I've been spending my free time searching for him. The field behind Paper Trail, Turtle Creek, White Rock Lake. That's their way. If he's dead they'll try to dump his body."

"That's how you got the poison ivy. You said you were giving me space but really you were waiting until the rash was gone." Our eyes connected. "We have to go back to the bank, Brad. A police lieutenant is going to be there and you need to talk to him."

"Forget the police lieutenant," said Grant Bonneville. He stood by the car pointing a gun in our direction.

Gone was the nervousness that had colored his appearance the first day he came to Mad for Mod. In its place was a cold determination, setting the angle of his jaw and the line of his brow. "Ms. Night, get into the car and drive back into the bank by yourself," he said.

"Don't trust him, Mads. He's not who he says he is," Brad said.

"I know he isn't, but I don't know what he wants from me."

"He wants the James Madison bill. Where is it?"

I looked at the car. My handbag rested on the seat next to the gift from Hudson. The bill was inside. I couldn't let them know how close they were to it.

"Why not give him one from the briefcase in your trunk? Because you know it's not there anymore?"

Brad was in front of me now. His expression changed from intense to hurt. "You know about the briefcase?" he asked. "Why couldn't you trust me?"

"You told too many secrets, Brad. Too many lies."

"Those secrets and lies were for your own good."

"I'm sorry, but I can't believe anything you say."

"You were never supposed to be involved," he said, like he'd been saying all along.

"Ms. Night, he's right. You were never supposed to be involved. The fact remains that you are. Now give me the bill," Grant growled.

"Give *me* the bill, Maddy."

"I don't have it."

"I know that you do. Hand it over, and nobody gets hurt," Brad said.

And then shots fired from behind us and a blossom of red spread across Grant's shirt.

TWENTY-SEVEN

"Get out of here, Maddy," Brad said again. "Call the cops, send an ambulance. The keys are in the ignition. Just go!"

"Who shot him?"

"I don't know."

"He's hurt—"

"I'll wait with him. You need to get someplace safe."

Brad eased Grant onto the ground and applied pressure against the wound. Grant closed his eyes but didn't make a sound, didn't fight Brad off.

"Know that I put you first, Madison. Always," Brad said.

I knew the best way for me to help was to meet Tex at the bank and bring him here. I ran to the car. I turned the key and peeled out of the parking lot.

The dirt road around White Rock Lake was designed for one-way traffic, but there was no time for that now. I spun the wheel as tight as I could and drove the wrong way to Garland Road. Halfway to the bank I pulled onto the shoulder and called 911 to report the shooting. I told her all that I could. After I hung up, I sat in the car, breathing in, breathing out. Calming down. Or at least, trying.

Flashing red and blue lights appeared in the rear view mirror. I watched them turn onto the dirt road around White Rock Lake. When the lights vanished from view, I pulled back on the road and turned into the bank lot. Tex's Jeep sat in one of the customer spaces. I parked the brown sedan next to him and got out of the car.

"Where did you come from?" Tex asked from somewhere behind me.

"White Rock Lake. Brad drove me—"

"Damn it, Night."

I held up both hands, and then pointed over his shoulder in the direction of the lake.

"About a quarter mile up East Lawther Drive. Grant Bonneville—the fake Archie Leach—was shot. Brad's waiting with him. I called 911. I don't know who the shooter was."

Tex stared at me.

"I am not your problem. Those two men at the lake are."

A wave of vertigo hit me and I stepped a few steps left, then right, trying to recapture my balance. Tex was immediately at my side with a hand on the back of my green tunic.

"Whoa. You okay?"

"I need to sit down."

"Come with me."

No sarcastic comments or reprimands came from Tex as he escorted me to his Jeep.

He unlocked the back and flipped the panel down. I turned around and leaned against it. He put his hands under my arms and lifted me up like an adult lifts a child, and then set me on the fuzzy black interior. My feet dangled above the ground, brown loafers swinging back and forth.

He pulled a bottle of water from the back of his Jeep and handed it to me. I twisted the cap off and drank half. When I finished, I recapped the bottle and held it against my forehead even though the water was room temperature.

"Didn't you get my text?" I asked.

"I got here as soon as I could. You want to tell me what the fuss was all about?"

"I came here to deposit the rent checks. Grant Bonneville was behind the glass like he worked here. He acted like he didn't recognize me, but it was him. I got out of line and went to the ATM machine and he followed me. He told me to act normal, that nobody else had to know we had unfinished business. I didn't know what else to do so I faked my password a couple of times and the machine ate my card. I ended up with the manager. I showed him the five thou—" I stopped abruptly.

"It's okay. I figured you kept the bill with the rent checks. I went by for them earlier today but they were gone. The next logical step was to look for you at the bank."

"Hudson picked them up." I looked down at my hands. "He's getting out of town and he went to the apartment to say goodbye. When he saw the box was overflowing, he picked up the checks. He asked me to come over and he gave them to me."

"Does he do that a lot?"

"Pick up the rent checks? Never."

"Did he know you kept the five thou in there?"

"No." I waited for more questions. When none came, I continued. "Something was up with the bank manager too. I felt he was detaining me until Grant could get to me, so I ran out the exit. Brad pulled up and told me to get in. He was driving the brown sedan. What does that mean?"

"I don't know."

"He pulled onto Lawther and parked under a row of trees. Somehow Grant found us. The two of them were having a Mexican standoff, and somebody shot Grant. I don't know who, but it wasn't Brad. There's a third man."

"Where are they now?"

"I don't know, Tex. I called 911 and reported the shooting and came back here."

Tex looked up at the sky for a couple of seconds and squinted. He ran a hand through his hair, and exhaled. He took a step closer, and then turned around and hoisted himself on the back of the Jeep next to me. Since I was in the middle, he didn't have a lot of room.

He bumped me with his hip and I shifted to the left to give him space. His legs dangled next to mine, his knees apart, and his thigh pressed against mine even though I had readjusted myself.

"There's this thing about you, Night," he said, shielding his eyes from the sun. "You try to make it clear you can take care of yourself, but I think you underestimate the effect that has on the men in your life."

"I don't know what you're talking about."

Tex kept talking as though I hadn't interrupted him.

"About a week ago, Hudson called me. Said he was worried about you and needed to tell me something. That was just about the last phone call I ever expected to take, but I have to say he got my attention. I went to see him that afternoon."

He studied my face. I hoped it was unreadable.

"He told me something was going on with you. Said you asked a bunch of question about counterfeiting. He felt guilty about something you asked him to do, but he wouldn't tell me what it was. I can probably guess, but it's neither here nor there. He told me he wasn't going to jeopardize his freedom, not now, but he wanted me to know he was pretty sure you were in danger, and that you might do something stupid."

"Hudson said that?"

"Those might not have been his exact words."

"Hudson's the person you had looking after me?"

"No, in fact, kinda the opposite. He asked me to keep an eye on you."

"But you said—"

"He told me he cared about you."

I blushed and looked down at the stripes painted on the parking lot asphalt.

"He said he was pretty sure I cared about you too, and that I was in a position to make sure you weren't in danger. Trouble was, there was only so much I could do while I was dating Donna." He rested on his palms and turned his face up toward the sun. "I've known for a while the thing with Nasty wasn't going to work out. I don't think she was all that surprised when I broke it off."

I didn't look at Tex.

"Hudson James is the last person I ever expected would come asking me for help. That's you. That's what you do to people."

"I didn't expect him to tell you about my problems. I thought that was just between him and me."

On some level, I was offended that Hudson had broken my confidence, but I knew I'd get over it. He was doing what was right for him. I couldn't hold that against him.

"I'm telling you what I can tell you. I'm not telling you everything because you're not a cop, and you're not working a case. I am. This part concerns you, and you have a right to know that I know."

"Do I have a right to know anything else?"

"Not yet."

"I can help you," I said.

"I know."

One of the uniformed officers called Tex's name, and he held up his hand. He jumped off the back of the Jeep, bent down and adjusted the leg of his jean, then stood up and looked me straight in the eye.

"I'm trying to decide if I want you to or not."

He crossed the lot and conferred with another officer. A few seconds later, he jogged back to me.

"Get in the car," he said.

"But I have to talk to somebody here."

"This trumps whatever you were told. Nasty just took a call from Stanley Mann."

"Stanley Mann? He's okay?"

"Not sure if he's okay, but he's alive."

"Brad told me he was being tortured at Paper Trail. That Philip and a guy in a mask tortured him to get him to do work for them."

"Which was what?"

"They wanted him to authenticate large denomination bills to sell to collectors. Nasty talked to him?"

"Yes. He identified himself, and somebody else came on the phone and demanded money in return for his safety."

"Demanded—but that means—"

"Yes. Looks like Turlington was telling you the truth. While you were hearing his version of things, someone else was making the ransom call."

TWENTY-EIGHT

"Did the caller identify himself?" I asked.

"No. He said, 'We want our money in return for the numismatist.'"

"How much?"

"Don't know. Cocky bastards, calling it their money."

"Did they say where they were keeping him?"

"No." Tex hopped into his Jeep and started the engine.

"Where are we going?"

"Your studio. Get in. We're losing time."

"I need my keys." I reached into the brown sedan. My handbag had tipped during the drive and rent checks spilled out onto the floor by the hundred dollar bills.

"Come on, Night, we gotta go."

"Why my studio?" I opened the door and looked at him, trying to read his cop face. I couldn't.

"You have a file on this Bonneville guy, right? Nasty saw it. I want to see it, too."

"What do you mean, Nasty saw it?"

"That day I took her to your place to use the restroom. She told me she saw the file on your desk and checked it out."

"Damn it, Lieutenant! Your girlfriend is going through my client files, and you're talking about me with Hudson behind my back. What about my privacy? Why doesn't your code about private citizens apply to me?"

"I didn't ask Nasty to check it out. I didn't know about that until just now. But a man is dead. Another's been shot. Sorry if you don't like my methods, but I'm going to catch these guys."

Judging from the way Tex avoided the speed limits on the way to my studio I half-expected to find Stanley Mann tied up to my desk. He pulled the Jeep around back and parked across the two spaces. We slammed our doors at the same time and even though I was walking as fast as I could, Tex reached the door before me. I flipped through a set of keys and unlocked the door. He followed me to the office. I pushed piles of paper around the top of the desk, looking for the file.

"It's not here."

"Did you take it home?"

"No. I was going to, but I didn't." I sat upright and looked past Tex to the corner trash can for no reason other than I wanted to focus on something unimportant.

"I got distracted. Why—wait a minute. It was on my desk after Donna was here. I remember. It was open. Then I went home to meet Connie and go over the plans for her atomic kitchen. When she left I went to Turtle Creek Luxury Apartments." At Tex's confused look, I continued. "That's where he lives."

"He lied about his name. What makes you think he didn't lie about his address?"

"Because the real Art Leach lives there too. He told me who the imposter really is. I'm surprised Donna didn't tell you any of this."

"I don't think she knows most of it. She looked in his file. She knows the kind of things about him that you would have written in there. His decorating tastes. His deposit. Not the fact that he's impersonating anybody."

"No, that's not what I'm talking about. She was at Turtle Creek Luxury Apartments. When I went there the first time, when I thought Grant's name was Archie Leach. The real Archie Leach—Art Leach—thought *I* was trying to pull something. He called the cops on me, and Donna arrived. She didn't tell you?"

Tex propped himself on the wooden desk, his hands fisted, his weight resting on the back of his knuckles. His head hung low. After a few seconds, he lifted his head, stood up straight, and looked at me. His blue eyes were dark, his voice low.

"She never mentioned any of this. What else was there for her to tell me?"

"I'm going to tell you something that happened at Turtle Creek Luxury Apartments. It was told to me in confidence. Please respect that."

Tex looked past me to the interior of my studio. When he spoke, his voice was cold, direct. "What happened out there?"

"There have been a few break-ins. Some staff members were robbed. When I showed up asking about Archie Leach, I ended up talking to an employee named Art Leach. Someone stole eleven thousand dollars in cash from his apartment. He didn't report it."

"Why not?"

"The money was tip money. He didn't want anybody to know about it. Building security took me into their office and asked me a bunch of questions. When they told me they called the cops, I thought you were going to show up, but Donna showed instead."

"Why wouldn't she tell me?"

"Because it was me."

"Give her some credit, Night."

"I keep trying to give her credit, but it's getting harder and harder to think of her as an objective cop. You have to see it. She's been acting like she has some kind of hidden agenda. I don't know what she knows or what's driving her. Half the time it seems like she's out to get me."

"She's out there now. You need talk to her, tell her what you know, try to help her."

"She doesn't trust me, Tex. I'm probably not the best person to try to help her."

"That's where you're wrong, Ms. Night."

I jerked at the voice. Tex spun around. Grant Bonneville stood in the doorway. His left arm was in a sling, a bandage visible through the torn fabric of his blood-stained shirt. A couple of buttons were undone down the front and a black protective vest covered his chest like armor.

"That makes you the perfect person to try to help her," he said.

TWENTY-NINE

Tex jumped to his feet and reached for his service weapon. Grant held out his gun with his fingers splayed, then set it down on the corner of my desk. I stood up and backed away from the two of them until I was pressed up against the wall behind me. Grant held his jacket open and pulled a small black leather item from inside. He flipped it open with his thumb, displaying a star-shaped badge and an identification card.

"I'm Secret Service." He held the badge holder out to Tex, who inspected it closely. "I've been tracking these guys, trying to get a handle on their counterfeiting operation for a while now."

"Why were you at the bank? They're counterfeiting bills that are out of circulation. I don't think they're planning to pass them," I said.

"Counterfeiting is my area of expertise. Working at a bank is standard cover."

"Why did you use a different name?" I asked.

"I wanted to establish a reasonable connection with you. I knew Turlington was here, and I knew he knew me from Philadelphia. I couldn't risk you using my name and blowing my cover."

"You've been undercover for two years? They just showed up a couple days ago."

He didn't answer. I suspected this man wasn't going to be as forthcoming with information as I would like, but I pressed on.

"Why 'Archie Leach?' Why that name?"

"You have a movie still from *That Touch of Mink* on the wall of your office." He stopped talking for a second, as if weighing how much he should tell me. "Archie Leach is Cary Grant's real name."

"I know that. But there's a real Art Leach, at Turtle Creek Luxury Apartments."

"That's probably why the name was stuck in my head. He's legit, aside from his income tax situation, and that's not my problem."

"Why did you charge me at the bank?"

"I wanted to get you somewhere where I could talk to you. I had to figure out what you knew so I could figure out damage control."

"I don't understand," I said.

"Sit down, Ms. Night."

I wasn't particularly fond of his tone of voice, but my knee had been throbbing for the past half hour, and I was even less fond of the feeling that I was the least informed person in the room.

I dropped into one of the Barcelonas. Tex sat in my chair. Grant leaned back against my cork wall of inspiration. A photo of the kitchen from *The Glass Bottom Boat* fell from the wall and floated to the floor by the corner of the desk. Grant looked at it but didn't pick it up.

"I understand you watched a piece of film that Mr. Turlington hid in your car."

"Yes."

"That piece of film gave us a solid lead on these guys. The men Mr. Turlington indicated on the film strip had been running a counterfeit operation in Pennsylvania. I'm not at liberty to discuss that case with you, Ms. Night. What I can tell you is that Mr. Turlington disappeared for a couple of years. He turned up in Dallas and a man involved in that case turned up on his heels. That man is now dead."

"Philip Shayne?" I asked.

"You know more than you should. I'm not sure I would have made the same decision to let you view that bit of footage."

"The footage was intended for me," I said. "Lt. Allen made the right decision. I had every right to see it."

Grant turned to Tex. "You shouldn't have let her get this involved."

Tex's nostrils flared, but he said nothing.

Grant looked at me. "Do you have any coffee?"

"In the cabinet next to the desk. I'll get it."

"Not necessary, Ms. Night. Tell Lt. Allen where it is, and we'll take it from here."

Heat crawled from the base of my neck up into my hairline. I was being dismissed from my own office. I fought the urge to snap or say something I might regret. Regardless of the number of things wrong with the way Grant addressed me, I knew this was a battle I wouldn't win.

I pointed to an electric Scandia coffee pot, a white plug-in-and-pour model most people forgot ever existed. I had bought it from a vendor in Canton who used it to hold plastic floral arrangements. She'd kept the plug and the internal components in a closet, never used.

"The coffee is in a canister on the first shelf. I'm sure you can figure out how to work it."

I left the office and sat in a round white ball chair I picked up a couple of months ago. I pulled my legs into the ball and spun the chair so Tex and Grant couldn't see me.

I didn't need them. I needed time to think. I had to process the pieces of the puzzle.

I once likened the skills of a detective to those I used when designing a room. Look at what was there. Figure out what doesn't fit and take it away. Determine what's missing. Unlike the drama used in a makeover show where decorators clear a room and start from scratch, I like to learn a client's personality by looking at how they live first. They might want me to redo a room that holds one lamp that they love, and that lamp might be the key to everything.

I had to find that lamp and turn it on. I had to figure out the key to everything.

The scent of coffee perked me up. The men were managing to do things on their own, which was fine by me. I was missing something.

I leaned back and closed my eyes and thought about what I'd been through in the past week since Brad had shown up. That had been the beginning of a rollercoaster ride that I seemed unable to stop. I'd found a body. I'd been chased from the restaurant. I'd been confronted in the parking lot outside of my building. And who had done those things? An anonymous person. A man in a mask. Someone who wanted to fly under the radar.

It didn't help that Brad didn't know the identity of the masked man either. It was almost too convenient. If Brad had admitted to knowing that other person, it would negate the entirety of his explanation of events.

Or...

Brad? Could he have been the man in the mask?

My eyes popped open. Did it fit, or did I just want it to fit?

Brad could have followed me from the restaurant because he had been with me at the restaurant. If he heard me leave the apartment, he could easily have pulled on a ski mask and slipped out the front, driven the brown sedan to the lot, and taken the briefcase out of the car. It was his car. He could have done anything with it he'd wanted to. The only reason I hadn't suspected him was because of the masked man decorating my apartment. That couldn't have been Brad. So Brad was working with someone else. Who? And why hadn't I realized this before now?

Had I been blind all along? Was it because deep, deep down, in a place I hadn't looked in a long time, I wanted to forgive him and believe the fairytale he offered me?

No. Tex was right when he said the person he knew, the Madison I was now, had been born the day Brad lied to me. The moment I turned away from him and skied down that mountain at Jack Frost ski resort in the Poconos, I'd established my independence. And the truth—the real truth? Despite my vintage wardrobe and mid-century modern business, I wasn't willing to go back in time.

I'd been wrong when I thought this all started when Brad sent me the five thousand dollar bill. This had all started before that, when I was still in Pennsylvania. And it wouldn't be over until I ended things.

I went back to the office where Tex and Grant were comparing notes. Grant stopped talking when he saw me.

"Lt. Allen, can I talk to you?" I asked.

"Ma'am, this is a confidential conversation. I think it's best we keep you out of this from here on out," said Grant.

I looked at Tex, then at Grant, then back at Tex. He and I had been through this before and I thought he'd back me up. He didn't.

"I need to borrow your car," I said to Tex, ignoring Grant. "My car was totaled. I have an animal in need of food and attention. If my help is not needed here, then it certainly is needed there."

Tex studied my face for a few seconds and narrowed his eyes. I knew what he was thinking. He didn't trust me. He was right not to trust me, but I didn't want him to know that. I held his stare.

"All I'm asking is to borrow your car so I can pick up Rocky and take him to my apartment. If you want me to bring your car back here when I'm done, I can."

"Give her the keys, Allen. We have my car now. Ms. Night, we'll take it from here," Grant said.

Tex tossed his keys to me. I caught them easily with one hand.

"I don't know your exact title, Mr. Bonneville, but you wouldn't have half the leads you do if it wasn't for me, so good luck 'taking it from here,'" I said.

My eyes jumped to Tex's face for a second. I forced myself to look away before he had a chance to read the secondary agenda in my own expression.

I unhooked the keys to the studio from my own key ring and set them on my desk. "Lock up when you leave." Before they could stop me, I was out the door.

I drove Tex's Jeep back to the bank. The brown sedan was parked in the lot. The trunk was open and empty. Hudson's ring of keys was on the corner of the floor mat, half hidden by torn envelopes and rent checks. The scattered hundred dollar bills and the box to Brad's watch were gone.

A piece of paper titled Referrals, with names and phone numbers, jutted out from under the pile of checks. A ball of wrapping paper rested by the center console, and a painting lay on the passenger-side seat.

I picked up the painting. It was a representation of a five thousand dollar bill with my image in the center where a president's image might have been. My name was lettered below it. I turned the painting over. Above Hudson's signature was one word: Priceless.

Someone had torn the wrapping paper from the painting and left the painting behind. In my opinion, he'd left the most valuable thing in the car.

I put the keys, referrals, and rent checks into my handbag and carried the painting with me back to Tex's Jeep. I didn't know where Brad went after the shooting with Grant. He might try to skip town. He might disappear again. He might do a lot of things to make it seem like we were over, just like last time.

Only this time, I didn't feel like it was over. This time, I knew it wasn't.

I drove the Jeep to Thelma Johnson's house and collected Rocky. He squirmed in my arms and licked my cheek. I drove home and went directly to Effie's apartment.

The door next to hers opened up after the second round of knocking. Mrs. Young peered into the hall. She wore an oversized Texas Tech sweatshirt and jeans. A piece of clear plastic imprinted with an XL was stuck to the side of her sweatshirt. Her hair was pulled into a ponytail and a smudge of paint was on her nose.

"I'm sorry to disturb you. I was hoping Effie could watch Rocky for a few hours. I have to go back out for a bit."

She stepped into the hallway and pulled her door shut behind her. "I've been wondering about you."

"Wondering, how?" I asked. I backed away from her and tripped over Rocky's leash.

"I've been wondering about why you're never here. It seems to be a waste of rent money, if you ask me. And you have that beautifully renovated apartment too. It doesn't make sense."

Mrs. Young had been more inquisitive than my other tenants. She'd picked up on the attraction between Hudson and me, and now she was telling me she kept track of my hours. Something about her was off. I wish I'd looked at her file, at the background check Hudson had mentioned. Clean as a whistle, he'd said.

"Tech?" I asked, nodding at her sweatshirt.

"Years ago, yes. I found this when I unpacked. I'd forgotten how comfortable it was."

I mustered up the closest facsimile to a smile that I could dig out of my arsenal of fake facial expressions. That sweatshirt wasn't old. The size sticker indicated as much. And if she was lying to me about something as minor as a sweatshirt, she must have been trying to hide secrets far more dangerous.

"I really do need to be getting home. Like you said, I haven't been here much lately, and I'm starting to forget what the place looks like. Busy with clients, which is a good problem to have. Sometimes I end up working late. You probably haven't heard me return because you're asleep when I get here." I coiled Rocky's leash around my right hand.

"No, I don't think that's it at all. I think you've been staying somewhere else, somewhere you don't want anybody to know. Avoiding someone. I have a pretty good idea why," she said.

"I don't know what you're talking about."

"I think you do." She reached a hand out and put it on my forearm. Effie bounded up the stairs and Rocky strained his leash to get to her.

"Effie, remember Lt. Allen? He specifically asked if you would be available to watch Rocky tonight. Can you do that?" I asked.

Effie's eyes grew wide, in the way a college student who believes that a favor for a cop might pay off someday.

"Lt. Allen asked? Um, sure, I guess so. Are you helping him with another case?"

"Thank you. He and I are..." I paused, unsure if Mrs. Young was still in the hallway listening to me. I suspected, even if she wasn't there, that her door was cracked and her ear was pressed to the opening. "... we're going on a date tonight."

"Is he coming here to pick you up?" she asked. "What are you going to wear?"

"I'm meeting him at the restaurant." I flipped through my keys until I found the one that unlocked my apartment. "I really have to run, Effie, I don't have a lot of time to get ready. Thank you, you're a lifesaver."

I headed into my apartment and dumped the bag of rent checks on the floor. I found the folder with Mrs. Young's application and opened it up. I scanned past her last known apartment, past her work history, to her education. And there it was: Oklahoma University.

It wasn't an everyday lie. No self-respecting OU grad would don a Texas Tech sweatshirt. Their rivalry was legendary.

I ran to the phone and called my studio. Nobody answered. I knew if Tex was still at my desk, he would hear my message through the machine.

"Tex, it's Madison. You need to get here, now. There's a woman who lives in my building. Mrs. Abigail Young. She showed up here right after Brad sent me the five thousand dollar bill. I'm going to the place where I was last night. I think I'll be safe there because nobody knows about it but you."

I hung up the phone, distracted by a corner of the new hardwood floor that was uneven from the rest. It wasn't like that two days ago. I'd marveled at the near perfect job that Brad's team had done in such a short amount of time. But what if the decorating job was a cover for something else? A clever hiding place?

I lowered myself to the floor and pried at the wood with my fingertips until I freed the uneven plank. I pulled it up and stared at a row of James Madison five thousand dollar bills, each tucked inside individual sandwich-sized plastic baggies.

And under the row of sandwich baggies were the uncut sheets of paper I'd found in the trunk of Brad's car.

Their money. That's what the man on the phone had called it. Stanley Mann's kidnappers weren't looking for a ransom. They were looking for these bills that had been hidden in my apartment. *This* was their money.

THIRTY

But even without proof, I already suspected that most of the bills were fake. The only one that seemed real was the one Brad had sent me from Pierot's Interiors. The rest did little more than downplay the value of the real one by making them all seem common.

A door shut in the hallway. I froze. Was Mrs. Young on her way over? She had maintained a nosy neighbor-style interest in my new living room. Was she was keeping watch on the money? I knew there were still questions I didn't have answered, but I didn't care. What I did know was that I had to get out of there before Mrs. Young had a chance to discover what I'd found. I knew the money wasn't safe at my apartment. I had to figure out a way to get it out and get it to Tex.

I moved to the bathroom and found half a roll of surgical tape relegated to the flotsam bin after my knee had healed. I pulled off my tunic and pressed the plastic baggies against my stomach, then wound the tape around me several times. I pulled my tunic back on, grabbed Tex's keys, and left out the back door, driving Tex's Jeep back to Mad for Mod.

Tex had set a standard for breaking speed limits. I decided to follow his lead. I would have welcomed a set of flashing lights in my rear view mirror as I drove back to the studio, but the lights never appeared. A white Lexus was pulling out as I pulled in. Tex was driving.

"Listen to me. The ransom call was code. The kidnappers don't want cash, they want the fake five thousand dollar bills."

"Get out of my way, Night," he said.

"I think the next door neighbor is in on it. She's been trying to get into my apartment since Brad renovated it and I found the money hidden in the floor."

"Where's the money now?" he asked.

"It's safe."

The back door to Mad for Mod opened and Grant walked out. "Ms. Night? I warned you to stay out of this."

He climbed in the shotgun seat. Tex glared at me, his forehead drawn, his eyes cloudy. He drove past the Jeep and left me standing in the parking lot.

I stormed into my studio and pulled the door shut behind me. I dialed information and asked for the Dallas Police department. A few seconds later I spoke to a dispatcher.

"My name is Madison Night. There's been a kidnapping and I have information that can help you."

"Where are you located?"

"Mad for Mod on Greenville Avenue."

"Stay there. I'm sending an officer. Don't trust anyone who doesn't show you identification."

I hung up the phone and paced around the office. I didn't know if I'd done the right thing, but if Tex wouldn't listen to me, then I didn't have any other options. I stood inside the studio and paced between the furniture, and then went to my office to wait. Within minutes I heard a car pull up to the front curb.

A fist pounded on the door. "Madison Night? I know you're in there. Come out now."

I knew the voice. It was Mrs. Young. She must have followed me. I dropped to my hands and knees and crawled from the office to the studio.

"Madison, this is no time to screw around. I'll explain everything after you come out."

I crawled across the floor, staying behind sofas and end tables that were staged for walk-in customers. The bills taped to my torso made it difficult to move. I peered out from behind a couch near the door and looked up. Mrs. Young's face was pressed against the glass. She was looking for me, but she hadn't seen me.

I grabbed a canister of pepper spray that I'd bought a few months ago and pulled the pin. My left hand gripped the keys to Tex's Jeep. I started a silent countdown and stood slowly. On three, I whipped the door open and hit the nozzle on the pepper spray. Mrs. Young screamed and put her hands to her face. I pushed her out of the way, yanked the door shut behind me, and ran around the side of the building to where I'd parked the Jeep.

Directly into the arms of a man in a black ski mask.

THIRTY-ONE

He dropped a bag over my head and spun me around. Handcuffs clamped onto my wrists, and I was pulled backward. I tripped and fell. Someone yanked on the handcuffs until I was back on my feet. I was picked up, carried a few feet, and dropped. My left shoulder and hip slammed onto a slightly padded surface. I tried to unbend my legs but my feet hit something. I heard a door slam. I was inside a trunk.

I kicked my feet against the interior. It didn't do any good. The car started to move. I screamed. I didn't know if anyone could hear me. The only hope I had was that the officer who was coming to get me would discover I was missing and would put out an APB or whatever they put out for missing people.

The car occasionally turned left or right, shifting me in the small space. My head bounced when we drove over something—a speed bump, I'd guess—and a couple of sharp right turns pushed my back into the depths of the compartment. The bag on my head smelled like onions. My empty stomach convulsed with nausea. I'd neglected my hunger for days but was thankful that there was nothing in me to come back up. I thought about the speed bumps and the succession of right turns.

The car slowed down. It glided over another set of bumps, twice, stopped for a couple of seconds, then started moving again. A few seconds later, the engine turned off. I braced myself for the worst. A car door slammed. I heard the key enter the trunk. I felt the fresh air against my right arm seconds before I was lifted out, set on my feet, and pushed forward.

I stumbled again, tripping over my shoe. I kicked the shoe off and hobbled awkwardly, the pace dictated by the person holding my arm. I felt gravel under my bare foot, then carpet. Fingers clamped around my left wrist. I balled my hand up into a fist. My arms were yanked behind my back, and the cold metal pressed against my wrists. I tried to pull away but couldn't.

The onion bag came off my head as suddenly as it had been dropped on. Light bit through my vision. I pinched my eyes shut, then blinked rapidly against the assault of light. Almost instantly, the lights went out, leaving dots in place of my vision. I barely made out a figure in a black ski mask leaving the room. There were no threats, no confessions.

"Who is that?" said a raspy male voice. Until that moment, I thought I was alone. I twisted around and slowly made out the figure of a man handcuffed to the metal leg of the desk.

"Madison Night." I said. "Who are you?"

The man coughed. "Stanley Mann."

As my eyes adjusted to the darkness in the office, I noticed movement from behind the file cabinet.

"Madison?" asked a female voice.

"Officer Nast?" I asked, surprised. "Is that you?" I blinked a few times to try to see better. "What are you doing here?"

Nasty ignored my question. "Where did you come from?"

"I was jumped outside of my studio. Somebody threw me into the trunk of a car and brought me here. Are we at Turtle Creek Luxury Apartments?"

"Yes."

Nasty squatted next to Stanley and unlocked his restraints with her police-issue handcuff key. I heard them click open. Stanley rubbed his right wrist with his left hand for a couple of seconds then switched. I hadn't thought much about how long he'd been trapped.

"Are you okay?" I asked him, my voice barely above a whisper.

I looked at him. A faded brown baseball hat was on his head. Dark circles, purplish-brown, stood out under his eyes. His skin was sallow. "My dog—I need to check on my dog. He's alone at my store. He's probably starving," he said. Tears welled up in his eyes.

"Your dog is okay, Mr. Mann. He's at my house," Nasty said.

"You have his dog?" I asked with surprise.

She didn't answer my question. "Does Tex know you're missing?"

"No. He sent me home."

"And you didn't listen. Figures. I bet you think he's going to bust through those doors and rescue you."

I ignored her and turned my attention to Stanley. "The police know everything. This is almost over."

The man's head hung low, his shoulders protruding up and out like a vulture. I wondered what this past week had been like for him. He coughed again, this time repeatedly. I looked around the office for a refrigerator or bottle of water. A pack of Orangina sat next to the printer. One bottle had already been taken from the pack.

Nasty followed my stare. She uncapped one of the bottles and held it up to Stanley's lips. A trickle of orange drink dribbled down his chin while he swallowed.

"Officer Nast, someone demanded a ransom for this man. Tex and a Secret Service agent are operating under the assumption that the kidnappers want cash, but they don't. They want the James Madison bills. I found them—I have the money. When Tex wouldn't listen to me to me, I called the station."

"You know about Agent Bonneville?"

Her reaction surprised me. She knew about Grant? She knew he was Secret Service?

"Tex doesn't know about this case," she said. "I was assigned to help Agent Bonneville but to keep the investigation confidential. I have the situation under control," Nasty continued. "You being here complicates everything."

Stanley's coughing resumed.

"I was jumped before anybody showed up at my studio. I didn't want to come here and complicate your investigation, and I don't intend to stay here, either. I don't know what issue you have with me, but I can help you."

"You said you have the money? Where is it?" she asked.

"The money is safe. Right now we have to get out of here."

Nasty leaned behind me and unlocked one of my handcuffs. "This man's safety is the most important thing right now."

A door opened in the hallway before I could respond. In a quick motion, Nasty pulled the open end of the handcuff around the leg of the desk and clamped it back on my wrist. She pulled the hat from Stanley's head and put it on mine.

"I'm going out there," she said. "I don't want you following me. You said the money was safe, right?"

"I said the money was safe." And it was, at least until I sweat through the surgical tape and a shower of five thousand dollar bills in sandwich baggies dropped out from under the hem of my tunic. "Officer Nast, there's a woman. She goes by Abigail Young. She was at my studio right before I was jumped. I hit her with pepper spray, but whoever she's working with caught me when I ran."

"You're way off base, Madison." She pushed Stanley toward the door and cracked it open. I watched her look both ways. She turned back to me. "Wait here and I'll come back for you." She and Stanley left me alone in the dark, chained to a desk.

Before I had a chance to figure out what to do next, two sets of footsteps resonated in the hall, headed my direction.

THIRTY-TWO

The footsteps proceeded past the door. Snippets of conversation were muffled. Something about the weather, I thought. When the sound dropped out of range, I started working on my situation. Yes, the handcuffs kept me bound to the leg of the desk, but the desk could be tipped.

I got on my knees, then put my feet underneath me. I was bent at the waist, thanks to the restrictions of the handcuffs. I stood, pulling the heavy metal desk with me.

A sheaf of papers fluttered through the air and fanned out around the carpet. When I got the leg off the floor by about six inches, I heaved it backward. For a moment, it tipped precariously on the back legs, until a firm bump with my hip knocked it over.

The computer and keyboard crashed to the floor. The leg of the desk stood straight out, parallel to the floor. I slipped the handcuff chain down the leg until I was no longer attached to anything but myself. That created a new problem, not as easy to solve.

I brought my hands from behind me to in front of me by stepping over the handcuffs. I looked around the office for something that could help me. The carpet was covered with paper and items from the desk. The trash can had turned on its side, spilling coffee cups, candy bar wrappers, and an empty bottle of hair dye for men. A Hawaiian shirt hung from a hook on the back of the door. It looked vaguely familiar.

I moved to the windows. They were shaded by plantation shutters. I adjusted the vertical bar that controlled the slats enough for me to see outside. Leaves from a tree partially blocked my view, but beyond it I saw a parking lot filled with cars. One of them was a white Lexus.

From a distance, I made out Harry, the valet attendant with the dyed brown hair. Another member of the staff took his place by the gate. They exchanged words, and Harry pulled his phone from his pocket, tapped the screen a couple of times, and walked in the direction of the building.

I needed to get his attention. If only he would look up from the screen of his phone. He tapped his screen a few more times. Before I could act, the door of the small office opened and a man in a black knit ski mask entered. He wore a red valet vest over a white shirt and black pants.

"Who are you?" I demanded. "Why did you bring me here?"

He stepped backward, away from me. A dog yipped from the hallway. The masked man stepped into the office and shut the door behind him.

I stepped forward but stopped when I saw his gun. I put my handcuffed hands in front of me and slowly raised them. The masked man didn't say anything, but I could tell from his eyes that he knew I got the message.

Someone knocked on the door. Through the textured glass pane nestled in the middle of the decorative wooden door I could make out the silhouette of Mrs. Bonneville.

The man in the ski mask kept his eyes and his pistol trained on me.

"My Gosh, I could have sworn I saw a man in a red vest go in there. Where did he go, Giuseppe? Where did the man in the red vest go?"

Despite my silent pleas that Mrs. Bonneville come in, I knew she wasn't the type of woman to enter an office that belonged to the service staff. Giuseppe barked twice. The shadow turned around and receded into the hallway.

The man in the ski mask reached up to his head and scratched his hairline through the wool. His sleeve rode up by his wrist and I saw the flash of a Submariner watch.

Slowly, I inched backward, until I was pressed up against the wall. I slid down the wall until my bent knee couldn't take the pressure anymore, and I fell onto the side. I planted my handcuffed hands on the floor and repositioned myself into a crawling position.

"The police know everything, Brad. Even if you try to run, you won't get far."

He set the pistol on top of the metal file cabinet and pulled the hat from his head.

"I'm sorry, Madison. I thought I could end this, but I can't. You'll never know how far I went to protect you. You'll never know how sorry I am."

He left the office. There wasn't much I could do to get away considering Nasty had left my hands locked together. I pushed my feet around the paper on the floor, trying to come up with a plan. My toe connected with a tape dispenser, and I got an idea.

I reached up under my tunic and tore the surgical tape from my body. One of the sandwich baggies fell to the floor. I pulled the tape dispenser toward me. I freed a piece and stuck it to the baggie.

I put my hands on the floor in front of me and pushed myself up so I could reach the window, then I taped plastic baggie with the James Madison bill to the glass under the plantation shutters. If I was right, and if anybody—*anybody*—walked past that window, they'd see it and wonder. And at this point, getting someone to wonder about was all I could do.

The grating sound of the doorknob turning pulled my attention to the entrance. Slowly the door pushed into the room. I half-crouched, half-stood, frozen in place. Harry stepped into the room. I wanted to hug him.

"Mr. Delbert? Yoo-hoo, Mr. Delbert!" Mrs. Bonneville called out. Through the distorted, textured glass I watched Harry run his hands over his hair and down the front of his vest. He smiled at her.

"Hello Mrs. Bonneville. How's Giuseppe today?"

The three of them moved down the hallway, outside, and into the parking lot. I watched them between the slats of the shutters.

Harry might come back, I reasoned. Or he might notice the currency I taped to the window.

Or neither.

Giuseppe strained forward in Mrs. Bonneville's arms and sniffed Harry's fingers. Harry pulled away and balled his hands into fists. Giuseppe barked at him. Mrs. Bonneville tried to calm him but was unsuccessful. Harry stepped away from the woman and her dog and scratched his left sleeve with his right hand. A streak of black stained the white fabric.

I looked away from the window at the Hawaiian shirt that hung from the peg on the back of the door. I remembered where I had first seen it. On the waiter at Trader Josh's, the night Brad took me to dinner, when I'd called him after finding the body at Paper Trail. Brad had been the one to suggest the restaurant.

I crossed the room and lifted the shirt from the hook. A piece of masking tape was stuck to the fabric above the manufacturer's label and Harry Delbert was written in blue ballpoint pen. Harry the valet attendant with the shoe-polish hair was Harry Delbert, the gray-haired waiter from the Polynesian restaurant.

I dropped back onto my hands and knees and crawled around the floor, pushing papers out of my way, hoping to find Nasty's handcuff keys while I had time.

As I sifted through the mess, I pushed stacks of paper under the desk. I could tell from the apartment application paperwork that this was where the building's landlord kept confidential tenant information. At first, I found it odd that so much of what people preferred to keep private could easily be found on the lease agreement.

But I was a landlord, too. And I knew what I was allowed by law to ask for on an application. Sure, my building paled in comparison to the luxury building I was captive in now, but laws were laws. If people were disclosing this kind of information, there had to be a reason they felt it was okay.

The staff of the building had access to their apartments and to their personal belongings. Harry had been the one to rob Art of the eleven thousand dollars he'd kept in his room.

Harry had used trust to violate these people—both the tenants and his coworkers. His willingness to feed me information about Grant Bonneville, his story about a counterfeit bill that was accepted by the bank. It was a package of carefully planted lies intended to keep me from looking too closely at him. He'd been keeping an eye on me since the night I found Philip Shayne's body.

I pulled a couple of papers close to my face. The light was fading and it was tough to make out the details, but not so tough that I couldn't read a request for personal information about a temporary tenant named Philip Shayne.

What was he doing at Turtle Creek Luxury Apartments?

They were in it together.

Brad said Philip Shayne had a partner in Dallas. That partner was Harry.

Everything about Brad's story made sense. Philip Shayne and Harry Delbert were the two men who had tracked him from Pennsylvania. But when Philip and Harry learned about me, they headed to Dallas. Brad had thought he was free. He thought he'd protected me.

But they put two and two together and came after me. The fight at Paper Trail, while they were holding Stanley hostage. The accidental murder of Philip Shayne, who had four bullet holes in his leg.

The very trouble Brad had hoped to protect me from by lying two years ago had followed him to my door.

I had to get out of the room before Harry Delbert came for me.

I grabbed Brad's pistol from the file cabinet and moved to the window. Harry stood outside of the valet station. His sweeping gaze scanned the street and the building.

And then he saw the James Madison I taped to the glass.

THIRTY-THREE

I dropped to the floor and crawled over piles of paper to the exit. I stood up and stepped onto the oriental carpet in the hallway. The double doors to the apartment complex stood to my left. Keycard access would keep me from entering. I ran to the parking lot on my right, my fingers wrapped around Brad's gun.

I got outside and raced for the street. I heard footsteps behind me. I turned around and raised Brad's pistol with my handcuffed hands. Harry was ten feet away. He held a gun.

I pulled the trigger on the gun I held. It clicked. I pulled it again and again. Click. Click. No bullets. Brad's gun wasn't loaded.

Harry smiled, the face of a deranged man who just recognized his own luck. He slowly raised his own gun and aimed at me. Nasty approached him from behind. She threw her arms around his arms. His gun went off. I screamed as a flash of heat tore through my upper arm.

"Madison!" yelled Tex, diving toward me. He knocked me to the macadam. More shots were fired, shots I didn't feel.

I squeezed my eyes shut, scared by the weight of Tex's body on top of mine, scared by the fact that he wasn't moving, scared by the silence surrounding us. I couldn't breathe, and my arm felt like it had been stung by a thousand bees. I opened my eyes and stared at the clear, cerulean sky.

The faint sound of sirens hinted that the worst was over. Two ambulances pulled into the parking lot, and I realized that the world had not gone silent, but that my hearing had been affected by the shots of the gun.

I tipped my head up and looked at the building. Nasty had handcuffed Harry and was walking him toward her patrol car. I lay back down and closed my eyes a second time.

Tex moved, slowly. He put a hand on either side of me and raised himself into a half-push-up.

"This is not how I pictured this moment," he said and rolled off. Blood covered his jeans and my green pants. He lay back on the ground and closed his eyes. I was only minimally comforted by the rise and fall of his chest.

A sea of people appeared to help. I felt woozy and couldn't make out faces, names, or sounds. Paramedics moved Tex onto a gurney and rolled him into the back of an ambulance. Someone unlocked the handcuffs still around my wrists. A man dressed only in white tended to my arm. I didn't want to look at it. I already knew I'd been shot.

I didn't need to know the details of the wound. I tried to stand, but dizziness made it near-impossible. Someone thrust a wheelchair under me. Despite my hatred for the metal contraption, I collapsed into it, like a marionette whose strings were no longer being pulled. I felt a needle in my arm and I melted into sleep.

"Looks like we're both members of the injured below the waist club now," said a familiar voice.

I opened my eyes and looked directly at Tex. I'd been sleeping in a chair in the waiting room outside of Emergency. My arm was in a white sling. It was bandaged and stiff. Tex was in a wheelchair in front of me. I didn't like what was familiar about the scenario, and I didn't like what was new.

"What happened?" I asked.

"We got shot."

"Both of us?" The details were cloudy in my mind. I looked at the ceiling and replayed the memories that had been filling my dreams. "That's not what I remember. Harry had a gun. Nasty surprised him. The gun went off."

"And shot us."

"No, shot me. Then you—"

Tex raised an eyebrow.

"Then you—" I tried again. *Then you jumped in front of me to protect me and got shot in the process.* I couldn't finish the sentence.

"And then I did my job," he said.

"You got shot because of me."

He shrugged. "All in a day's work."

"You know this is going to change the way I see you."

"How's that?" he asked. His face hinted at nothing.

It was a crossroads for Tex and me. There was no way I could see him as the playboy like I once had, but I knew him too well to adopt hero worship. Here was a chance for us to start fresh and rewrite the basis of our relationship. I took a couple of seconds before responding.

"For starters, until you're out of that wheelchair, I'll be looking down."

He shook his head and smiled. There was a purplish bruise by his right eye and a cut over his brow that was held shut by two small butterfly Band-aids.

"Harry Delbert killed Philip Shayne, didn't he?"

Tex nodded. "Harry Delbert's locked up now, and he'll stay that way for a long time."

"Do you understand what it was all about?"

He shook his head slightly. "I don't know the details of what happened in Pennsylvania. I do know that Delbert and Shayne tracked Mr. Turlington to Dallas. He had something they wanted."

Mr. Turlington. Tex's formality established a barrier. I tensed up, wondering if I could talk about Brad in calm, formal terms.

"The James Madison bill."

"It would seem so."

"Brad said they were holed up at Paper Trail," I said. "Harry and Philip forced Stanley Mann to authenticate counterfeit bills so they could sell them to collectors."

"That's where the Secret Service came in."

"But this was a whole different kind of counterfeit scheme. They weren't passing fakes, they were selling fakes. It's not like a collector was going to do anything with the bill other than save it or display it."

"Still, the Secret Service has jurisdiction over counterfeiting crimes—doesn't matter what they were planning to do with the money they made. Spend it or sell it, either way it's a federal felony. They probably could have gotten away with it if they didn't get greedy."

"I think they did get away with it, at least for a while. That's why I was told Brad's video message was evidence to a crime in Pennsylvania, wasn't it? And why Grant said I shouldn't know as much as I do?"

Tex nodded. "The one thing that made their whole plan work was your James Madison. It's the only one that was real."

It started to make sense. "So if anybody ever called them on what they were doing, they could pull a switch and look legit."

"Yep. Too bad your—Mr. Turlington—had the romantic notion to send the real bill to you."

"How did Harry find out I had the real bill?"

"I don't think he knew at first. Mr—"

"If you insist on calling me by my last name, you can drop the formalities when it comes to Brad."

Tex raised one eyebrow and continued. "Turlington had your business card. Not sure where he got it, but I imagine you have them around town. We think he was at Paper Trail earlier, before Philip Shayne was killed. Maybe he dropped your card. Once Harry found out about you, he figured he had Turlington's soft spot."

"But Brad took me to the restaurant where Harry worked the night Philip Shayne was killed. Why would he do that?"

"We already checked Harry's schedule. He wasn't supposed to be working that night. He needed an alibi, and the best he could come up with was to show up at work. Turlington knew about the restaurant because they'd met there before. He might have been planning to tell you the truth then. Would have made things easier if he did, but seeing Harry probably shut him up."

"So Harry left when I left and followed me home in the brown sedan."

"Seems that way."

"And he was the guy in the ski mask who took the briefcase from Brad's trunk. Why didn't he come after me then?"

"You were the only one who knew where the real five thou was. Coming after you at that point wouldn't have done anything other than draw attention to them. He needed you."

As I reasoned out what I knew, I compared people to parts like I was casting a movie. Tex sat silent, allowing me the space to figure it all out for myself.

"Harry was the one who jumped me outside of my studio." My eyes moved around the interior of the waiting room, over framed paintings in shades of aqua, salmon, coral, and white. "They must have been at Paper Trail across the street from the bank. That's how Brad got the brown sedan and took off with me. And Harry followed us on foot and shot Grant."

Tex nodded once.

"So that's it. It's over?"

"It's over."

I wanted to believe what he said, but I knew it wasn't over. Not by a long shot. I knew all too well that there was a strong possibility that I'd never know the extent of Brad's involvement. If Brad had vanished a second time, it would never be over. I'd always wonder when or if he'd pop back up in my life. It was time for me to relegate him back to a small corner of my memory, to start pretending that he hadn't violated my trust and confidence a second time.

The doctor approached us from a long narrow hallway.

"Are you going to explain the money?" he asked me.

"What money? I don't have any money," I said.

"That's not exactly true," the doctor said.

Tex looked up at him, and I tipped my head to the side, confused.

"We had to remove your clothes to give you a physical, make sure there were no internal injuries," the doctor continued. "When we stripped you, we found something interesting."

I remembered the sandwich baggies taped to my midsection. "The James Madisons."

I looked at Tex, not sure how much he knew about that. He didn't look surprised, but he didn't look happy.

"Where are they?" I asked.

"Grant Bonneville has them now."

"All of them?"

"We don't know. Nobody knows how many there are."

It made sense. "How long are they going to keep you here?"

"With any luck I'll be out later today."

"How are you getting home?"

"I'll work it out." Tex spun himself backward and raised his hands. "What? This is the perfect opportunity for me to abuse my power. I'll get a rookie to drive me around Dallas for a while."

A man in blue scrubs approached us. "Are you his ride?"

"No. Actually, I don't have a ride myself."

"Yes, you do," said Tex. "There's an officer waiting out front. She knows where you live. When you're ready to leave, she'll take you home."

"It's not—" I stopped. I assumed he meant Nasty but refrained from saying so. She'd been rude and hostile toward me, but she'd also saved Stanley Mann's life and reunited him with his dog. Acknowledging I didn't like her would mean more than it should.

"Fine. I guess I'm ready to go." I stood from the plastic chair and walked to the exit.

"Hey, Night," Tex called behind me. I stopped walking and slowly looked over my shoulder. "Don't freak out on me, okay?"

I turned away from him and walked out the door. The sun was bright. I shielded my eyes and scanned the parking lot for a police cruiser amidst the small army of ambulances. I saw none. What I did see was my nosy neighbor, Mrs. Young, leaning against the back of her minivan.

"I knew you had to come out sooner or later," she said.

She stepped away from the car and adjusted her tweed blazer. I saw a holster under her jacket and the butt end of a gun before she pulled the jacket shut.

THIRTY-FOUR

"NO!" I screamed. She reached inside her blazer and I turned around, heading for the entrance. Tex, in his wheelchair, blocked my path.

"She's been watching my apartment—she's going to kill us!"

"She's not going to kill us." He put his hands out to my hips and slowly turned me around until I was facing her. "She's a police officer," he said.

I looked at Mrs. Young. She held a badge, confirming what Tex had said. "To be fair, you were half-right," she said. "Lieutenant Allen asked me to watch your apartment. But for the record, I'm not in on anything, and I'm not trying to kill you."

I turned back around and faced Tex. "You did this?"

"Get in the car, Night. Officer Young will drive you home and explain everything."

I pushed the arms of Tex's wheelchair backward. It rolled a couple of inches into the man in blue scrubs who had followed Tex outside.

"This is so not over," I said to him, pointing a finger in his face.

"That's what I'm counting on," he said with a smile.

If it wasn't for my current lack of funds, I would have stormed past Mrs. Young to a waiting taxi, but at the moment I didn't have any other choice. Reluctantly, I climbed into the car and sat next to her. I wanted to ask a thousand questions, but I didn't want to admit the depths of my ignorance. She pulled out of the parking lot and drove about a mile down Gaston before she spoke.

"You impressed me, Ms. Night."

"Why Ms. Night? You've called me Madison up till now."

"That was part of my cover as one of your neighbors. As a police officer, it's policy for me to call you Ms. Night."

"Call me Madison."

"Only if you'll call me Abby."

"Fine."

"You impressed me, Madison. Lt. Allen said you were a strong woman who could take care of yourself, and he was right."

"So why were you there?"

"No offense, but he suspected your judgment might be clouded when it came to your ex-boyfriend."

"So I've been told." I looked out the window at the passing trees. "The day I found you out front—you'd been waiting for me. Your application, everything—all made up."

"Yes."

"Tex set that up?"

"Yes."

"Did Hudson know?"

"Yes."

"And all of your questions, all those times you tried to look into my apartment, that was to keep an eye on Brad? When you showed up late that one night? And the times I heard a door open in the hallway but no one was there?"

"Pretty much."

"All Tex's idea?"

She nodded. I was quiet until we stopped at a traffic light.

"What about the times you asked me about Hudson?"

"Let's just say inquiring minds wanted to know your answers." She smiled.

I didn't say anything for a couple of minutes. "He told you I owned the building, didn't he?"

She nodded again.

"So I'm not really going to get a rent check from you."

"As it turns out, I really am in need of an apartment. Maybe we can work something out."

I accepted Abby's newfound friendship while she parked the car and walked with me to the back of the building. She kept up polite chatter about superficial subjects that required little more than a nod, a smile, or some other vague acknowledgement that I was half-paying attention. I didn't think she was fooled by my minimal attempts, but she seemed to appreciate the effort.

I went straight to Effie's apartment and knocked on the door. When she opened it, Rocky bounded out and stood up on his hind feet, paws in the air. I scooped him up, and he showered me with puppy dog kisses. I wrinkled my nose at the contact of his little pink tongue but didn't pull away. I thought about what Mrs. Bonneville had said about puppy kisses. It was just Rocky and I again. Only this time it felt different.

He put his paw on my upper arm by the bandage, and I flinched and repositioned him, cradling him in my other arm like a baby.

"Looks like he really missed you," Effie said.

"I don't know who missed who more."

When we reached my apartment, I unlocked the door and set Rocky down on the floor. I scanned my living room. Planks of the hardwood floor stood like sentries propped against the wall, leaving a hole where the James Madison bills had been hidden. I didn't bother returning the planks to the floor. I didn't bother folding the blanket that had been tossed to the side of the sofa or picking up the pillow and sheets from the nights Brad had slept there.

Instead, I went to the hall closet and pulled two vintage turquoise Samsonite suitcases trimmed in white from where they'd been stashed. I carried them to the bedroom and filled them with underwear, clothes, shoes, an overnight bag, puppy toys, blankets, my laptop and power source, books, pajamas.

For the next day I wandered around, randomly adding my favorite things to the suitcase. It wasn't a well-thought out plan or anything concrete, but I knew what I was doing. I was preparing to leave my building, and I was making sure I wouldn't have to come back for a while.

When the suitcases were stuffed, I clipped Rocky's leash to his collar and started loading the car. After the second trip, I knocked on Abby's door. The officer opened it a crack, recognized me, and held it open wide.

"Madison," she said as her eyes swept me and my loot. "Come in."

"No, thank you. I'm getting out of here. Right now, it's too much. I'm taking what I can carry. Everything else is nobody's business but mine. Here are my keys. Do what you gotta do."

"Where are you going?"

"I'd rather not say." I set my keys in her hand and walked away.

"He's going to ask, you know," she said to my back.

"I figured as much."

"Good luck, Madison."

I took a taxi to Thelma Johnson's house. Only one person would think to look for me there. But Tex's case was solved. He'd have no need to talk to me. On the other hand, if Brad was out there and wanted to find me, he'd never think to look there, and that was the space I needed.

My phone rang every day for the next two weeks. The number was blocked. After the first four days, I turned off the ringer. After ten I powered it off. On day fifteen, I turned it on. There was one message.

"Madison, this is Officer Young. I need to talk to you regarding Brad Turlington. Please call me at your earliest convenience."

I ignored the message for three more days.

I spent a lot of time lying in the twin bed from Joanie's store, staring at the ceiling. Rocky slept by my thigh. We took walks around the neighborhood three times a day, and I met a few of the neighbors.

When the pet food ran low, I knew I had to leave the house. I pulled a navy blue tunic over a white turtleneck and navy and white plaid pants, tied a yellow scarf around my hair and slipped into yellow patent leather shoes. I walked to the grocery store and pushed a cart up and down the aisles, so lost in my thoughts that I almost crashed carts with Connie Duncan.

"Madison!"

"Connie, I'm so sorry."

"Don't apologize. If I were you, I'd be preoccupied, too."

"This is a nice coincidence. I've been meaning to call you, to see how you're doing."

"It's not really a coincidence. I saw you walking along the road and followed you." She tipped her head to one side. "You were going to check on me?"

"Since the car accident. How are you?"

"Madison, I'm fine. I've been to the studio about a hundred times. It's never open. I've been calling you too. When the news broke, about the counterfeiting and about Brad, I couldn't believe that Ned and I had pushed you to be with him. We've both been worried. I didn't know if we'd ever see you again."

I didn't want to admit I'd been living in solitude for the past few weeks, that I'd essentially shut out the outside world. I didn't want Connie to know that Brad had vanished into thin air, but I also didn't know how to go about pretending everything was normal.

"Can I give you a ride home?" Connie asked.

"Sure."

After I checked out, I pushed the cart to the parking lot and loaded the bags into Connie's trunk. I gave her directions to Thelma Johnson's house. I considered it a good sign that I was allowing another person into my private Idaho. A good sign, that is, until she pulled up to the front of the house and parked behind a police cruiser.

"Who's house is this?" Connie asked.

"Mine. I don't live here ... well, I guess I kind of do live here. I'd explain but I don't think this is the right time."

We both got out of the car. Connie popped the trunk and unloaded my groceries. She helped me carry them to the front door, then hesitated for a second.

"Do you want me to come in with you?"

"Not yet. Soon, but not yet." I hugged her. "Thank you, Connie. When I get everything sorted out, if you want, I'll give you that kitchen we've been talking about."

Connie hugged me back. "I'm going to hold you to it."

I fumbled with the front door keys. Officer Young appeared from around the side of the building. She was in her uniform. A canvas shopping bag hung from her shoulder.

"I brought your mail," she said.

"How did you know I was here?"

Tex stepped out from around the side of the house. I looked at him, then at her. He put his hand up and shook it side to side, as if telling her not to answer. She set the canvas bag on my porch by the screen door and walked away.

Tex approached slowly. If I hadn't been looking for a limp, I might not have noticed the change to his walk.

"Abby? She's your chauffeur?"

"I don't need a chauffeur anymore. Department cleared me for regular duty."

"So why is she here?" I asked.

"This was her idea."

I looked past Tex to Abby, who was unwinding Rocky's leash from around Connie's legs.

"I'm surprised it took you so long," I said to Tex.

"You didn't leave town. That's a good sign."

"It's not a bad idea. Get lost, start over. There are some people I'd rather didn't find me."

"You might get your wish."

"Do you have a lead on Brad? Do you have any idea where he went or if he even went anywhere? I keep thinking I'm going to walk outside and he's going to be sitting on my doorstep, or worse, hiding in my studio. I have nightmares that he's going to show up again."

"Night, we found a body in a hotel room about a hundred miles northeast of Dallas. Gunshot wound to the head. Messy." Tex paused for a second, and his voice dropped. "It was Turlington."

"You're sure?" I whispered.

"We're sure."

I closed my eyes as Tex's words sank in. Brad was dead. By killing himself, he'd admitted his guilt. And that guilt tainted every single memory I had of the good times with him. A numb sensation radiated from my chest and spread through my arms and down my thighs. I wondered if I'd ever feel anything again.

"Night? You still with me?"

"I'm not with you, Tex. I'm not with anybody."

"That's funny, because it feels like you're with me even when you're not. And that's not something I ever saw coming."

"I can't talk about this right now."

"Then call me when you can, because I don't see this changing. You know the number." He walked past me and headed down the street to the waiting police car.

I carried the canvas bag into the dining room and emptied a stack of envelopes, magazines, color circulars from the grocery store, and a tortilla-chip colored padded envelope onto the table. The handwriting on the front of the envelope was Brad's.

I sank into one of the chrome-trimmed kitchen chairs and stared out the window. The view from the kitchen included a small sidewalk that led to the separate garage. On the right hand side were the flower beds I'd caught Tex watering. The sun shone on the green grass and the wooden stakes that supported tomato plants starting to bud. The social garlic was blooming next to it, the purple flowers standing two feet tall.

I took a deep breath, tore the envelope open, and tipped it until the contents fell onto the table. A bundle of white tissue paper hit the Formica tabletop with a *thunk*. My hands shook as I unfolded the layers. When I reached the middle, I sat back in my chair and stared at it.

Brad's Rolex.

I picked up the watch and held it for a couple of seconds. The crystal was broken, but the watch still kept time. When I turned it over and read the inscription, I knew it had been right. Time had been the one thing that told me the truth. I set the watch between two small clay pots of African Violets and noticed a slip of paper that had been tucked into the tissue paper under the watch. I unfolded it and read his note. *You deserve more.*

I left the watch on the sill while I carried the plants to the sink. I watered each one and let them drain, then collected the layers of tissue paper and carried them to the trash can. When I let go, the layers fell apart.

Between the tissue paper was a plastic sleeve. On the top left were the letters PMG next to a picture of a scale. Below that were the words Paper Money Guaranty. To the right of the logo were the words $5000 1928 Federal Reserve Note Atlanta. Under that was a series of numbers and letters that meant nothing to me. Inside was a slightly weathered, but otherwise new, James Madison bill.

I knew the bill was evidence.

I knew it didn't belong to me.

I knew the right thing to do would be to contact Secret Service and arrange to turn it over to them.

I flipped the plastic over and stared at the back. The simplicity of the design, vibrant green ink more beautiful than an emerald. It had been created in a time when the need for magnetic strips and holograms to prohibit counterfeiting would have sounded like science fiction. One bill, that, if proven to be real, was worth about hundred thousand dollars to someone.

I sank back into the dining room chair and propped my elbows on the table, holding the plastic envelope in front of my face. I looked back out the window and watched the police cruiser idle by the curb. After a few minutes, it pulled away and drove down the street.

I picked up my cell phone and called information for the number to Paper Trail.

"Paper Trail, Stanley Mann speaking."

"Mr. Mann, this is Madison Night. I wasn't sure if you'd be back at work yet."

"Life goes on, Ms. Night. Won't do me any good to pretend it doesn't, just because I lived through a nightmare."

"About that nightmare," I started. We exchanged what we knew about the case. I asked about his dog, he asked about my injury. It was as if I was talking to a friend.

"How late are you open today?" I asked. It felt like déjà vu, that familiar sensation of knowing I'd spoken those same words the last time I called this number. "I have something I want to give you."

I made arrangements to meet the numismatist at his temporary office in the Lakewood Antique Mall. I hung up the phone, tucked the plastic pouch with the collectible bill back into the mailing envelope, and set it on the corner of the counter.

The front door opened, and Connie stood in the doorway. "I overheard part of your conversation. Do you need a ride to the Lakewood Antique Mall?"

"Actually, I do. Do you mind?"

"I'm sorry, I can't. Ned's waiting for me. But I know someone who can take you if you want."

She pushed the door open wider, and Tex stepped into view.

"I thought you said I should call you when I'm ready to talk? Because I'm nowhere near ready."

He stepped through the doorway and approached me. His blue eyes sparkled.

"Who said anything about talking?"

Reader's Discussion Guide

1. Madison has established an independent life for herself, but when Brad returns, she is thrown off-kilter. Do you think she is as independent as she portrays herself, or do you think she has merely shut out the world to avoid emotional entanglements?

2. Madison waffles back and forth on whether or not to trust Brad, based on how she used to feel and how she feels now. Do you think both sets of feelings are justified?

3. Do you think Brad truly cares for Madison, or do you think he is a manipulator and sees her as a means to an end?

4. Madison's relationship with Brad is exposed in *That Touch of Ink*. Do you feel like you have a better understanding of what made Madison the woman she is, or do you think she is still hiding behind the Doris Day image?

5. Many of the characters—including Madison—engage in subversive behavior in this book. Consider Madison drugging Brad, Brad lying to Madison, Hudson confiding in Tex, and Tex not telling Madison that Brad is a person of interest. Do you think their behavior is justified? Do you think any of the characters has more reason for acting the way they do than others?

6. How did you feel when Hudson left Dallas? Did you want him to stay, or were you happy that he was moving on with his life after what happened in *Pillow Stalk*?

7. Madison finds herself confiding in Lt. Tex Allen about Brad. Do you think he is a smart choice for confidant? Does he put his job as police lieutenant above his attraction to Madison, vice versa, or neither?

8. Both Madison Night and Officer Donna Nast are strong female characters. Are they more alike than they would admit? Or does one have traits the other aspires to have herself? Does the animosity between them stem from their individual relationships with Tex, or do you think there's more at the core?

9. Is it creepy or a sweet gesture that Brad makes over Madison's living room without consulting her?

10. Even though he hurt her, Madison lets Brad back into her life. Do you think she is looking for closure on her past or nostalgic for what was a defining relationship in her life? If it were you, what would you have done differently? What would you have done the same?

From the Author

This is a mystery about a counterfeiting scheme, but it's also about broken trust. How easy is it to accept someone back into your life after he or she has lied to you? What if there is an explanation for the lie? Even if a person can find their way to forgive and forget, can trust ever really be reestablished?

Diane Vallere

Diane Vallere lives in a world where popcorn is a breakfast food and Doris Day movies are revered for their cultural significance. After over twenty years in the fashion industry, she now writes full time, juggling the Mad for Mod series, the Style & Error series, and the upcoming Material Witness series. She launched her own detective agency at age ten and has maintained a passion for shoes, clues, and clothes ever since. Visit her at www.dianevallere.com.

In Case You Missed the 1st Book in the Series

PILLOW STALK

Diane Vallere

A Mad for Mod Mystery (#1)

Interior Decorator Madison Night has modeled her life after Doris Day's character in *Pillow Talk*, but when a killer targets women dressed like the bubbly actress, Madison's signature sixties style places her in the middle of a homicide investigation.

The local detective connects the new crimes to a twenty-year old cold case, and Madison's long-trusted contractor emerges as the leading suspect. As the body count piles up like a stack of plush pillows, Madison uncovers a Soviet spy, a campaign to destroy all Doris Day movies, and six minutes of film that will change her life forever.

Available at booksellers nationwide and online

Visit www.henerypress.com for details

Be sure to check out Madison's prequel novella
MIDNIGHT ICE featured in

OTHER PEOPLE'S BAGGAGE

Kendel Lynn, Gigi Pandian, Diane Vallere

Baggage claim can be terminal. These are the stories of what happened after three women with a knack for solving mysteries each grabbed the wrong bag.

MIDNIGHT ICE by Diane Vallere: When interior decorator Madison Night crosses the country to distance herself from a recent breakup, she learns it's harder to escape her past than she thought, and diamonds are rarely a girl's best friend.

SWITCH BACK by Kendel Lynn: Ballantyne Foundation director Elliott Lisbon travels to Texas after inheriting an entire town, but when she learns the benefactor was murdered, she must unlock the small town's big secrets or she'll never get out alive.

FOOL'S GOLD by Gigi Pandian: When a world-famous chess set is stolen from a locked room during the Edinburgh Fringe Festival, historian Jaya Jones and her magician best friend must outwit actresses and alchemists to solve the baffling crime.

Available at booksellers nationwide and online

Visit www.henerypress.com for details

Henery Press Mystery Books

And finally, before you go...
Here are a few other mysteries
you might enjoy:

LOWCOUNTRY BOIL

Susan M. Boyer

A Liz Talbot Mystery (#1)

Private Investigator Liz Talbot is a modern Southern belle: she blesses hearts and takes names. She carries her Sig 9 in her Kate Spade handbag, and her golden retriever, Rhett, rides shotgun in her hybrid Escape. When her grandmother is murdered, Liz hightails it back to her South Carolina island home to find the killer.

She's fit to be tied when her police-chief brother shuts her out of the investigation, so she opens her own. Then her long-dead best friend pops in and things really get complicated. When more folks start turning up dead in this small seaside town, Liz must use more than just her wits and charm to keep her family safe, chase down clues from the hereafter, and catch a psychopath before he catches her.

Available at booksellers nationwide and online

Visit www.henerypress.com for details

DOUBLE WHAMMY

Gretchen Archer

A Davis Way Crime Caper (#1)

Davis Way thinks she's hit the jackpot when she lands a job as the fifth wheel on an elite security team at the fabulous Bellissimo Resort and Casino in Biloxi, Mississippi. But once there, she runs straight into her ex-ex husband, a rigged slot machine, her evil twin, and a trail of dead bodies. Davis learns the truth and it does not set her free—in fact, it lands her in the pokey.

Buried under a mistaken identity, unable to seek help from her family, her hot streak runs cold until her landlord Bradley Cole steps in. Make that her landlord, lawyer, and love interest. With his help, Davis must win this high stakes game before her luck runs out.

Available at booksellers nationwide and online

Visit www.henerypress.com for details

BOARD STIFF

Kendel Lynn

An Elliott Lisbon Mystery (#1)

As director of the Ballantyne Foundation on Sea Pine Island, SC, Elliott Lisbon scratches her detective itch by performing discreet inquiries for Foundation donors. Usually nothing more serious than retrieving a pilfered Pomeranian. Until Jane Hatting, Ballantyne board chair, is accused of murder. The Ballantyne's reputation tanks, Jane's headed to a jail cell, and Elliott's sexy ex is the new lieutenant in town.

Armed with moxie and her Mini Coop, Elliott uncovers a trail of blackmail schemes, gambling debts, illicit affairs, and investment scams. But the deeper she digs to clear Jane's name, the guiltier Jane looks. The closer she gets to the truth, the more treacherous her investigation becomes. With victims piling up faster than shells at a clambake, Elliott realizes she's next on the killer's list.

Available at booksellers nationwide and online

Visit www.henerypress.com for details

DINERS, DIVES & DEAD ENDS

Terri L. Austin

A Rose Strickland Mystery (#1)

As a struggling waitress and part-time college student, Rose Strickland's life is stalled in the slow lane. But when her close friend, Axton, disappears, Rose suddenly finds herself serving up more than hot coffee and flapjacks. Now she's hashing it out with sexy bad guys and scrambling to find clues in a race to save Axton before his time runs out.

With her anime-loving bestie, her septuagenarian boss, and a pair of IT wise men along for the ride, Rose discovers political corruption, illegal gambling, and shady corporations. She's gone from zero to sixty and quickly learns when you're speeding down the fast lane, it's easy to crash and burn.

Available at booksellers nationwide and online

Visit www.henerypress.com for details

ARTIFACT

Gigi Pandian

A Jaya Jones Treasure Hunt Mystery (#1)

Historian Jaya Jones discovers the secrets of a lost Indian treasure may be hidden in a Scottish legend from the days of the British Raj. But she's not the only one on the trail...

From San Francisco to London to the Highlands of Scotland, Jaya must evade a shadowy stalker as she follows hints from the hastily scrawled note of her dead lover to a remote archaeological dig. Helping her decipher the cryptic clues are her magician best friend, a devastatingly handsome art historian with something to hide, and a charming archaeologist running for his life.

Available at booksellers nationwide and online

Visit www.henerypress.com for details

THE AMBITIOUS CARD

John Gaspard

An Eli Marks Mystery (#1)

The life of a magician isn't all kiddie shows and card tricks. Sometimes it's murder. Especially when magician Eli Marks very publicly debunks a famed psychic, and said psychic ends up dead. The evidence, including a bloody King of Diamonds playing card (one from Eli's own Ambitious Card routine), directs the police right to Eli.

As more psychics are slain, and more King cards rise to the top, Eli can't escape suspicion. Things get really complicated when romance blooms with a beautiful psychic, and Eli discovers she's the next target for murder, and he's scheduled to die with her. Now Eli must use every trick he knows to keep them both alive and reveal the true killer.

Available at booksellers nationwide and online

Visit www.henerypress.com for details

PORTRAIT OF A DEAD GUY

Larissa Reinhart

A Cherry Tucker Mystery (#1)

In Halo, Georgia, folks know Cherry Tucker as big in mouth, small in stature, and able to sketch a portrait faster than buck-shot rips from a ten gauge -- but commissions are scarce. So when the well-heeled Branson family wants to memorialize their murdered son in a coffin portrait, Cherry scrambles to win their patronage from her small town rival.

As the clock ticks toward the deadline, Cherry faces more trouble than just a controversial subject. Between ex-boyfriends, her flaky family, an illegal gambling ring, and outwitting a killer on a spree, Cherry finds herself painted into a corner she'll be lucky to survive.

Available at booksellers nationwide and online

Visit www.henerypress.com for details

FRONT PAGE FATALITY
LynDee Walker

A Headlines in High Heels Mystery (#1)

Crime reporter Nichelle Clarke's days can flip from macabre to comical with a beep of her police scanner. Then an ordinary accident story turns extraordinary when evidence goes missing, a prosecutor vanishes, and a sexy Mafia boss shows up with the headline tip of a lifetime.

As Nichelle gets closer to the truth, her story gets more dangerous. Armed with a notebook, a hunch, and her favorite stilettos, Nichelle races to splash these shady dealings across the front page before this deadline becomes her last.

Available at booksellers nationwide and online

Visit www.henerypress.com for details

CIRCLE OF INFLUENCE

Annette Dashofy

A Zoe Chambers Mystery (#1)

Zoe Chambers, paramedic and deputy coroner in rural
Pennsylvania's tight-knit Vance Township, has been privy to a
number of local secrets over the years, some of them her own. But
secrets become explosive when a dead body is found in the
Township Board President's abandoned car.

As a January blizzard rages, Zoe and Police Chief Pete Adams
launch a desperate search for the killer, even if it means uncovering
secrets that could not only destroy Zoe and Pete, but also those
closest to them.

Available at booksellers nationwide and online

Visit www.henerypress.com for details

39153087R00145

Made in the USA
Lexington, KY
10 February 2015